T0365669

THE OTHER SIDE OF THE DOOR

VERN THIBEDEAU

THE OTHER SIDE OF THE DOOR

iUniverse books may be ordered through booksellers or by contacting:

iUniverse
1663 Liberty Drive
Bloomington, IN 47403
www.iuniverse.com
844-349-9409

ISBN: 978-1-6632-4460-4 (sc)
ISBN: 978-1-6632-4459-8 (e)

Library of Congress Control Number: 2022915965

Print information available on the last page.

iUniverse rev. date: 08/24/2022

Contents

Preface

I wish to state that this novel is completely fictional. All names of people, locations and things are strictly from my imagination.

Most of the novel takes place inside a penitentiary. I should also note that my story is set several years ago. However, I have been informed that even though several institutional routines have changed since I was a correctional officer, the incidents and staff difficulties are still similar.

Due to many misconceptions regarding prisons—which, in my mind, are due mainly to outlandish movies and the manner in which the media report incidents—I was advised that it would greatly assist readers if I gave a short version of the day-to-day routine of an institution. I have done this and have included a glossary at the end of the novel.

Hopefully, this novel, even though it is fiction, will take some of the mystery out of what I term "a society within a society."

Chapter 1

The gavel came down with a bang. The old bitch, who was dressed in black, took a minute or two to stare down at the young man standing in front of her before uttering the words "Mr. Mac Shipley, I sentence you to eight years and six months in a federal prison."

Shipley couldn't believe it. He was almost in shock. He'd thought he might get two years if the judge was in a bad mood, but never in his wildest dreams had he figured on eight and a half years. He honestly didn't believe it was his fault that the old man had been entering the store just as he was running out with the stolen money. However, his fault or not, the guy was presently lying in a hospital bed, full of tubes and on life support, after hitting his head on the sidewalk when he was knocked down. Shipley still thought that once again, he had been shafted. He firmly believed his lawyer was useless, and the judge was an old dried-up biddy. As usual, everyone was blaming him for everything. He was positive about one thing, though: there was no way in hell he was going to spend that much time in prison. *Screw the whole damned lot of them*, he thought. *I don't know how or when, and I don't care if a pig has to go down, but one way or another, I'm gonna be gone within a year or so.* Shipley just figured it depended on where he was locked up. Naturally, he couldn't have realized what was in store for him or known he was just dreaming.

Vern Thibedeau

The provincial officials were fast, though. It took them only four days, and there he was on Monday morning, hooked up in a belly chain and leg irons, sitting on a bench in a van with four other rough-looking cons and admitting to himself that he was scared shitless. *God, I'm actually going to a federal pen with murderers and every other type of asshole they can lock up. How in the hell can I ever get out of this? What a bunch of pricks.*

The inmates had been told they were heading for Mountainview Prison, which was commonly called the Mount. It was a four-hour drive with no stopping. They were also informed that if it was really necessary, they would be supplied bottles to piss in. *So nice of them!*

He stared out the window at the traffic and hoped the rain and the wind that was swirling water all over the place weren't signs of what was to come. Every now and again, he sneaked a look at the guards sitting on the other side of the wire mesh, who looked as if they were half asleep.

Shipley had just turned 26. At about 6 foot 1 inch tall and a little over 200 pounds, he was easily the largest inmate on the bus. But even so, he was scared witless. All his life, Shipley, even though he was usually the largest person in a crowd, never had been able to exert any authority. Unfortunately, he had always lacked self-confidence. This was likely due to the brutal discipline of his alcoholic father and his submissive mother, who never raised her voice to her husband. So as usual, he kept his mouth shut and listened to the others bragging about how tough they were and how they'd outwitted the cops for years. *Christ*, he thought. Most of them didn't look over 25 or thereabouts. *Oh yeah, real tough guys, probably in for raping young girls or something.* But no matter what he was thinking, he was smart enough to keep his mouth shut.

The inmate who was sitting beside him was easily the oldest one on the bus. He appeared to have a tough self-confidence and a calm aura surrounding him. After a half hour or so, he turned to Shipley and said with a smirk, "Boy, ain't they a tough lot? I bet they'd shit themselves if someone screamed out loud. What'd they nail you for anyway?"

This was Shipley's first time staying with the feds, but he knew enough not to get too free with his information, so he replied, "Oh, just an armed robbery where some jerk got hurt. How about you?"

"Ah, I don't want to yap too much. Let's just say I did some jobs for the Gennetti family and let it go at that. The goofs have hung a murder rap on me, and believe it or not, it's one murder that I didn't even do. But I guess that's life, and we might as well make the best of it, eh?"

Christ, the Gennetti family—that's big time. He must have a lot of contacts if he isn't full of shit. Shipley gave him his name and said, "They got me for eight and a half years."

"I'd shake hands with you if we weren't chained up. I'm called Joe Dominic. It's nice to meet you. Now let's quiet down and have a rest."

Shipley went back to listening to the idiots carrying on about how tough and experienced they were. To help pass the time, he watched the cars and trucks whiz by in the rain with their windshield wipers slapping back and forth, chilled to the bone and half hoping there'd be a small accident or something. In a bit of a daze and with his stomach clenching tighter by the minute, he sat and waited for whatever was in store for him.

Within a couple of minutes or so, Shipley's mind was somewhere between dreamland and a catatonic state. For one reason or another, he began to relive an episode that had taken place when he was around 10 years old. It was winter and was very cold, and since he didn't have any mitts, he decided to steal a pair. Naturally, a store clerk caught him and placed a phone call to his father, and within a short time, his angry father arrived at the store. Shipley was made to apologize to the manager, and his old man hauled him out to their aged car. The car didn't want to start, and his old man cursed, banging on the steering wheel. Eventually, the wreck started, and once they arrived home, Shipley's father dragged him into the house and pushed him down onto a kitchen chair.

"Well," he yelled at his shaking son, "you want to be a thief, do you? I'll show you what happens to thieves. For a start, you get your ass outside, grab that shovel and get the driveway and sidewalk cleared out. And don't you dare step foot inside until it's bloody well done."

While he was shoveling snow, Shipley sneaked the odd look through the living room window and saw his mother, who, with a sad face, was watching him work. She was not saying anything but was watching him. As soon as Shipley finished shoveling, his old man ordered him to get a sandwich and get his ass up to his bed.

Vern Thibedeau

During his younger days, Shipley hadn't realized that the house they lived in was just barely above being called a shack. As far as he had known, it was normal to live in a house that was heated with a wood stove and to have a television that only worked occasionally. He also had thought it was normal to go outside and use an outhouse for a bathroom. He'd thought everyone lived like that. He had been shocked the first time he was at a friend's house and realized that most people certainly didn't live like that. He also had discovered that most fathers were actually nice to their young ones.

He did have one positive memory of himself and his father being together, though—well, at least part of the memory was positive. One day his father had looked down at him and asked if he'd like to go to a movie. An excited son had looked up at his father and, almost dancing, replied, "Oh yes, yes! That would be so much fun!"

Shipley didn't remember much of the movie; apparently, for some reason or another, they'd had to leave before it was over. But he was pretty sure it had been a western of some sort; he did remember people with wide hats on horses and some shooting. But there was one thing he did clearly recall: a swarm of big black birds flying over an area and making a lot of noise. He believed they had been vultures trying to decide if the person or thing lying on the ground was dead or not. In his mind, they had seemed hungry. Later in life, when he was under stress or concerned about a major happening in his life, those damned vultures always tended to return in his dreams.

Unfortunately, Shipley always seemed to get into trouble. Luckily, at least up until he had done the attempted robbery, the problems had been relatively minor. At times, he was a bit of a bully, and that had seemed to upset the teachers at school. He also had a habit of picking things up if he felt like he wanted them. Sometimes he took things from a yard while walking past a house or even from a store, but it was just when he felt the need for a certain article, so it wasn't too often.

But after that awful night of shoveling snow, Shipley never had seen or heard from his father again. Heck, he still didn't even know if he was alive or dead. To be honest, he wasn't overly concerned. His mother, when he'd gotten up in the morning, had told him his father was gone, and that had been it. However, that had made big changes in the household. There certainly was a little less to eat, but there were fewer punishments and no beatings, at least not at home. Sadly, about five years later, Shipley's older sister had taken off, and neither he nor his mother ever had heard from her again. But Shipley just figured that was life, and he didn't realize that not all families lived the same way.

Chapter 2

After what seemed like several hours, with a bit of a jerk, Shipley came out of his daze and realized they were on the Mountainview reserve. *Boy,* he thought, *what a fancy name for a stupid prison.*

He was wide awake now and staring at his new home. As the bus driver drove around the fence to the rear of the prison, Shipley spotted three towers and what he figured were two patrol vehicles. He also knew damned well the staff in the jeeps and towers were armed with rifles and revolvers. As if that weren't enough, there was a high double fence with coils of razor wire along the top circling the whole damned place, and by the looks of all the lights, he figured the nights would be about as bright as the days.

With that first shocking view of the place, it suddenly hit Shipley like a ton of bricks that he'd reached the big time. *God,* he thought, *what in hell have I gotten myself into this time?* As he stared at the mobile vehicles driving around the fence and the towers, he believed the guards were praying that some foolish con would try to get out so they could take a shot at him.

The bus pulled up at the sally port, and the gate slid open so the van could enter and get checked out. There were only the five inmates in the van, so it didn't take long for the overweight guard to step on, give them all a nasty look, get off again and then wave to the tower to open the inside gate so they could get on their way. As the bus headed for a loading dock, Dominic looked over at Shipley and said with a sarcastic grin, "Well, we'll soon be in reception, and at least we'll have clean sheets tonight."

Dominic was right. Once they got off the van, stumbling and falling all over the place—leg irons were not the best thing to strut around in—they entered a large room that held several wire cages. Most of the cages had cardboard boxes stacked in them, but a couple of the larger cages were empty. They soon found out that one of the larger cages was reserved for them. In the cage they sat like animals in a zoo. Shipley, for one, felt like an animal in a zoo.

The guard who seemed to be in charge of the place—Shipley didn't think he was too big of an asshole—called them out one at a time to issue them their bedding, clothing and all kinds of effects. Once that was finished, he said to them, "You guys just have to sit and wait for a while until someone from A unit gets down here to escort you up to your new home."

Dominic looked over at Shipley and, with a wink, said, "I told you we'd have clean sheets tonight, eh? Hell, we won't even have to wash our own clothes; they do it for us. Just like a hotel that's free. Now, how can you beat that?"

So they just sat there and felt like a bunch of idiots. The inmate sitting beside Shipley looked at him and asked, "Hey, what the hell you in for? You're really quiet; must be your first time in a joint."

Shipley simply stared at him for a couple of seconds and then replied, "Oh, I just stomped on an idiot's head for asking too many stupid asshole questions." Shipley thought he should try to act like a tough guy and prayed it would earn him some respect.

* * *

At 7:15 on Monday morning, Bill Richards was on his way in to work and was concerned he might be a little late in getting in. *Christ,* he thought to himself, *what a way to start a new week. And I'm likely going to be spare, so God only knows where I'll end up working. Oh well, at least it stopped raining, so that's something.*

Richards was a corporal posted to Mountainview, which meant he was in charge of whichever area he happened to be assigned to. At the present time, he was usually posted to A unit, which served as a reception centre. All new inmates were processed through it, which could take up to a month or two.

It was only about a 20-minute drive, but Bill was a little later than usual in leaving the house and was slightly concerned about the time, thinking, *Hell, a boss is supposed to set an example for the other staff. Ah hell, stop worrying about little silly things; Greg and Steve are often late, and no one says dick-all to them. I should just calm down and stop worrying over nothing.*

The drive was along the lake, and except for the winter drive, he found it relaxing, especially if there had been a problem at the Mount, such as a murder, a hostage situation or something similar, which, sadly, wasn't all that uncommon.

He cruised off the highway onto the reserve. As he coasted around the curve, he realized he was going to make it in on time, which was a relief. As usual, he gave the parking lot a quick scan, looking for any police cars, and was thankful he didn't spot any. His next habit was to take a glance at the flag pole. The flag was happily flapping at full staff. That little bit of information told him there had likely been no serious incidents over the weekend—always good news!

Bill parked his car, and as he headed in to work, he looked at the sun and thought, *Hell, I'm not even going to get wet.* He passed through the ID building with a wave to the officer in charge of the place, walked through both gates once they opened up for him and continued on inside. He hustled over to the sergeant, also called a supervisor, who was taking roll call, to find out if the sergeant wanted him anywhere special or if he was still spare.

"Yep," the sergeant said, "still spare, Bill. Just go down around A unit, and give them a hand. Then I'll know where to find you if I need you for something."

"OK, but I'd just as soon have a job as hang around with dick-all to do."

With a little laugh, the supervisor replied, "Hell, Bill, I'll do my best for you."

Richards walked around the main control and started down the corridor for A unit. Several minutes later, after chatting with a few staff and passing through a couple more barriers, he finally reached the unit. He waved to the control officers and strolled around to the unit office. Entering the office, he spotted Art behind the desk, talking on the phone. Once Art hung up, Bill looked at him and said, "Morning, Art. Just wanna let you know I'm spare, and so far, I haven't been given a job. It looks like everyone showed up for work."

"Hey, Bill. Good to hear. Can you get down to reception and pick up five newcomers who just came in? I've got their cells ready on 1B, but my two guys are tied up, and I can't find anyone else to go down."

"Sure, at least it'll give me something to do for a while."

Richards walked out of A unit and swung left. He waved to the staff in a couple of controls, passed through their barriers and entered reception. He spotted Norm in his office and headed toward him to see what was going on. As he walked across the large, cluttered room, he couldn't help but notice five inmates locked in one of the wire cages. They were just sitting there, clutching their goodie bags, looking a little lost but gazing around and trying to take everything in. Richards figured they must be the newcomers and thought, *Well, by the looks of them, they must be the cons I'm picking up. They do look lost, but I'd bet a day's pay that lost look won't last long. Pretty damn soon, they'll be putting on their tough "Screw you too" act.*

Bill entered the office, which was actually more of a storage room than an office, and as he settled into the chair on the opposite side of the desk, he told Norm he was there to pick up the newcomers.

With a nod toward the five inmates, Norm said, "Glad you're here, Bill. The sooner you get them the hell out of here, the sooner we can get to the rest of our work. They don't actually seem to be a bad lot. The one exception may be the tallest one. His name's Shipley, and he's got a hell of a chip on his shoulder. Christ, the asshole went into some corner store and robbed the place, and then, when he was running out the door, he pushed an elderly guy over. When the guy went down, he hit his head and ended up on life support. Now, for Christ's sake, this guy's pissed off because the judge gave him eight and a half years. The asshole should've been given life. At any rate, he's gonna to be a problem, and he's a big sucker."

"Oh well, we've had them bigger, and we've managed. I hope you're wrong, though; I'm getting too old to be wrestling with these idiots. Anyway, I'll just grab the paperwork for the unit, have a chat with them and get them out of your hair."

Bill ambled over to the cage with the files, had an officer unlock it and stood there looking at the new inmates for a minute or so before saying, "My name's Richards, and I'm one of the officers in charge of A unit. You likely know that this unit is the reception unit. Staff will decide what level of security you'll be classified at, and then you'll be transferred to whichever institution is decided upon. One of the things to remember while you're here is that this is a maximum-security institution, and no matter what security level you consider yourself to be, you are considered a maximum inmate while you're in here. All staff in control centres, towers and mobiles are armed and under orders to use those arms to stop escapes, disturbances or whatever else pops up. So consider yourselves advised."

They just sat there looking at Bill as if they hadn't heard a word he'd said, except for Shipley. Shipley threw a look at Richards that reinforced everything Norm had said just a few minutes ago.

Richards, one of the reception staff and the five newcomers headed out for A unit. The reception guy had to take the files up front and figured he might as well go with them at least as far as N area. They crossed the corridor, Bill waved at the officer in unit control to open the barrier and they headed up to N area. He couldn't help but chuckle to himself as he watched the five cons gawking around. A person would have thought their heads were on a swivel. He also noted that Shipley appeared to be highly interested in the system, especially the armed control points and the empty food carts sitting on the loading dock, waiting to be loaded onto a truck.

They reached N barrier, and Bill, who was now leading the group, waved to the control officer to let him know they needed through. Bill, with the inmates in tow, turned toward A unit. They entered the unit and went straight to the office, and Bill instructed them to wait at the door. He went inside to inform Art that his five newcomers were there and were all his.

Art glanced at his two staff and said, "You know which one goes where, so just take them down on lower B, and stick each one into his assigned cell. Make sure you tell them the routine for lunch, and let them know each one will be interviewed sometime this afternoon."

* * *

Shipley and his newfound friends just stood there looking at one another, staring at their new environment and patiently waiting while Richards went into the office. Within a couple of minutes or so, two guards came out, and with a nod and a wave, one said, "Follow me, and I'll show you your new home."

The five inmates and the two officers trooped down the range, and as they walked down, Shipley's stomach sank even lower. The range appeared huge and scary. There appeared to be about 25 cells on each side of the range. The doors were solid steel, and each one had a little window in it that was about five by six inches. Shipley had been in enough jails to know without being told that the little window was for staff to peek into the cell at them. The floor was tiled, which he assumed was to make the place look less menacing, but in Shipley's mind, if that was the intent, it failed miserably.

As they walked farther into the strange, ominous place, Shipley couldn't help but gawk at everything he saw and flinch at every noise. As they hustled along, he continued to feel more hemmed in and felt a more pressing weight pushing him down. To make matters worse, just as they were passing a closed cell, he looked toward the little window and spotted some movement. Suddenly, they heard pounding on the door. Shipley jumped and did a little spin-around, which gained him a few grins from his newfound buddies. He almost did the same thing again when the inmate, who was pounding on his cell door, started to scream about being let out to the common room. The only reply the inmate received was from one of the guards, who hollered, "Shut your stupid mouth and quit pounding on the door, or your next stop will be the hole!"

Likely due to several large light fixtures in the ceiling, the place suddenly struck Shipley as being extremely bright. There was also a foul odour. Shipley assumed it was from dozens of guys living in a fairly small area, several of whom likely weren't overly concerned about showering.

As they strode down the range, each time they came to an open door, one of the guards would look at a card in his hand and call out a name. Once the inmate replied to his name, he was told this was his new home and to get in. As soon as the inmate was inside, the door would slam shut, and the guard would stick the card into a holder attached to the door. That explained why Shipley didn't see any locks on the cell doors; they were controlled by the guards in the unit control.

When they reached the third open cell, the guard called out, "Shipley, this is yours. In you go."

Shipley stepped in, looked around his new home, jumped when the cell door slammed shut behind him and apprehensively tossed his bedding and clothing onto the mattress. Then he walked over to the window at the back of the cell. He didn't realize it yet, but he had sort of lucked in. His window, even though it had three large horizontal cement bars, looked out onto an open field of grass. Once he managed to ignore the fencing with the razor wire along the top, the huge guard tower in his view and the mobile vehicle that constantly drove around and around, he actually found it kind of pleasant and relaxing.

But all the same, he still felt a crushing pressure on his chest, and he knew there was no way on God's green earth he could ever spend years in that place.

He didn't realize it at the time, of course, but he was not going to be in Mountainview nearly as long as he or the officials expected. The problem for Shipley was that he was not going to exit the place in the manner he had hoped or planned, so maybe it was just as well that he couldn't see into the future.

* * *

Back in the unit office, once the two staff and the newcomers were on their way down the range, Art looked at Richards and asked, "Hey, Bill, any problems or anything we should know about with these guys?"

"Nope, but we'd better keep an eye on that Shipley; he's the big one. He certainly doesn't like it in here, and I have a feeling he's going to be a problem." Richards didn't realize it at the time, of course, but Shipley and he were going to have several serious run-ins over the next little while.

"OK," Art replied. "I'll make a note of it in the logbook, and we'll see how it goes. Thanks for the help."

"Sure. No problem, Art. I'm going to go up front to see if anything is going on. If anything else comes up, give me a holler."

That was about it for the day. He helped out here and there, and at the end of the shift, he took off for home. As staff liked to say, "One day closer to retirement, and everyone got to go home." But all day at work, Richards kept thinking about Shipley and those looks he was throwing around. He knew in his gut that the con was going to be a problem. And he was right!

Bill was about halfway home, when he remembered that a babysitter was coming in, and he and his wife were going out for dinner and then to a movie. He immediately forgot—or almost forgot—about work and proceeded to think about having a nice evening out with his wife and no kids hollering and running around.

Chapter 3

In a way, it was Shipley's birthday—one whole week locked up in the Mount. He had to admit to himself that it wasn't as bad as he'd thought it was going to be. Even the guards weren't all that bad. Except for a couple of them, most left the inmates alone as long as they did what they were told. But boy, if an inmate acted up, they didn't mind jumping on a con and muscling him off to the hole. The few guards who were pricks seemed to go out of their way to stir things up, and then if the cons reacted, they'd be charged with some asshole offence. He admitted to himself, however, that some of the cons deserved everything they got.

Shipley and the four inmates who'd gotten off the bus with him didn't do much; actually, newcomers didn't seem to do much of anything. One of the bosses took them around to show them how the areas that were relevant to them operated. But Shipley didn't get too excited and soon forgot most of what he'd seen.

However, he did note how the meals were brought into the prison. Well, actually, he paid much closer attention to how the empty food trays were taken out of the prison. He soon found out the trays were piled into same enclosed hot carts that brought the food in. He tossed around the idea that he could somehow hide inside a cart, behind a pile of trays that could be hollowed out. He was smart enough to realize he'd need some help and would certainly have to lose some weight, and even then, he would have to curl up into a small ball to fit behind the trays. But with planning, and if he paid someone to help, he figured it just might work.

After a few days in A unit, Shipley was told to visit his case management officer. He nonchalantly strolled into the office for his third visit, sat in the chair and just stared at the officer.

The CMO started the interview by saying, "Once again, I need your number and name to verify my paperwork. Once we get that out of the way, we'll get down to work. Remember, I told you that due to your crime and the length of your sentence, you'll likely be classed as a maximum-security inmate, at least for a while anyway. But remember, I also told you that if you stay out of trouble and get along with everyone, an eight-and-a-half-year sentence will not keep you here for long. I would imagine in a few years or so, you will likely be cleared for medium security."

That was about what Shipley had expected. He answered by asking what he thought were a bunch of dumb questions, signed a couple of forms and left the office, thinking, *Big fucking deal, and they convict me of robbery while he sits there doing bugger all and likely earning more every month than I tried to take from that stupid store.*

It didn't take the staff long; the next day, he was in J unit, classified as a real maximum-security con.

J unit wasn't really much different from A unit or E unit. Just like the other two units, it had three ranges, which were named K, L and M. K and L had two tiers, and M had one tier. After the morning, noon and afternoon counts were certified correct, inmates were allowed out, one range at a time, to file down to the servery area to pick up a meal tray. Then they had the option of going to their cells or to a common room to eat. After their supper meal, they had a choice of going to the yard, the gym or a common room or staying in their cells. *Boy*, Shipley sarcastically thought, *nothing but decisions, decisions. Ain't life a bitch?*

He also had to get a job. They didn't actually do much work, but if an inmate didn't work, he had to stay in his cell during working hours. In addition to that, he was also put on bottom pay. Some of them even got paid to go to school in an attempt to learn something. Shipley wasn't too sure just what it was, and he really didn't give a damn anyway. He tried to get a job working in the servery. He figured that working there would give him a better chance to see just what the hell went on with the food trays once they left the servery, but he wasn't that lucky. Shipley, like all inmates, went in front of the work board, and the officer in charge looked at him and said, "We need a cleaner in J unit, and since that's where you live, that's where you will be working."

With a smart-ass grin, Shipley sarcastically replied, "Well, thank you very much. I'm looking forward to it. I always wanted to be a big-shot cleaner." He knew by the look thrown at him that the officer knew damn well he was being a wise-ass. *Ah, what the hell could the guy say to me anyway? Nothing. Absolutely goddamn nothing.*

On the whole, though, Shipley didn't think J unit was all that bad. He was in a regular cell with a single bed, a desk, a chair, a stainless-steel sink and a crummy toilet, but it was fairly large and bright, and it even had an outside window, although the bars on it kind of pissed him off.

One of the things that did upset him, and the other inmates, was the light from the night lights in the cells. Granted, they weren't very bright, but they never went out. Staff claimed the night lights were left on so the midnight staff could tell if an inmate was having a medical problem. But inmates believed the reason was so staff could look through the little window in the door and make sure the inmate was still there and hadn't somehow managed to escape. God, they all hated those lights! He could understand why inmates told him the night lights were usually the first things to get ripped out every time there was a smash-up.

The cell doors were solid steel. No one could get through the doors unless they were opened from the unit control. Inmates complained about them, but staff stated they'd heard inmates say on different occasions that the only place they really felt safe in the Mount was in their cells with the doors closed. And Shipley did feel safe in his cell. Unfortunately, at times, when he was daydreaming and his mind slipped away to an earlier time in his life, he suddenly felt as if the walls were closing in on him. There were even times when he had difficulty breathing. After the feeling occurred a couple of times, though, he realized that if he stood in front of his outside window and stared out, everything seemed to settle down somewhat.

* * *

Another day at work was coming up. Richards and his wife, Shirley, had been out fairly late the night before, and now he was on his way in to work with a bit of a headache. They'd had to celebrate their 12th wedding anniversary. Bill was 36 years of age, had been married for 12 years to a lovely wife, was the father of two children, had spent eight years in corrections, and felt like he was turning into an old man.

He was in a reflective mood and couldn't help thinking, *Christ, I must be due for a change. Hell, I've been at the Mount for something like five years and most of those in A unit.*

Bill and Shirley, mostly at the urging of Shirley, had discussed the possibility of Bill looking for different employment. They had talked about it three or four times, and Shirley didn't think it would hurt Bill to at least look around. Little did he know he was going to walk in to work and be notified that a change was going to take place. Not a large change but at least a change.

With a quick glance at the flag and a look for any police cars, and thankfully not spotting anything out of the ordinary, he pulled into a parking spot and headed toward the ID building. He threw Joe a good-morning wave on his way through and started toward the fence's two large gates. Once they slid open for him one at a time, he hustled into the institution. When he reached the sergeant taking roll call, Bill gave him a wave and kept walking—that was, until the supervisor gave him a holler and told him to take a couple of minutes to go to Lockhart's office.

"I'm not sure what he wants, Bill, but he said it would only take a couple of minutes."

Richards replied, "OK. On my way." He swung to the right and headed down to the staff sergeant's office, all the while wondering what the heck the meeting could be about. He was sure he hadn't screwed up, at least not lately. When he reached the office, the door was open, so he just walked in and said, "Hi."

"Hey, Bill," Ray replied, and he waved him to a chair. "Glad you could make it. I know you're due in the unit, so I'll only keep you a few minutes. I just want to run something by you to see what you think. I imagine you've heard about Bishop in J unit wanting to transfer out to another institution. Anyway, it's been approved, and he leaves next week. Management was wondering if you'd be willing to transfer over to his position."

Vern Thibedeau

Well, Bill thought, *so much for the big change. On the other hand, what the hell? At least it's something.*

"Aw, why not?" he replied. "They say a change is as good as a rest."

"Glad to hear you agree, Bill. I really think a bit of a change will be good for you. I don't doubt you'll be putting in for the next sergeant's competition, and this'll give you a little different look at the system."

After a couple more minutes of chitchat about Bill's schedule and whatnot, Bill left the office and continued on his way to A unit to relieve Andy.

As soon as he walked in, Andy greeted Bill with "Hey, Bill, did you hear Bishop is transferring out, and word says management's gonna ask you to transfer over to fill his spot?"

Holy hell, Bill thought, *everyone knew about it before I did. Nothing ever changes in these places.*

Bill didn't verbalize much of a reply; he just said they'd already asked him, and he was starting in J next week. After a short chat, Andy filled him in on the past shift and then took off for home.

The rest of the week floated along, and thankfully, it was rather quiet—no suicides, stabbings or smash-ups, just the usual petty problems and whatnot. Of course, then the staff started to complain about being bored. Whenever the job was quiet, the staff enjoyed it for a few days and then started to bitch and complain about being bored. Then, when the shit hit the fan and the staff were fighting cons, putting out a fire or trying to save an inmate from bleeding out because he'd been stabbed or slashed up, they complained and wished things would quiet down and get back to normal.

Bill finished his week in A unit, and after his days off, he headed in to work and straight to J unit. The job in J unit wouldn't actually be a big change. There would be different routines, and the inmates wouldn't be on their best behaviour, because they'd been classified as maximum-security inmates and sent to a maximum unit. At least in A unit, they were trying to impress staff with their behaviour and attempting to be classed as medium- or even minimum-security inmates.

But once they were designated maximum, they'd be in the Mount for however long, and some really didn't care for it. In fact, several would be there for a good many years and were well aware of that fact. The life of a criminal could be a real bitch at times.

The morning rolled along normally until the noon count, and then, suddenly, things were not quite as normal. Bill and his staff went out to N area to observe the inmates returning from their jobs, and when they were notified by the unit control that the inmates were all in the unit, they headed back in. Before they even reached the office, the control notified them that there was a problem on 1K and that all inmates were locked in their cells, except one, who was refusing to go in.

All three staff headed onto lower K, and sure enough, all the cell doors were closed, which meant they were locked, but one inmate remained out at the end of the range.

As the staff started toward the inmate, one of the officers looked at Bill and said, "Uh-oh, that's Pezzio. He's a nutbar with a very small brain; in fact, he's on the far side of stupid. And one other thing: he seems to enjoy pain. On top of all that, he's built like a brick shithouse, and he's all muscle. For some reason, at times, he just refuses to go into his cell. This usually ends up in a big fight, with us eventually lugging him to segregation. Other than these episodes, though, he's usually not a problem."

Christ, just what I need on my first day in J unit. Bill told the staff to go back and wait at the range barrier and have the control radio N area to tell them to send in a couple of guys with a can of mace. He also informed them that he was going to try to talk Pezzio into going into his cell.

"Sounds good," one of them replied. "Especially the mace part. Just don't get too close; that bugger is very unpredictable. Good luck, but for Christ's sake, watch yourself!"

Bill nonchalantly walked down the range toward Pezzio. He had always found that a nonthreatening approach, if it were possible, helped to settle things down. Once he was close enough that he didn't have to raise his voice, he tried to start up a conversation by saying, "Hey, Pezzio, what the hell you doing? We have to get the count in, and if we're late, everyone will be late in getting lunch. Why piss everybody, including your buddies, off?"

Vern Thibedeau

"First off, I got no buddies. Secondly, I'm not gonna go in my cell. I'm sick of it. Hey, I remember you; you work in A unit. What the hell you doing over here? Making a bunch of overtime or something?"

"Nope, the powers that be got pissed off with me and transferred me in here to work. You'll likely be seeing a lot of me."

The conversation carried on back and forth for a short time, but it didn't take Bill long to realize it was an exercise in futility. In fact, he'd just said to himself, *This is nuts. We might as well get on with it*, when Pezzio interrupted his line of thought.

Pezzio bellowed, "Go screw yourself, Richards! I'm sick of talking!"

Once Bill made it back to the unit control, he saw that he had five staff plus himself. He quietly gave them their instructions. "We'll go down the range together, but I want whoever has the mace to be on the side farthest away from me. Once we're very close, I'm going to distract him by yelling. As soon as he looks my way, give him a couple of good bursts of mace. Then everyone pile on, and we'll hope for the best."

Everything worked as planned: Bill yelled, Pezzio got maced and the staff piled on. Then, as usual, all hell broke loose, with yelling, screaming and cursing. Pezzio was strong; even a punch in the stomach didn't slow him down. In between puffs, Bill thought, *God, I know we can't shoot the sons of bitches, but would a Taser ever be handy!*

As usual, the incident made the inmates on the range go nuts. They started screaming, cursing, banging on the cell doors and threatening staff with all kinds of mayhem. Within a few seconds, staff could hardly hear themselves think, let alone talk.

But they lucked in: as soon as Pezzio grabbed for his eyes, Bill managed to grab an arm and, with help, got an arm bar on him. Then, with some twisting, pulling, choking, more puffing and yelling, they managed to force him down onto the floor and snap the cuffs on him. So far, as near as Bill could tell, no one had been injured, including the con. With two guys hanging on to each leg for dear life and with more panting and puffing, they started to half carry and half drag Pezzio to the front of the range.

However, they didn't make it far before one of the officers started screaming, causing the others to almost wet themselves. Someone, between gulps of air, yelled, "Jesus Christ, the asshole has Greg's finger in his mouth, and the bastard won't open up!"

Staff started yelling and pounding on Pezzio. While that was going on, Bill somehow managed to take a moment to glance up at the control. He spotted a control officer, and even though he likely wouldn't be able to use it, the officer was standing there with a rifle all set to go. Later, once he had time to think about it, Bill felt sorry for both control officers. They were up there locked in, watching Greg being injured and listening to the screaming and the staff yelling and pounding the con, and they could only stand there clutching a rifle and watch.

After what seemed like 10 minutes to the staff but actually was only a few seconds, one of the officers who was struggling with a leg swung his fist into Pezzio's crotch area, at which time Pezzio let loose a bloodcurdling scream. Once he finished screaming, all the fight appeared to evaporate out of him. He kept saying through his tears, "Oh, you bastards. Oh, you bastards. You fuckers all fight dirty!"

At any rate, staff continued lugging him up to the front and handed him over to several other staff who had stormed into the unit. Away went Pezzio to the hole, where Bill hoped he'd stay for several years to rot. *Well,* he thought, *there is no harm in dreaming! Jeez, not even a full day in J unit, and I'll be filling out reports for a bloody hour. Hope it's not a sign of things to come.*

Once things settled down and Greg was off to the institutional hospital, Bill filled out the relevant reports and had them taken up to the sergeant's office. The inmates still had to be counted, fed and released for work, so Bill, after thanking the staff, sarcastically said, "We'd better get back to work. You guys know that above all, the bloody routine must continue at all costs."

That ended Bill's first day in J unit. It could have been much worse, though. Greg's finger had been chewed up a bit, but it wasn't broken, and the injury gave him some time off. No one else had been injured, including Pezzio (at times, to staff, that seemed to be management's major concern), and Bill was also informed that the situation had been handled correctly. So all in all, it had been a successful shift, and he was a day closer to retirement.

Chapter 4

Shipley had been in J unit for a week now and had been a cleaner for almost that long. He still wasn't a happy camper. His stomach was in knots almost all the time, and any unusual noise caused him to give a little jerk. But there was no way he would admit to himself or to others that the place scared the crap out of him. He knew he had to keep showing everyone how tough he was.

He hadn't made any friends either—not that anyone really ever did in those places. He knew enough not to get overly friendly, and he was careful about not borrowing anything from anyone. He wasn't the brightest light in the chandelier, but he knew enough not to get into debt. He'd already watched an inmate get badly beaten because he was in debt to a couple of the heavies. He didn't know how much the guy owed, but he'd heard the debt was two cartons of smokes. True or not, it didn't really matter; the guy was in the hospital for a few days and then put into protective custody at another institution. The guy was likely just sitting there hoping to get his teeth fixed, and Shipley had been around long enough to know that getting classified as protective custody, commonly called PC, was about the worst thing that could happen to any inmate. *Christ, that's where they send the baby killers, cops, guards and every other kind of goof there is.* Just thinking about it made his stomach quiver even more than normal.

Once again, another Monday rolled around. The inmates finished breakfast and dropped their meal trays off at the servery on their way out to work. Nonworking inmates were locked back into their cells, and the cleaners started their daily grind. It wasn't as if they were overworked. It didn't take a lot of effort or mentality to push a broom and swing a mop, but the cleaners were out doing their work such as it was.

As usual, Shipley started his cleaning job at the appropriate time. But also as usual, before starting work, he hung around the servery while he had a coffee and chatted with the inmates working there. He also made a point of watching the trays being returned, washed and stacked into the food carts. He was doing his best to get to know the workers by chatting them up but wasn't having a lot of success. He was finding out that it was a little difficult to get chummy with fellow inmates in a federal joint. But he also realized he was going to have to keep at it. So far, hiding in a food cart seemed the only possible way to get out of the place.

After a couple of hours, Shipley had worked his way around to the office area, and as usual, he asked permission from the officer at the desk to come in and start cleaning.

The guard looked up from what he was doing and said, "Sure, come on in. Not much going on this morning anyway." Little did he know that situation was going to change shortly.

Shipley came into the office, took another look at the guard and said, "You're Richards. You picked us up when we first came in. You said you worked in A unit. You over here now?"

Bill looked up and replied, "Well, good morning to you too. Yep, that was me. I remember you were there with four other newcomers. I was transferred over here for whatever reason; in fact, it's my first day. How you doing? All settled in?"

"Oh yeah, didn't take too long; I expected to end up here anyway. I'm doing eight years and a bit, so it was bound to happen."

"Well, it's not too bad in this place. I imagine they've mentioned that you can get to a medium by just doing your job and staying out of trouble."

"Yep, that's been driven into my head several times. Easy to say, but I'll do my best."

"Hope so; the fewer problems we have, the better we like it. Anyway, remember, when there's a problem, the inmate pretty well always comes out on the losing end of the stick, eh?" With that bit of advice, Bill looked down to his desk and went back to work.

Shipley threw a dirty look that Richards couldn't see and went back to his cleaning. He finished the office and continued on to the common room. He had just finished, when staff rattled the cell doors to signal that everyone was on his way back from the shops and that it was time for the noon count.

Shipley headed for his cell, thinking, *Christ, it's about time; I'm starving.*

He was sitting on his bed, contemplating life, when, shortly after the doors slammed shut, he heard what he thought was the officer coming down the range to do the count. For some odd reason, he stood up to look out the little window and spotted Richards walking down the range. *Strange. The boss doesn't usually count us poor slobs, and he's not looking into any cells anyway. What the hell's going on?* Shipley became a little more alert and tried to hear what was happening. Listening carefully, he heard a couple of different voices carrying on a conversation at the end of the range. Inmates hated any break in their routine, and two people, including the unit boss, carrying on a conversation during count time was a big break in routine.

Suddenly, the conversation stopped, and Shipley heard footsteps coming his way. He stood at the window, staring out onto the range. Within a few seconds, he spotted Richards stalking past the cell door and looking pissed at something. Shortly after Richards was out of sight, except for some murmuring, everything was quiet for a few minutes, and then Shipley could hear Richards giving instructions. Unfortunately, except for a few words, such as *mace, jump* and *hole*, he couldn't tell what was going on, but there was no doubt something was in the air.

Shipley continued standing at the window with his nose pressed up against the glass, and within a short time, he spotted several staff hustling past his cell and heading for the end of the range.

Because the window was so small and the door was solid steel, he could see only four or five feet on each side. That was one of drawbacks of the solid doors. The cell doors at several institutions were made of vertical bars, and because the doors were inset a foot or so, most inmates had small mirrors glued to the end of sticks. If an inmate wanted to see what was happening on the range, he simply stuck the mirror out between the bars and had a clear view. But not at the Mount; it was difficult to stick anything through solid steel, so they had to depend on their ears and imaginations. At times, imaginations could run wild.

Shipley remained at the window, trying to hear what was going on. Everything was more or less quiet for a few minutes, and then he heard Richards let out a yell. Then, immediately, he could hear different voices yelling.

"I got him!"

"He's down!"

"Christ, grab that leg. Hold his arm so I can get the cuffs on the shithead; watch he doesn't head-butt you."

Then, for a short time, everything was more or less quiet, except for the sound of people shuffling around. Then more yelling started up, and suddenly, someone began screaming.

Shipley's first thought was *Jesus Christ, the pigs are beating someone up. Can't be a fire, 'cause there's no smoke, so they must be laying a beating on one of us. God, I hate those bastards; they really think they're something!*

Just as he was processing the realization, the banging started. Inmates started kicking and pounding on their cell doors while screaming and threatening to kill every pig they could get their hands on as soon as they got out. The noise was deafening. It almost drowned out the screaming.

Shipley stood quivering at his door, staring out the window, scared and almost in shock. He was positive that at least one person was being killed. He couldn't believe the noise and was sure he was in the middle of a riot. Suddenly, a piercing scream that didn't sound human emanated from the range. Shipley gave a jerk just as several staff, panting and puffing, struggled into view, lugging an inmate. As Shipley watched, one officer bent over and grabbed the inmate's leg, which had been dragging on the floor, while he screamed, "Keep going! He's let the finger go, and I've got the leg again!"

At the same time, Shipley heard the inmate say, "Oh, you bastards. Oh, you bastards."

Vern Thibedeau

The inmate mumbled something else, but Shipley couldn't make it out. But he knew the inmate had been beaten up. *Jesus Christ, these people work just like the cops out on the street: "I don't like you, so I'm going to put cuffs on you, kick the shit out of you and then take you to jail."* Luckily, things like that had never happened to him, but he'd heard the stories and knew they were bloody well true. *Boy*, he thought, *you just can't trust anyone. Stupid me. I thought Richards might be OK, but he's just another goddamned screw!*

Once the staff and the inmate were off the range, it only took a couple of minutes for things to quiet down and get back to normal, or at least what was normal for a prison. Within a short time, an officer was on the range, taking the count, which was soon verified. Inmates were then allowed out one range at a time to pick up their noon meal, and within an hour or so, they were on their way back to work. It appeared as if nothing unusual had happened at all. And really, if a person reflected on the environment, the incident hadn't been all that unusual.

In the middle of the afternoon, Shipley had just finished cleaning the common room and decided to have a coffee break. He was sitting at a table relaxing, or trying to relax, which was difficult because he couldn't get the shemozzle that had happened on the range out of his mind, when an inmate who lived on same range sat down at the table. Patterson gave Shipley a sour look and said, "Boy, wasn't that a screwed-up mess this morning? Those pigs just maced Pezzio and then beat him down and snapped the cuffs on him for no reason at all. The bastards just enjoy beating us up."

Shipley looked over at Patterson and replied, "Jesus, I know. The buggers lugged him right past my cell as if he were a slab of beef or something. What the hell did they treat him like that for?"

"You never know what the assholes are gonna do. I saw one of them drive his fist into Pezzio's balls for no reason. One of the guys told me he was just standing at the end of the range and couldn't get into his cell because the pigs had closed the door on him. Then they stormed down, used the gas and pounded the shit out of him. Then, when the pigs were done with that, they lugged him off to the hole and charged him! Oh yeah, they're just a bunch of bastards."

"Well, I gotta get back to work, or they'll be kicking the shit out of me and throwing me in the hole. Talk to you later, eh?" With that bit of wisdom, Shipley grabbed his mop and left the area.

A few days later, after the supper meal, Shipley was out in the yard, walking around, thinking about the food carts and still trying to figure out a way to use them to get the hell out. He'd discovered that it wasn't feasible to tunnel out, because the fencing didn't end at ground level. Apparently, it was buried several feet down. He also knew he couldn't climb over both fences because of the height and the coils of razor wire that ran along the top of the fences. And, of course, who could ignore the armed guards in the towers? He'd found out several days ago that the guards in the towers and controls had .38-caliber revolvers, plus high-velocity semiautomatic rifles. A couple of inmates told him they thought they were AR-15s.

Shipley was just strolling along, minding his own business and dreaming of his great escape, when he accidentally bumped into the back of another inmate, who was standing and chatting with a few of his buddies. With a jerk, Shipley looked up and saw four tough-looking guys who were covered with tattoos, had shaved heads and were big enough to make him feel small. At that same split second, he noticed the one he'd bumped into spin around, and then he felt his stomach explode in pain. As he went down, he was sure he'd been stabbed, but within a second or two, he realized the inmate had rammed an elbow into his belly.

Shipley just lay there on his back, moaning, trying to catch his breath and looking up at the inmates staring down at him.

"Hey, asshole," one of them snarled, "why the fuck did you punch me?"

Shipley couldn't even breathe, let alone grovel for his great error. All he could do was look up and watch them closing in around him. He also noticed they were looking around, and he had enough on the ball to know they were making sure they hadn't been spotted by the guard in the tower. He also knew damned well a lot of inmates carried weapons of one kind or another, and the chance of a guard realizing something was going on before it was too late was small. Shipley knew he was, at the least, going to receive a bad beating. He also realized that all he could do was hope he'd survive it. While his mind was processing that information, he watched one of them draw his foot back and felt a white-hot pain stab into his right leg and shoot up to his hip.

Shipley shuddered with the pain as he watched them look around while one reached under his shirt and muttered, "Ah, screw this; I'm gonna stick him."

Shipley felt another presence, and through a haze of pain, he heard a quiet voice say, "Hey, guys, what's going on? I think he's had enough of this shit, so back the hell off."

Shipley watched them spin around while the one pulled a shank out from under his shirt. He saw Dominic standing there staring at them. As soon as the gang saw who it was, they immediately relaxed, mumbled a few words and walked away.

"Jesus," Dominic said while he bent down to help Shipley up, "what the hell are you doing? You're going to get yourself killed, for God's sake."

By that time, Shipley was on his feet but still bent over and in a lot of pain, but he breathlessly managed to reply, "Jesus, all I did was bump into the big one, and you'd think I was trying to kill the bugger or something."

"Christ, man, I've told you that you have to keep your eyes open in these places and know where you are and what's going on around you all the time. That group you bumped into is part of a larger gang. They also think they have to prove how tough they are so the other cons will kowtow to them."

Shipley and Dominic strolled around the yard and chatted while Shipley got his breath back and tried to walk the pain off.

"God," Shipley said to Dominic, "I'll never get a handle on this place; I don't know if I'm coming or going. I gotta admit that I'm scared all the time. The damn cons are as bad as the pigs, if not worse. Hell, a few days ago, the guards beat up a guy at the end of the range for no reason at all—and I thought that asshole Richards was OK. Or at least OK for a guard, and then he went and pulled that stunt. And now a jerk's going to shank me because I bumped into him. This is fucking nuts!"

"If you're talking about that Pezzio thing that happened at the end of our range, he deserved everything he got. He refused to go into his cell, and apparently, for no reason, he does this every once in a while and then refuses to do anything except fight. He's kind of nuts, I guess. And this time, he chewed a guard's finger and wouldn't let it go until one of the guards punched him in the nuts. It's a wonder they didn't lay a real beating on him, but they didn't. If that'd happened to the group I hung around with on the street, he would've been lucky to just have his stupid throat cut. And it woulda looked good on him."

"Hell, I didn't know all that. I was just told they locked him out of his cell, came down the range, gassed him and then beat him up."

"I'll tell you once again, Mac: you believe nothing you hear in here and about half of what you see, and even then you'll likely just have part of the truth."

"God, I have to get out. There's no way I'll be able to do all my time. I've been looking at different ways, and there must be something I can do. I've even thought of hiding in the food carts when they go out."

"It's up to you, but your best bet is to do your time and get out free and clear or behave yourself, get to lower security and try it from there. There's been plenty of guys try to take off from here, and all they get is more time added on and a transfer to a special handling unit for a while. But like I say, it's up to you."

Chapter 5

Several boring months crawled by, and other than a few inmates getting transferred out and several new ones coming in, a few fights, one suicide and one inmate getting stabbed, nothing much happened. Shipley was even getting used to the place and could sleep almost a whole night through, even with the damned night light burning all the time.

Then, one night, he decided to go to the gym during the second changeover. He was striding down the corridor without a care in the world, when he felt an ominous presence behind him, and a low, menacing voice whispered, "Hey, punk, just wanna remind you that I ain't gonna forget how you came at me in the yard. When that wop buddy of yours gets out of here, you're going to have a shank up your ass. Just giving you fair warning of what's coming, you jerk-off."

Shipley whipped around, and there was the con who had put him down in the yard. He had learned that his name was Crothers, and he was the head of one of the gangs in the Mount. Shipley had also found out that he was dangerous, was a little crazy and likely would never get out of the place. He'd been sentenced to life several years ago, and so far, he had spent about half his time in the hole.

Shipley watched Crothers and one of his idiot buddies continue on toward the gym while he started to sweat and get shaky, and his stomach started its clenching all over again. He also realized he had to keep going to the gym because a couple of other inmates had overheard the conversation and were staring at him and shaking their heads. Shipley had been there long enough to know that he couldn't look like he was backing off. If that happened, he might as well go to the hole and put in for protection. He felt he would rather be dead than do something like that, but he also realized that being either dead or being a PC con was a distinct possibility.

Shipley shuffled into the gym, shakily eased his back up against a wall and stood there looking around. While he was looking around, he kept one eye on Crothers and his gang, hoping they wouldn't notice him. Shipley spotted Dominic glancing his way, and with a wave, Joe started through the crowd of inmates toward him.

"Hey, Mac, how's it going? Getting all settled into your new home?"

"Hi, Joe. Yep, starting to feel like I've always lived here. You doing OK?"

"Oh, you know how it is. I was talking to one of the guys, and he was telling me you had a run-in with Crothers just now. What the hell's he up to? Still giving you a hard time?"

"Oh yeah. Told me I'll be dead or worse within a few hours after you're out of here. Jesus, Joe, I don't know what to do, but if I'm still around and Crothers isn't dead, please let me know if you are going to get transferred out."

"I will, Mac; don't worry. But you know that's about all I can do for you. He sure as hell won't do anything while I'm here, but after that, who knows? Anyway, you'll likely be gone long before I go anywhere, and Crothers and his pack of idiots sure as hell won't be going anywhere. On another note"—Dominic quickly looked around to make sure no one was listening—"I can tell you're still thinking of trying to get out of here. Any plans other than that food cart thing?"

"Nothing else has popped up yet, Joe. I know I'd never get over those damned fences, and I can't go under because they're dug in too deep. About all I can do is keep thinking about it and, hopefully, come up with something. Besides, it keeps me from going crazy in this shit box."

"Here's a couple of ideas you could work on. Don't know how they'd ever work, but you never know. I'd think the easiest way would be to try to get a uniform, change the way you look and maybe just walk out with a shift change. The other thing is out in left field, but two guards go into the ducts each shift to check the area out. If you and a couple others could get down there, you could maybe whack them. You'd have to watch it, though, because one is always armed, and I've heard they're nervous going down, so they'd be wide awake. But if you did get them, one of you could put a uniform on and maybe sucker your way into that main control up front. Not sure what you'd do after that, though; guess you'd have to play it by ear. They aren't supposed to let anyone out of here, even if it's a hostage situation, but you never know. But I still think you'd be better off just doing your time."

Mac and Joe continued to chat while Shipley kept his eye on Crothers and his gang, and then Shipley said to Dominic, "Well, that's it for me. I'm going to head back to the range to see what's going on there. See you later, Joe."

"OK, Mac. Just take it easy, and watch your back. You'll be OK."

With that bit of advice in his ear, Shipley, feeling as if there were a hundred eyes boring into his back, headed out of the gym and back to his cell.

A few nights later, Shipley ran into a huge chunk of luck. During a changeover, one of the inmates he had become fairly friendly with invited him into his cell. In Shipley's mind, he eventually would become a very good friend, but the friendship was also going to lead to dire circumstances for Shipley. Shipley was aware that there was a strict policy of one inmate to a cell, but he had been invited in, so there wasn't really a hell of a lot he could do except slip in. As soon as he entered the cell, he spotted two other guys sitting with their backs against the wall, and his first thought was *Oh God, what now?* They were both situated so that if a guard glanced in, they wouldn't be seen, or at least they hoped they wouldn't be seen; the hole was not a comfortable spot, and that was where they would likely end up if they were spotted.

Shipley had just made it in, when the cell doors rattled and then slammed shut, signaling the end of changeover, which meant he was in that cell for at least 40 minutes or so. After seeing two other guys in there, Shipley was one scared con. As soon as the door slammed shut, Owen, who resided in that cell, waved Shipley over to the wall so he'd be out of sight of the door and said with a smirk, "Hey, buddy, wanna drink of brew? It turned out really good this time. In fact, I think it's the best fucking brew I've made yet. Hell, you don't even have to pay me for it. At least this time you don't."

"Holy Christ," Shipley replied. "You talked me into it. I've never had any brew in this place, but I'll tell you one thing: it smells damned good. Just get it done?"

"Yep, it finished during supper. We got a whole pail of it to get down. Now," Owen said with a laugh, "all we need are some real pretty dancers in here without their clothes on."

Owen was pretty much a typical inmate. There wasn't anything outstanding about him physically; he hardly ever worked out on the weights. He had a good family life. His main problem was that at a young age, he had become addicted to gambling. It didn't matter what the situation was; he could bet on it. His parents had done what they could, such as counselling and paying some of his debts off. But eventually, Owen had owed too much money and tried to pay it off by becoming involved in illegal activities. Naturally, that eventually had landed him in prison, with a five-and-a-half-year sentence.

Unfortunately, Owen's gambling habit was going to get him into serious trouble on the inside and also have dire consequences for Shipley.

Shipley accepted a mug of brew and was proud of himself. He managed to reach out, accept the mug, not spill a drop, take a sip and keep it down, and the other cons didn't even realize how hard he was shaking inside. He sat there with the three cons, shooting the shit, and had two more mugs of brew, and at every second, he expected the cell door to crash open, when the guards would rush in, cuff them and haul them to the hole. Or if that didn't happen, he was concerned his three buddies would jump him and do God knew what to him. But nothing happened, so he just relaxed and almost enjoyed himself.

The cons, as usual, were curious about how much time he was doing and what he had done to earn the time. Shipley gave them a rough idea of his great robbery. Of course, according to Shipley, it had been an armed robbery, and the old guy he'd knocked down while running out suddenly became much younger and had attempted to stop him from leaving, so he'd had to pull his gun on the idiot and whack him over the head. "Hell," he said to end his great story, "I could've shot him!"

Vern Thibedeau

Just before the cell doors were due to open, Shipley thanked Owen for the drinks and told him he didn't want to drink all his booze and thought he had better head back to his cell. "Christ, that's good booze, but I'd better take off. See you all in the morning." Shipley didn't know it then, but he wouldn't see them in the morning; in fact, it would be several days before he saw them again.

The door slid open. Shipley waited until there were several inmates on the range between the cell and the control, and with a wave to his new buddies, he slipped out onto the range and, with a little stagger, headed back to his cell. Shipley staggered a couple of times, but he made it back without a problem. He walked in, flopped onto his bed and didn't intend to get off it until morning.

Shipley lay on the bed, daydreaming and thinking about his life, and half dozed off. He was aware of the cell doors shutting, and a short time later, someone looked in his window and then walked past his cell. Without opening his eyes, he knew it was a guard doing his patrol and checking the cells, so he never gave it another thought. A few moments later, though, he heard the same footsteps returning and hazily thought, *Jeez, that was a fast trip; he couldn't have made it to the end of the range that quickly. What the hell's going on now?*

A few minutes later, Shipley, who was now a little more alert, heard several footsteps coming back his way. He stood up and looked out his little window, and a whole pack of guards rushed past his cell and continued on down the range. *Oh Christ, I bet that prick looked into Owen's cell and saw the guys in there. Glad I took off. Hope to hell no one rats me out.*

Shipley stood at his door, listening and trying to see whatever he could. After several minutes of listening to a lot of back-and-forth discussion and the odd yell, he watched his three newfound buddies being marched past his cell. As soon as he saw them in handcuffs, he knew they were on their way to the hole. Owen glanced toward Shipley's cell and gave him a little grin, and then they were gone. *Oh my God, am I ever glad I took off when I did.*

Owen wasn't a bad person, at least not compared to several inmates locked up at Mountainview.

Chapter 6

Several weeks passed, and one evening, after the count came in, Shipley decided to go to a common room and have a coffee and a couple of smokes before going back to his cell to watch TV. He'd just gotten settled in with a coffee and gotten a smoke going, when he spotted Bentley, who lived in the cell beside him, coming in. He hoped he'd sit somewhere else, but instead, Bentley gave him the eye and headed toward him. So Shipley, pretending to have just seen him, threw him a wave and said, "Hey, how ya doing? Come on over, and grab a seat." By then, Shipley had been at Mountainview for more than six months, and he felt like an old pro.

Bentley came over, flopped down and said, "Hey, neighbour, how they hanging?"

"Oh, you know, same old, same old. Nothing much changes around this place. You doing OK?"

"Ah, not really; things are a bit rough right now. Thought I'd give that goddamn parole board another try; naturally, the pricks turned me down. But I guess it's about what I expected. The case-management slug didn't even want me to try for another six months, so I guess the old bugger was right after all. And then, as if that wasn't a big enough hit, I had a letter from my wife today, and with it, I got divorce papers. She says she doesn't give a shit if I sign them or not, because she isn't coming back in again, and what's more, she's taking off with the kid. She also told me I'll never see either one of them again."

"Jesus, Larry, that's rough. I haven't even tried to get to a medium pen yet, let alone a parole. What happened with your wife? You were always carrying on about her and how she was going to wait for you. So now she just up and leaves? Christ, man, I'm sorry to hear that."

"Ah, I don't know what the hell I'm gonna do. I borrowed some dope a while ago and then tried to win more by playing cards and lost everything. So now I owe twice as much. And they said they want it all back, or else. And I don't have dick-all to give them. My so-called wife was in for a visit the other day, and I asked her to buy some dope, put it in the kid's diaper, come in for a visit and pass it over to me. Jesus Christ, she got herself all huffy, told me to go screw myself and took off. Now I don't know what the hell I'm gonna do. I did everything for that bitch and now she shafts me."

Mac and Larry talked over their problems until the doors opened up, and then they started back to their cells for the night. Bentley went on about his problems during the few minutes it took to reach their cells, and Shipley mostly grunted in agreement, but he was thinking, *Jesus, I wouldn't wanna be in his shoes. Christ, that's tough; thank God it's him and not me. Christ, I don't wanna listen to him yap on and on about it all day tomorrow.*

Sometime around two in the morning, Shipley sensed, rather than heard, the guard pass his cell on his regular patrol. Suddenly, he heard him yell out, "Oh shit!" and start running back toward the control. He also heard him call on his radio to get some extra staff and medical to 1K right away.

Shipley jumped over to his window and tried to see what was going on. Within a few seconds, he could hear guards running back toward him, and just as they reached his cell, he heard one yell at the control, "Open K15!"

Holy Christ, that's Bentley's cell. What the hell's going on? He must be sick or something. Just as they rushed past his cell, he heard Bentley's door slide open. Then he spotted the nurse running past and heard her go into Bentley's cell and order the staff to stand back so she could check his signs.

After a minute or so of quiet, Shipley heard the nurse tell the staff it was too late, and there was nothing she could do for him. By that time, the sergeant was close enough to the cell to hear the nurse's comment, and Shipley saw him take a quick glance into the cell and heard him agree with the nurse by saying, "You're right about that; we're too late again. Damn! I'll make a few phone calls to let them know we have a hanger, and the police will likely be in with the wagon shortly. You make your calls, and I guess that's about it, except for someone from region coming in in a few days or so to do their investigation."

Then the sergeant, throwing a looks toward Richards, said, "Hey, Bill, make sure the cell door stays closed until the police and the wagon get here, and when they do show up, I'll have them escorted down. It shouldn't take me long to do my phoning, and I'll be back down. In any case, make sure your guys complete their walks; you just never know."

Shipley was almost in shock and flopped back onto his bed. *God, we were just talking. I can't believe he was that messed up; I should've paid more attention to what he was saying, and maybe I could've talked him out of it. Christ, it's these damned nuthouses; there should be a law against them.*

Shipley would never have admitted it, being a tough con and all, but he felt a little like crying. Once he managed to doze off, those damned vultures once again returned with their screeching and hungry looks.

* * *

Richards was beginning to think working J unit wasn't that bad after all. Naturally, they'd had a few problems, but nothing that couldn't be handled, at least not yet anyway. Unfortunately, Bill was going to have a major problem on his third morning shift, which was called midnight shift on normal jobs; he just didn't realize it yet. But at least his first two mornings had been relatively quiet.

Bill pulled into the parking lot for his third morning shift, did his usual quick look at the flag and checked out the parking lot. All looked OK. He headed in to work. With a yawn, he gave the sergeant his usual wave and continued on to J unit. Richards relieved the other corporal, and when his two guys reported in to the unit, he informed them there was nothing special going on, so as far as he knew, they just had to do the regular walks and counts.

Bill and his two staff carried out their normal duties and had a chat with the sergeant on his trip into the unit, and other than that, it was an uneventful shift, at least up until the two o'clock walk. The three staff were sitting and having a coffee, trying to stay awake, when Richards said, "Christ, it's almost two. You'd better get the ranges done and make sure they're all still here and alive."

With that bit of instruction, the two staff headed out to check their assigned ranges. Bill, as was his usual practice, gave them a few minutes and then started out of the office to check the one range he usually walked. He had just reached the office door, when he heard Tom yell at the control to get some extra staff and the nurse. Tom reached the office and excitedly yelled to Richards, "We've got a hanger in K15, and he's not moving!"

"Oh crap. Let's get down there; maybe we can still do something for him!" As Bill started down the range, he took a moment to glance up at the control to make sure they knew what was going on and received a wave of acknowledgment. His stomach, even though he had been involved with a few suicides, started bouncing around, and he knew he was in for a rough night.

As soon as they reached the cell, Bill took a quick look inside. He spotted the inmate against the far wall with a cord around his neck and his feet sticking out in front of him. After that one look, he gave the control a wave to open the door, and the staff stormed in. He took a quick glance around to make sure no one else was in the cell and rushed toward the inmate. By that time, he remembered the guy's name was Bentley, and the few dealings he'd had with him flashed through his mind, but he couldn't think of anything that would've been a clue that the con was having problems.

Bill was the first officer to reach Bentley, so it was his job to cut him down. As he started cutting the boot lace, Bill knew Bentley was dead. He had seen enough hangers to know. The thought flashed through his mind that whatever had been bothering him wouldn't be bothering him any longer. By the time he'd cut the boot lace and they'd lowered Bentley to the floor, the nurse had reached the cell and rushed in.

The nurse, in a clipped, professional voice, ordered the staff back so she could check Bentley for any signs. Richards glanced her way and said, "I hope you find some, but I'm pretty sure we're too late." Then he looked at the staff as he said, "You guys might as well step out of the cell, but try not to touch anything on your way out. The cops will be in shortly, and they'll want everything left as it is."

The staff had just cleared out of the cell, when the officer in charge of the institution reached the area and stopped in front of the cell. The nurse looked at him and reiterated that there was nothing they could do for the inmate.

The nurse headed out of the cell, and when she reached the sergeant, he looked at her and said, "You're right about that; we're too late again. Damn! I'll make a few phone calls to let them know we have a hanger, and the police will likely be in with the wagon shortly. You make your calls, and I guess that's about it, except for someone from region coming in in a few days or so to do their investigation."

Then the sergeant said with a harried look, "Hey, Bill, make sure the cell stays closed until the pen squad"—the police—"and the coroner get here, and when they do show up, I'll have them escorted down. It shouldn't take me long to do my phoning, and I'll be back down shortly. In any case, make sure your guys complete their walks; you just never know." With a wave to the staff, he was off.

Bill waved to the control to close the cell door, and the staff headed back toward the office. On their way back, Bill said to the staff, "That was good work, guys. The inmate was spotted as soon as possible, we were less than a minute in getting to him and the nurse made excellent time. You'd better go ahead and finish your walk, and when you get back to the office, fill out your reports. And for Christ's sake, don't leave anything out, especially if you have any idea why he topped himself."

That was the end of anything unusual happening for the rest of the morning shift. For that, Bill was happy. He figured one suicide on his shift was enough. Bill also figured that once he got home, even though it was early morning, he might have a drink before climbing into bed.

Chapter 7

A couple of weeks passed, and things settled down. Heck, one would never have known anything had happened. Another inmate was in Bentley's cell—the cells didn't stay empty for long. The staff had handed in their reports, the police had completed their investigation and eventually an inquest would be held, but for now, everything was back to the daily grind.

Bill was back on the day shift and was standing out in N area with the other staff, watching the inmates come back from work for their lunch. He was chatting with one of the guys working for him in the unit and noticed inmate Johnston come through the barrier. Johnston gave Bill a quick look and a slight shake of his head. Bill sent back a short nod and carried on his conversation with the officer as if nothing had occurred. Except for Bill and Johnston, nothing unusual had occurred. But as the staff headed back into the unit to do the count, he thought, *Christ, now what? Johnston's a good informant, but like all of them, he's usually out for himself; on the other hand, he's given me a lot of good info. I guess just to cover my ass, I'd better arrange a trip to the hospital for him, even if it means more problems. Shit, as if I don't have enough to worry about.*

Bill had worked in prisons long enough and had enough dealings with informants to realize staff had to be careful when dealing with them. The most important reason, especially for the inmate, was that it was dangerous for an inmate to be seen whispering into an officer's ear. If other inmates thought one of their own was, in prison terminology, a rat, he'd better get into protection because he would likely be seriously injured or dead in short order. Secondly, most inmate informants, even when their information was good, were usually out to further their own agenda. However, Bill and most of the other staff realized that just like police officers on the street, they would have been in a difficult position without informants.

After thinking about it for a while, Bill decided to interview Johnston in the hospital. He trusted his staff explicitly, but in prisons, there was a lot of time for staff to sit around and chat with one another, and inmates loved to listen in on those chats. Hell, inmates usually knew more about what was going on on the inside than the guards ever did. But he knew he had to see Johnston. He'd given him good information in the past, and he could know something important; one never knew.

During the lunch hour, Bill made arrangements to have a relief come into the unit for him for a half hour or so. He also instructed one of his officers to inform Johnston while taking the count on 1k that the nurse wanted to see him in the hospital before he went back to work.

Just before workup was called, Bill headed for the hospital. Once there, he approached the guard posted to the area and said, "Hey, Joe, a con by the name of Johnston's coming to see the nurse; just send him down to number-eight cell."

Bill made sure the head nurse knew he was going to be in number eight to interview an inmate, went in, moved a chair to make sure he couldn't be seen from the corridor and waited for Johnston to show up.

Within a few minutes, Johnston entered the room, and with a wave at the other chair, Bill said, "Hey, how's it going? I assume that with you taking a chance like this, it must be important."

"It is, and I don't need payback this time. I thought I'd fill you in on this, even though you're kind of new to the unit. Your other buddies don't seem too concerned about things, and I don't want the unit locked down because some idiot goes and gets himself killed."

"Well, that sounds rather important, and I agree with you; I really don't want anyone killed either. Are we talking staff or inmate?"

"Oh, as far as I know, it's one inmate that Crothers and his bunch of assholes are after."

"Damn. That prick's at it again, is he? The shit just never stops. We'd love to get enough on him to ship him out to the special handling unit."

"Well, I don't know if this'll help, but they're gonna either put a guy in the hospital or kill him, and he's not really a bad guy, just kind of stupid. We really don't need all the crap that goes on after something like—"

"Well," Richards said, interrupting, "let's be honest here. I would guess your range doesn't want to be locked down and searched over the course of a few days. In any case, we'd better get at it. I don't want to keep you here too long; it wouldn't look good."

"Yeah, OK. You know Shipley on 1K? Well, he got into a beef a while back with Crothers and his bunch, and Crothers was going to put the word out to dump him. The only thing that saved Shipley's ass was Dominic. He's got a lot of respect in here. But it looks like things on the street are getting a little dicey for the crowd Dominic works for. I really don't know what's going on out there, except a few of them have gone missing or have been found tits up. In any case, Crothers is feeling braver, and I heard talk they're gonna go after this Shipley guy."

"Jesus, I do know Shipley, and he wouldn't stand a chance. Actually, not many in here would, except maybe for the bikers. Do you have any guesses on the timeline here? Don't wanna jump the gun and put the poor bugger into PC if we don't have to."

"Na, no clue. I do know it won't happen for a while. Everyone still has a lot of respect for Dominic. You guys have no idea how many problems that guy has saved you. In any case, if I hear anything about it going down, I'll give one of you a heads-up."

"OK. Look, I'm not going to let this thing die. I'll have to have a chat with the IPSO, and if you hear anything else, get a message to me. Either send a note, or if you want a meeting, I'll arrange one. That sound OK with you?"

"Yep, sounds fair. Oh, one other thing before I take off. If I remember correctly, you were on when Bentley topped himself, right? Anyway, part of his problem was that he owed Crothers for some dope. He couldn't pay him back, so he tried some gambling and lost big time. He'd been told to pay up but didn't have anything to pay his debt with. I imagine the poor fuck was likely at the end of his rope in more ways than one. Well, I'd better get to work. Talk to you later."

With the conclusion of the discussion, Johnston closed the door on his way out, and Bill, after waiting for a few minutes, headed back to the unit. On his way back, he pondered the problem that had been dumped into his lap.

He knew he couldn't ignore it. If he did and something happened, it would only take a short time for Johnston to let management know he'd told Richards all about it, and then there'd be hell to pay, never mind about Shipley being injured or dead.

Bill had been around this business long enough to know he and Johnston were not buddies, and regardless of what he said, one way or another, Johnston would probably come out ahead in the mess. On the other hand, an inmate couldn't just be scooped up and dumped into protective custody because some other inmate said he was going to be killed. Hell, if that had happened, the PC joint would have been full, and a bunch of pissed-off do-gooders would have been swarming all over the place.

But there was no getting around it; this was serious. If an inmate would rather top himself than take on Crothers, then Crothers was a lot more dangerous than they realized. *Christ, why couldn't Bentley have come to me and gotten locked up? There must have been more to his problems than just Crothers.*

During the rest of the week, Bill had a couple of meetings with Jordon McDonald, the institutional preventative security officer, to discuss the situation. He was happy to do so because it took the responsibility, if something did happen, off his shoulders, or at least someone else would have to help him wear it. But there really wasn't a lot they could do. So they decided to try to keep an eye on things, and Bill was to attempt to get to know Shipley a little better. Maybe if they chatted a bit, Shipley would open up to him a little.

They also decided the IPSO should be the one to inform the other corporals in J unit about the problem. They thought if the IPSO did the explaining, the corporals would realize the situation could be serious, and there would be less chance of them babbling about it in the unit. So that was the plan, such as it was—that and keeping their fingers crossed.

The following week, Bill finally had an opportunity to have a reasonably private chat with Shipley. Shipley came into the office to do his cleaning, and since no one else was around, Bill grabbed his chance. He started the chat with "Hey, how you doing? Looks like you're surviving this place all right."

"Oh yeah. At least I'm still alive."

"Listen, I know you hung around with Bentley a little; that was really tough what he did. I'm not sure what all was going on with him, but I do know he owed drugs and some money to Crothers. I was thinking that likely had something to do with it. I was told he had to pay up or else."

When Shipley heard that bit of news, he gave a little jerk. He couldn't help thinking about his own beef with Crothers and what Crothers had said to him. "Oh, I don't know anything about that. He just told me his wife was going to leave him, and I figured that was the reason. Jeez, owing anything to Crothers is a real screw-up."

"You said a mouthful there. I've heard a rumour that you've had a run-in with Crothers yourself. Is that true?"

"Oh, it wasn't a big deal, just a little misunderstanding. I think it's all straightened out now. I'm not worried about anything."

"Don't you screw around here; you know what he's like. I've also noticed you and Dominic do a lot of chatting. Dominic is an OK guy, but I think he's also about to have a problem in here. He just doesn't have the power he used to have, and we're worried either he or someone else is going to end up in the hospital, dead or at least locked up. I just want to give you a heads-up and to tell you not to get involved with this crap. It's much better being locked up than dead."

By then, Shipley was almost shaking, but he just said, "Nah, I'm all right. I stay quiet, do my time and don't get in nobody's way, and they leave me alone. I gotta get going. Gotta finish my work, and I start in the servery tomorrow." With that, Shipley abruptly left the office.

* * *

Shipley was getting antsy. He'd just picked up his food tray and was heading into a common room to eat, when suddenly, he could feel someone staring at his back. Nonchalantly, after sitting down and starting to eat, he managed to sneak a look behind him and spotted a couple of Crothers's buddies giving him the eye. Shipley didn't know what was going on, but he had felt a change toward him from the Crothers crew over the last few weeks. Now, after his chat with Richards, he was really nervous; in fact, he was downright scared, almost terrified. He'd seen what cons could do to someone, and they seemed to get away with it in most cases. His thoughts slipped back to few weeks ago, when he was in the yard.

He'd heard some guys were out to get an inmate from A unit, but he hadn't thought too much about it. Heck, it didn't affect him, and there was always talk about someone out to get somebody, so after a while, he just sort of ignored the yapping.

During that particular evening, Shipley was just strolling around, talking to an inmate from his range, when they saw five or six inmates in a circle and one inmate in the middle of them, who looked terrified. There was some pushing and a bit of hitting, but then Shipley spotted one of the inmates holding a short iron bar. He said to his buddy, "We'd better turn the hell around and walk the other way. I don't think we wanna see what's gonna happen, and the less we see, the better off we are."

Just as they turned around and started walking in the opposite direction, they heard some yelling and a muffled scream.

The long and short of it was that the inmate in the middle had ratted out a con, or at least they thought he was the one who had. There really wasn't any requirement for proof in prison. The inmate they thought was a rat had one of his knees shattered. The iron bar was found, and an investigation was completed, but staff never did find out who was involved.

Shipley knew there was nothing Crothers or his idiots could do at the moment. In maximum, there were armed guards all over the place. In fact, there were two of them slouching around in the control, staring at them right now. Shipley had to admit he was damned glad they were there. He also figured he'd better talk to Dominic during recreation to find out what the hell was going on. All he could do was hope that Dominic went out to the yard after the count and that nothing happened before he could talk to him, and hopefully, Dominic could fill him in on what was going on.

It took two days before Shipley managed to track Dominic down. It seemed if he went to the yard looking for Dominic, Dominic went to the gym. If Shipley went to the gym, Dominic either stayed in his cell or hung out in a common room. It was starting to seem like Shipley didn't have any luck at all, or Dominic was avoiding him. But why would he have done that?

Eventually, Shipley finally caught up to him in the yard. When he spotted Dominic, he noticed he was just standing in a corner with his back against a wall, looking around while he had a smoke. Shipley strolled up to him and, while lighting a cigarette, said, "Hey, Joe, how you doing? Haven't seen you for a while. I was beginning to think you'd been transferred out or something."

"Oh no, still here. It's such a grand place to live that I'd hate to have to leave. You doing OK, Mac?"

"Oh, I guess. Just the same old, same old. I'm worried about Crothers and his asshole idiots, though. A couple of the guys have whispered to me that I'd better watch my back because the buggers are after me. I must admit that shook me up a little bit; in fact, every time I hear a loud noise, I almost piss myself. Hey, Joe, you're the only one I've said that to, so please don't let it get around."

"Nah, don't worry about that. I was going to tell you to watch your back. There's some crap going on outside that will likely cause both of us some grief if it doesn't switch around. Apparently, the guys I did some work for are in a takeover fight with another family, and it looks like my side, at least at the present time, may be on the losing end of the shit stick. They've already found a couple of bodies of guys I know, and they didn't go pleasantly. To be honest, I'm not sure what the hell is going on. I'll tell you one thing, though: I'm not going anywhere without a weapon!" With that statement, Dominic tapped his side, and Shipley realized he had a shank or some other weapon under his shirt. "I'll tell you one more thing. If my side loses, we're both in a tough spot. You'll either have to go PC or complete that escape plan you're working on. If it works and you get out, good for you; if you get caught, you'll be sent to the SHU, and you'll still be better off. At least you'll be away from these assholes."

Shipley and Dominic chatted for a while. Both made sure they kept their backs to the wall, and they watched the other inmates in the yard as they wandered around in their little groups. Shipley glanced up at the tower once in a while but knew the guard wouldn't be able to help them if something did happen. *Christ,* Shipley thought, *if we do get jumped, it'll be over before the guard can get his rifle up. That is, if the bugger's even awake—who the hell knows? On top of that, if there were enough cons involved, the tower guy probably wouldn't see anything go down anyway.*

As soon as changeover was called, he told Dominic he was going to head back in and said, "See you later, Joe," as he was on his way toward the barrier. As he trudged up to his unit, all Shipley could think about was his great escape. For a heavy price, he'd talked Jacob, one of the guys who worked in the servery with him, into giving him a hand, and now he was suddenly in a rush to get the plan going. He knew damn well he had to get the hell out quickly, or he'd never get out except in a box.

Chapter 8

Shipley reported for work in the servery the following morning. The food steward showed him what had to be done for the day, and it wasn't much different from what had been done the day before. *Now I just have to find out how Jacob and I can be left alone in this place, so we can get the trays cut out.* But even with the food-tray escape uppermost in his mind, he couldn't help thinking about the information Dominic had given him about staff checking the ducts at night. He had tried to get more information regarding the ducts but had had little or no luck. He had found out only that checks usually took place once during the night shift and once during the morning shift.

Several days after Shipley started working in the servery, he was lounging around in a common room during the evening, when the guard in the control yelled at him that he was wanted in N area.

Once he made it to N area, naturally not in a rush, the corporal in charge of the place pointed to a pile of broken cardboard boxes and some old clothes and told him to get a dolly and take the crap to the garbage room.

Just as he made it back to N area, he spotted two of the officers who were working in N area entering N control. Once they were in the control, he watched one reach down below one of the windows and come up with a firearm. Shipley wasn't an expert with firearms, but he knew damn well that one wasn't a rifle. It was a 12-gauge shot gun! Then the two guards headed for the stairwell and disappeared.

No one had to kick Shipley in the head for him to realize the two guards were on their way to check the ducts out. Once he spotted the 12-gauge going down the stairs with them, he immediately dropped any idea of using that area for an escape. He figured a rifle might miss one or more shots, but he didn't think there was any way in hell a shotgun could miss, not even if a guard tried. So back to the old food-tray escape.

Chapter 9

A couple of weekends later, Shipley was pacing around in a common room, waiting for his visitor to show up. Shipley and his girlfriend, Jennifer, had made arrangements for her to come in for a visit in the afternoon. Their visits had to be in the afternoon because she had to come by bus, and it was a long three-hour ride. And of course, there was also the cost of the bus ticket.

While Shipley paced around, he couldn't help thinking about Jennifer, how they'd met and how much she meant to him. He still remembered sitting in the coffee shop that sunny afternoon almost three years ago and seeing a lovely young lady sitting at the table next to his. He tried to keep his eyes off her but knew he had failed when she looked his way and gave him a smile before looking back down at the magazine she was reading. When he saw that smile directed toward him, he felt his heart give a little lurch, and he knew he had to meet her.

It took some fumbling around, and Shipley felt he was making a fool of himself, but somehow, they ended up sitting at the same table and chatting with each other. And that was all it took; Shipley was smitten by the lovely girl with the deep, expressive brown eyes and especially her bright, sexy smile.

During their discussion, Shipley discovered that Jennifer was a couple of years younger than he was and that she still lived with her parents. She also told Shipley she was working at a grocery store but was looking for another job that paid a little more money. However, she was also debating, at her mother and father's insistence, going back to school.

Shipley felt a little ashamed when he mentioned to Jen that he wasn't working or going to school. But he made sure to mention, even though it wasn't really true, that he was looking for a job and had a lead on a good one.

Over time, Jennifer and Shipley frequently met at a mall and at a park in the area. They enjoyed each other's company. Naturally, the little meetings worked into several dates and eventually to his meeting Jennifer's parents. However, that did not go well. In fact, once her parents realized he wasn't working, going to school or very ambitious, they had a difficult time speaking to him. Actually, they weren't even comfortable looking at him.

Later, Jennifer tried to explain to Shipley that they were just concerned about her, and it wasn't really that they didn't like him. "Don't forget," she told him, "Mom and Dad are great parents, and they just want the best for me." Then, making Shipley's blood beat a little faster, she added, "But to me, you're the best thing that ever happened!"

Shipley ended up working at a service station, and to the disgust of Jennifer's parents, he and Jennifer moved into a small apartment. The split with her parents was rough on Jennifer. Money was tight, and then Jennifer discovered she was pregnant. But love was a powerful force, and they stuck it out. Once Jennifer told her parents she was pregnant, a bit of reconciliation took place, which made Jennifer and her parents happy.

However, as Shipley paced around the common room, waiting for Jennifer to show up, he couldn't help but remember that the reconciliation didn't include him, and he hardly ever saw Jen's parents. But he really didn't give a damn. He knew they were slipping Jen some money every once in a while, and he wasn't going to complain about that. It wasn't as if he and Jen were floating in money or anything.

Jennifer wasn't aware of it yet, and Shipley didn't know how he was going to ask, but during their visit, he had to try to talk her into bringing in a wad of cash for him. He had to pay at least one guy to help him with his great escape. But he was worried about her being willing to bring it in. He knew she loved him, or so she said, but money was tight, and if she got caught, who knew what would happen?

Vern Thibedeau

She now had a job as a waitress, and of course, there was the baby they'd had about 18 months ago. Money was a big problem. There was some money in a savings account, but that was for rainy weather, or so Jennifer said. He wasn't sure if she'd consider escaping from prison to be rainy weather.

In addition, when they were on the run, she would have to leave her job and find another one whenever they managed to settled down again. As Shipley paced in the common room, waiting, he thought, *God, this is worse than worrying about being shanked. What'll I do if she tells me to bugger off? Christ, I'll really be screwed!*

The guard in the control finally gave the window a hard rap to get Shipley's attention and, through the gun port, told him his visitor was up front, and he'd better get going. Shipley waved a thank-you and headed out. He still had different ideas swirling around in his mind but was sure he would come up with something to get her to lug the money in for him.

Shipley made it through the usual barriers and, after being cleared by a guard, entered the visiting room. Looking around for Jen, he spotted several inmates sitting with their girlfriends and a few others sitting with families. There were even a few kids noisily playing with the toys that had been set up in a corner and looked a little worn from use. Then he saw her, the love of his life. *God*, he thought, *is she ever beautiful!* She was at a table, sitting on the metal chair bolted to the floor, looking lost and more than a little nervous and flinching at every little noise. She looked up when she heard the door slide open, and when she looked at him, he saw her deep brown eyes light up.

With a huge smile, Shipley plopped down onto the other chair and grabbed Jennifer's hands, and for a few moments, he just held on for dear life. Holding on to Jennifer felt like holding on to a piece of real life, and if he let go, he would sink back into the abyss.

For several moments, they just clutched hands and stared into each other's eyes. Then they both started talking at the same time. Jennifer and Shipley both gave a little laugh, and then Mac kept his mouth closed and listened to her chat. He just sat and continued to stare into her eyes, not really hearing anything she said.

Jennifer continued talking. She spoke about their son, Timmy, who was growing like a weed. She then spoke about her job, her friends and how tired she was of the little dinky apartment they were living in. Shipley thought she would never stop, but he also realized it was mostly nerves that kept her talking. And who could have blamed her? Thankfully, visiting a penitentiary was completely alien to her.

Their precious time was spent chatting, holding hands, dreaming of the life to come and gazing at photographs of Timmy; in fact, he took one to have in his cell. Suddenly, Shipley realized their time was getting short, and he knew he had to bring up the subject of the savings account. He carefully and quietly outlined his problems; naturally, he omitted the worst details, but he emphasized some other difficulties. Finally, staring down at the table, he worked his way around to his requirement for their savings.

Jennifer, with a sinking heart, listened quietly to everything Shipley had to say. Her eyes never left his face and started to become damp with sadness. Eventually, Shipley completed his story, and when Jennifer finally found her voice, she said, "That's all well and good, Mac, but what am I supposed to do if I get sick and can't work for a while or if Timmy needs some medicine? I can't just pull money out of thin air. God, Mac, I don't make that much, you know."

Their conversation carried on for a little longer, with Shipley trying to ease Jennifer's mind about every problem she brought up. Finally, because it was getting close to bus time, the visit had to come to an end. Jennifer said she'd have to toss his request around in her mind for a while and try to sort things out. Just before leaving, a disappointed Jennifer arranged a time and date when she was off work for Shipley to phone so they could talk a little more about their problems.

The rules stated that inmates had to stay seated in the visiting area and wait until their visitors left, so Shipley just sat there and watched Jennifer stride out, turn the corner and disappear into her other life.

His feelings were mixed. Jennifer, due to the cost and time involved, could hardly ever come for a visit, and Shipley missed her terribly. He'd suggested she move to the area so she could visit on a regular schedule, but she didn't like that idea due to the cost of moving; plus, she would have had to leave all her family, her friends and her job. In any case, he felt an overwhelming sadness. He knew, or at least was pretty sure, she loved him, and he felt a deep love for her, but he was concerned that she was drifting away from him; after all, eight years or so was a long time to be separated.

Even when he got out, there was nothing for them, other than trying to get a job and earn some money. As he sat there, those thoughts and others whirled around and gave him an added incentive to get the hell out. In his mind, it was either that or lose Jennifer for good.

Several days rolled by, and Shipley, even though he hadn't had the phone conversation with Jennifer yet, had talked himself into believing he would have the money to pay Jacob for helping him. Unfortunately, he and Jacob realized they'd need one more guy to help with the great plan. They also needed some type of saw to cut the food trays, and one of Jacob's buddies claimed that for a price, he could smuggle one out of his shop. Shipley had also come to the realization that once he was out free and clear, he would have to rob a store or a bank. He had to get money to live on until they could get settled somewhere else.

The great escape plan was coming along, though, and it was well thought out, at least up to a point. They'd figured out when, where, and how they could hollow out the trays. They also knew exactly where Shipley could slip in to hide among them, but from there on, everything was sort of unknown. After the trays were wheeled from the dock onto the truck, did the truck stop before entering the minimum-security camp? Could Shipley wiggle out of his hiding spot and jump out before they reached the camp? Or should he wait until the truck was inside? There was no wire or perimeter security, but would he be seen, and if he was, would anyone notice that he wasn't supposed to be there? And once he made it to the highway, where in hell would he go from there? *Ah*, Shipley thought, *what the hell? I'll worry about it then. I'm sure it'll all work out.* Shipley really wasn't big on making definite plans for the future.

But he was getting antsy. The guys who were helping him with his great escape were insisting on payment before he took off, not after. He couldn't blame them. What idiot would have helped someone escape from prison and believed that the escapee, once he was out and safe, would worry about smuggling money back into the joint to pay his bills?

Shipley tried to carry on as if everything were normal. He did his work in the servery, made sure he was in his cell for each count and picked up his meals, which he usually ate in the common room. He also made sure he was in his cell for the last count at 2300, and he usually spent some time during the evening in the yard or the gym. But actually, he was going through life in a bit of a daze.

He did more planning with Jacob, and everything was pretty well set to go, especially once Jacob's friend smuggled the saw out from the shop and gave it to them. When he handed the saw over to Jacob, he had his other hand out for the payment that was coming to him. Shipley had to assure him that he would receive full payment as soon as it came in from the outside. At the same time, he thought, *please, Jen, don't let me down, or I'm in more trouble. God, I wouldn't know what the hell to do. Jesus, another week before we talk to each other; how am I ever gonna wait?*

*   *   *

Richards and the rest of the unit officers working the evening shift were standing out in N area, chatting with one another. The inmates were straggling back from the shops and heading into their units for the count and their supper meal. Bill was just about to turn away and say something to one of the guys from J unit, when he noticed an inmate from lower L use the inside of his arm to give his side a little rub. *Jeez, that's the second time he's done that since he entered N area. I wonder if he's carrying something.*

Bill looked at the officer standing next to him, and when the guy glanced his way, Bill gave him the look and received a short nod in return. Bill then threw a look toward the control and received a small head nod. At the same time, the control officer took a couple of steps to his left, and Bill knew he was reaching for one of the rifles.

Even after all Bill's years in the service, he was still amazed at how an officer, with just a simple look, could alert other staff, and they would realize something was going on or would be going on. The staff might not realize what it was, but they would know something was up. Bill knew the inmate's name was Emerson, and as he glanced toward him, Bill felt the familiar tightening of his stomach. He'd been hurt a few times during his career, but so far, he'd had just minor injuries, and he hoped it would stay that way.

One never knew how an inmate was going to react. Would he do what he was told and lean into the wall? Would he suddenly become aware of what was going on and react by pulling a weapon? Or would he maybe just take a swing at one of them? They never knew and could only hope for the best. Bill thought, *at least this turkey's a normal size and doesn't seem to be one of the empty-headed weightlifters. At least that's a positive.*

Bill nonchalantly eased closer to Emerson. He knew he had to act before the inmate entered the unit, or whatever he had on him would be long gone, but at the same time, he was hoping most of the inmates would be cleared from the area. Even with the control officer standing there with a rifle, he didn't want a fight with a bunch of inmates, especially if Emerson wasn't carrying anything. Bill could sense one or more staff behind him as he and another officer continued their conversation while they sidled closer and closer to their target.

Apparently, Emerson sensed something wasn't quite right, and just before staff could grab him, he tried to speed up and get into the unit. However, the control officer was watching and managed to slam the unit barrier shut a second or so before he could reach it. At the same time, the officer closed the corridor barrier, which stopped any more inmates from entering N area. The inmates who were already in the area took a look at the control officer, saw him standing next to the gun port with a rifle and decided to back off and not get involved.

By that time, Richards and two other staff had crowded the inmate and had him facing a wall with his arms up against it. Bill, in a low voice, said to Emerson, "I know damn well you're lugging, so don't you make a move while I pat you down. I really don't want anyone getting hurt!"

"Ah, all you fucking guys want are problems. I don't know who ratted me out, but I'd like to find him so I could—"

"Ah, shut your mouth, and stand the hell still." Bill, even though he knew what he was looking for was likely around the waist area, started a normal frisk by checking the arms and working downward. When he reached the inmate's waist, he felt something unusual on the right side and, pulling up the shirt, found a sharp homemade shank. With only a glance, Bill could tell it likely had come from the machine shop. The weapon had been crafted out of a large table knife and was about six inches long. It'd been sharpened on both sides of the blade and honed to a sharp point. All in all, it was a deadly piece of equipment. He carefully eased it out, handed it off to an officer and completed the frisk, but he didn't find anything else.

Once he was finished, Bill told Emerson to put his arms down and turn around. "I imagine you know I'm taking you to the hole. Jesus, man, you know better than to pull a stunt like this. Somebody could've really been hurt."

Emerson just looked at Bill and replied, "Yeah, let's go. That's all I'd expect from a prick like you anyway—you and all your hero buddies."

Bill watched the con as he spouted off and thought, *He's talking tough, but he looks more scared than anything else. Something more than just getting caught with a knife is going on.* "OK, tough guy, let's go." Looking at one of the other officers, Bill said, "Tom, you come with us; it'll only be a couple minutes, and then you can get back to your unit." Bill felt relieved that it was over and that no one, including the inmate, had been injured.

Off they went, two officers and one inmate heading down the corridor. As was the usual practice, the inmate, who knew exactly where he was going, walked in front, and the two officers followed close behind. Also, as usual, the segregation area received more than one phone call informing them of the fact that they were about to receive another inmate and of the reason why he was being locked up.

During the short walk to segregation, Bill couldn't help going over the episode in his mind and feeling there was more to it. *Why in hell didn't he seem a lot more concerned about getting caught with a very dangerous weapon? Also, how come he didn't put up a fight or at least make a grab for the shank when he knew we were onto him? If the idiot had put up more of a fight, at least he'd be a bit of a hero to the other inmates. Ah, what the hell? At least he seems to have settled down a little; I think I'll try to have a chat with him in the hole. He might open up a little to me; hell, you never know.*

Just before the three of them reached the segregation door, it magically opened, and Bill knew staff had been watching as they walked down the corridor. It was a gratifying feeling. They entered the room, and while one officer locked the door, another one dropped a change of clothing onto the desk. He then looked at Emerson and told him, "There's your new wardrobe. Get changed while we check your other clothes. It's not nice to carry knives around this place."

Emerson started stripping, and one of the segregation staff grabbed each article of clothing as it was removed. Once each item was checked, it was thrown into a pile on the floor, and eventually, Emerson had a complete change of clothing on. Bill, along with the three segregation staff—he'd told the other officer to head back to the unit—watched Emerson to make sure he didn't have anything else on his person and didn't try to act out. Once the procedure was completed, Bill told the corporal in charge of the area that he wanted a minute with Emerson before they locked him up.

"Sure, no problem. We'll be just on the other side of the door if you need us." The corporal stared at Emerson as he spoke, and Emerson knew damned well he was being told not to cause any problems, or they'd be right back in, and he'd get his ass kicked.

Bill waved Emerson to a chair while he sat on the corner of the desk. Bill sat and looked at Emerson for a minute or so and then started the conversation by saying, "I don't know what your problem is, but I know it's a hell of a lot more than just carrying a knife around or lugging it in for someone else. Jesus, man, you could have been shot. As far as I know, this is the first jackpot you've been in, and make no mistake: this is serious. What the hell's going on? Is there anything I can do to help straighten things out?"

"Nah, not really. Sorry about mouthing off out there; you're really not one of the assholes, but I had to act up a bit."

"Don't worry about that; I know what you're saying. I'm just glad that's all you did."

"Look, I can't say too much. I don't want word to get around that I'm a rat. You know what—"

"Listen, nothing you say to me will ever get back to the other cons. I've been around long enough to know about that shit. And I certainly don't wanna make your problems any worse than they are now."

"All I can say is that I owe some money to a jerk named Crothers, and I can't get it back to him. I really thought I'd be able to, or at least I figured I'd be able to help him out with a job or something, but he just wants the money. And I don't wanna end up dead. Do you think I'll have to go running for protection? God, I don't want that. What the hell do I do now?"

"For starters, you're crazy to borrow money in this place. What in hell were you thinking? As for protective custody, that has to be up to you. You'll be locked up here for a while anyway, and depending on your record, you may end up in the special handling unit for a while. But after that, I really don't know. What the hell did you want the money for anyway?"

"Not saying anything else. Just lock me up. Screw the whole mess."

With that, Emerson stood up. Bill waved to the staff behind the door and then looked toward Emerson to wish him luck, but he'd already turned his back and was halfway through the doorway. Bill thanked Kelly, who had come in to let him out of the segregation unit, but before he could step through the door, they both heard what sounded like someone getting smacked, followed by yelling and scuffling. Bill and Kelly both gave a jerk. They looked at each other, and Bill, knowing there was a fight going on, with his heart pumping, took off for the other door while Kelly threw the lock on the exit door and followed Bill on the run.

They made it into the segregation unit, tore around the corner and came to a stop. They spotted an officer on the floor with blood running out of his nose onto his uniform shirt. Emerson was up against a wall with his hands up, and the other two officers looked as if they wanted to lay a beating on Emerson. But at least everything appeared under control, and no one was injured badly, although Bill didn't think the poor guy moaning on the floor would have agreed with that assessment.

Bill approached Emerson, who looked at him and said with a smart-ass grin, "I guess they'll have to send me to the SHU now, won't they?"

"You stupid idiot. What the hell were you thinking? Yep, you'll be going to the SHU and with an assault charge, but believe you me, you won't enjoy it." Bill looked at Rob, who was being helped up from the floor, and said, "I'm on my way back to J; want me to walk you over to the hospital on my way?"

"Nah, I'm OK. I'll clean up a bit and then head over. Thanks anyway."

That was the reply Bill had expected. Staff didn't want inmates to see them bleeding all over the place unless it was really necessary. "OK, guys, if someone'll let me out of here, I'll get on my way." Being a bit of a wise-ass and because he was leaving anyway, he said, "I'll see you all later. Don't forget to get those reports filled out. I didn't really see anything, so I guess you don't need my input."

With that little bit of wisdom thrown out, Bill headed for the door, and once Robinson unlocked it, he took off up the corridor for J unit. But regardless of his smart-ass remark to the guys in disassociation cells, he started thinking about the new information and knew the preventive security officer would have to be brought up to speed on it.

He entered J unit and found out that the count was in and that the inmates were about to be released for their supper meal, so all was good. Bill informed the staff of what had gone on in disassociation and told them that he was going to stay in the office to do some writing while the inmates were being fed. He also knew he'd have to contact the IPSO about Crothers and knew he'd have to get a hold of him at home, but even so, Bill figured Jordon should have firsthand knowledge of the episode rather than just reading the report.

Once the inmates had finished eating and been released for recreation, Bill headed up front to hand his report over to the sergeant and to phone the IPSO.

The sergeant looked the report over and said, "Thanks, Bill. That's a lot of info. I know you're doing a little work with the IPSO over this Crothers thing, and since you're not in until tomorrow afternoon, maybe you should give him a call to let him know about this. I imagine he'll find it quite interesting."

"Yeah, you're right about that. I thought I'd give him a dingle while I'm up here. This place is a little quieter and a hell of a lot more private. I don't know if Jordon's home or not, but I'll give it a try, and if I can't reach him, I'll try again later. In a pinch, I can always phone him here before the morning meeting."

"Sure, that sounds good. Hope it works out. Lemme know how it goes."

Bill lucked in and had a chat with Jordon on the first try. He explained everything that had gone on, making sure he told him that Emerson had decked the officer only to get to the handling unit. They both realized Emerson, like a lot of inmates, would rather be in higher security than go into PC, which was a last resort for most of them. The staff couldn't blame them for it.

When Bill was finished up front, he headed back down to the units. He knew it was almost changeover time, and he wanted to be back in the unit before the changeover started. They never knew when an extra hand would be needed.

Bill finished off the rest of his shift, which, thankfully, other than the usual problems, stayed quiet. As soon as the final count was in and his relief showed up, Bill headed out. He decided to take the longer way home and drive along the lake. He figured that particular drive might help him settle down a bit.

Chapter 10

Even though he hadn't spoken to Jen yet, Shipley had talked himself into firmly believing that Jen would agree to bring the money in. It never entered his head that she would put herself and their son ahead of him; he'd never thought that way. He was a bit of a self centred guy.

The escape plan had progressed to the extent that they'd done everything they could do. Now it was just a matter of waiting for the money to be ferried in. He still didn't know what he was going to do after he jumped off the back of the truck, hopefully without breaking a leg or anything else. But he figured it would all work out one way or another. They were also pretty sure Jacob's part in the escape was covered, and he wouldn't get jerked around. Jacob wasn't worried. He just said, "What the hell can they do to me anyway? I'm already locked up."

The date for the phone call to Jen slowly crept up, and while waiting for that big day and time, Shipley just stayed with his routine and made sure, as best as he could, to stay out of trouble. He couldn't help wondering what he'd do if he screwed up and ended up in the hole; there were no phone calls from that place. He also tried to stay as far away as possible from Crothers and any of his gang, but it seemed that everywhere he went, he would spot one of them and get the stare. He couldn't help wondering if they were just hanging around waiting to get him. *Jeez, what if that asshole Crothers spotted me spitting in his lunch last week?* Sometimes it was kind of nice to work in the servery; it was a great way to get even with jerks, even if they didn't know about it.

Shipley's big day for the phone call to Jen finally rolled around. *God, he thought, it feels like it's been weeks since we had our visit. Jesus Christ, I miss her so much, and I just feel that I can't go on like this.* He piddled around, working in the servery, until the agreed-upon time approached. Then, with a wave to the control officer, he headed to the inmate phone.

With his heart pounding, he shakily dialed Jen's number and listened while the operator informed Jen that she had a phone call from a federal prison and asked if she would accept the charges. Jen agreed, and the all-important conversation started with Jen saying, "On my God, Mac, I miss you so much."

With a quivering voice, Shipley replied, "I miss you too, Jen. I can't even explain how much. This is almost more than I can take."

The conversation continued for a lengthy time, with both parties exchanging terms of endearment, undying love and, unfortunately for Shipley, plans for the future, or lack thereof. Finally, they had to say their goodbyes and hang up.

As Shipley shakily hung up, his only thought was *Oh my God, what in hell do I do now?* Jen, while emphatically stating her love for him, had told him she couldn't bring the money in for him. She'd explained that her hours at work had been cut, and she had given other reasons that Shipley couldn't understand. In fact, by that time, he could hardly understand what she was saying. But Jen had made it clear that the only contact they could have until he got out was by letter and the odd phone call during Christmas and, once Timmy was older, on his birthdays. However, she had been emphatic that she and Timmy would be waiting whenever he was released from the prison.

Shipley, after hanging up, once he was able to calm down a little, began to process that information and figured Jen must have been getting advice from some asshole. There was no doubt in his mind that she had planned on bringing the money in. It never entered his head that maybe Jen was putting the welfare of their baby ahead of him. *Nah*, he thought, *that just wouldn't happen.*

In a daze, Shipley made his way back to the servery, poured himself a mug of coffee and headed to a common room to try to sort out the devastating news. He also had to try to stay alive while figuring a way out of this mess. A couple of inmates spoke to him as he meandered over to the common room to sit down, but he couldn't even process what they said, let alone make a reply.

The two inmates looked at each other, and one said, "By the looks of Mac, I'd guess another one of us just got a Dear John, or he's in one hell of a lot of trouble over something."

Shipley just sat there staring at nothing and taking the odd sip of coffee, which soon became cold. *Christ, do I tell Jacob there's no money coming in? Do I try to talk them into helping me escape without a payoff? Do I run for PC, or should I take a swing at a guard and get locked up? Good God, one thing I'd better do is make a shank and start carrying it around.* Shipley really didn't have a clue what he could or should do.

He didn't realize it, but his decision about the great escape was going to be made for him shortly.

Shipley was still sitting in the common room, contemplating life and holding on to his cold coffee, when the speaker system gave a squeal, and a loud voice ordered all inmates to their cells for an immediate count. Shipley jumped, spilling his coffee all over the place. He looked at his watch and noted that it wasn't even close to count time. But even so, he started to make his way to his cell, and at the same time, he spotted inmates coming back from work and heading for their cells. *Holy hell,* he thought, *something's sure going on. This never happens. If it's a fight or a stabbing, everyone's just locked down wherever he is. Jesus, this must be really big!*

Shipley had been in his cell for only a couple minutes, when the cell doors were given a couple of shakes to notify inmates they were about to close, and *bang*—close they did. At the same time, the speakers told all inmates to stand during the count. *Aha*, Shipley said to himself. *They must think a con got out. I hope he did and that he makes it all the way out of this hellhole.*

Shipley stood in his cell, waiting to be counted, and as soon as the guard looked in at him, he flopped onto his bed and tried to figure out what he was going to do. It had finally sunk in that he wasn't getting the money, and he also realized he had to keep that little point to himself, at least for as long as he could. It also hit him again that he'd better get his hands on a shiv and carry it with him all the time. He was still hoping he could escape, but he kind of doubted that was going to happen. So, his options were likely to get a shiv, run for protection or deck a screw—not much of a choice.

The inmates were locked in their cells for almost two hours before the doors opened, and they were told to continue their normal routine. Since the work in the servery was finished until the supper meal, Shipley decided to get another coffee and hang out in a common room. He picked up a coffee and sat down with a couple of guys he worked with.

One of them looked at Shipley and asked, "Hey, Mac, you got any idea what the hell that was all about?"

"Nope. Don't know what the hell's going on, and don't give a damn. But I'm sure we'll find out soon enough. I'd bet someone took off, and the pigs had to do whatever in hell it is they do when something like that happens."

The three of them chatted for some time, and then Jacob wandered in. One of the inmates looked at him and asked the same question he'd asked Shipley.

Jacob looked directly at Shipley and replied, "Oh yeah. I was just told Mackenzie from E unit took off. The talk is that he hid in a pile of food trays and got a ride out through the fence. Ain't that something? Haven't heard if they caught him or not, but I bet we'll hear all about it one way or the other very shortly. Hell, it'll be all over the news by tonight."

Shipley's mouth fell open, and he felt as if he'd been punched in the gut. He couldn't believe it. *Jesus,* he *thought, how much bad luck can a guy have?* He knew one thing, though: if the rumour was true, there was no way in hell he could get out, at least not with the plan he had intended to use.

Jacob gave another look toward Shipley and strolled over to an empty area of the common room, and Shipley joined him within moments. "I'm pretty sure that's how Mackenzie got out, Mac. And now there's no fucking way you can get out using the food trays. Got any other ideas?"

"Nah. That's about it. Christ Almighty, I don't know what to do now."

They discussed the problem for several more minutes, and then Shipley asked Jacob, "Do you think what's-his-name will take the saw back to his shop and forget about it?"

Vern Thibedeau

"Christ, Mac, of course he'll want his payment. It was a big risk to sneak that thing out of the shop, and if he'd been caught, he'd have been in big trouble; at the very least, he'd be in the hole." With that bit of knowledge, the conversation ended, and they both headed back to their cells.

Shipley made it back and curled up on his bed. He was at the end of his rope and didn't have a clue what do now. He had no escape plan, no money and a saw he couldn't use but would still have to pay for. Crothers was out to dump him, and in all likelihood, he'd even lost Jen. He'd told Jacob he still expected the money to come in, but he knew that little lie wouldn't last for long. Soon he'd have to come up with the money—that was, if he was still there and not in the hospital or someplace a lot worse.

Chapter 11

Another couple of weeks slipped by, and nothing unusual happened, at least nothing unusual for a prison. Shipley kept saying to himself, *I'm still alive. I'm still alive and not a PC con.* But he was careful and made sure that he was never by himself and that no one could get close to him without his being aware of it. In other words, he took Dominic's advice to heart. He went to the yard and the gym once in a while but spent most of his time in a common room or his cell. He figured the safest place he could be was in his cell, but he could only stay there for a while, and after a couple of days, he felt he had to get out and do something, or he'd go nuts.

Around that time, Shipley had a couple of exciting episodes come his way. Over the course of three days, he received two letters. Usually, he didn't receive that many letters in a month or more.

The first letter was from his mother. She didn't write often, so the message was a nice break for him. It was a short letter but still nice to read. She was having a bit of a hard time financially but managing to get along. The good news was that she'd met a nice man, and they were debating if they should move in together to save money. At the present time, Tom wasn't working, so the plan was for him to move into the old house with her. However, his mom reiterated several times that he was looking for a job, and she was excited about the future. But as usual, there was no mention of Shipley's sister. He read the letter over a few times, and all he could do was shake his head and hope for the best for his mom. He also hoped she realized he couldn't send her any money.

The second letter, which he received the next day, was from Jen. This one was a little longer and filled with new happenings. Jen's job was going well; in fact, she'd received a promotion, which meant a little more money for her and Timmy. The other big news was that Jen and her parents were finally speaking and getting along well.

Shipley could tell Jen was excited about the whole thing. "Jeez," she wrote, "they even want to look after Timmy, which means I won't have to pay a babysitter anymore. This will really help Timmy and me." At least the letter was signed with "Love, Jen." That made him feel a bit better.

He wasn't sure if he was happy about Jen and Timmy moving in with her mom and dad, though. He could imagine the pressure she'd be under to leave him. *Oh well*, he thought. *There's nothing I can do about it anyway, and I have my own problems to worry about.* And he certainly did have problems.

One evening, when the weather had finally cleared up, he decided to go to the yard for a change of scenery. As usual, he kept a lookout for any of the Crothers bunch and for the guy he owed money to for the saw, who was starting to give him a hard time. Shipley walked into the yard and looked around, hoping to see Dominic. But he had no such luck, so Shipley figured Dominic must have gone to the gym or maybe a common room. He did spot Owen, who'd gone to the hole a while back because of the brew, and he made his way over to say hi to him. As he approached Owen, he started the conversation with "Hey, how you doing? Glad you made it out of the hole."

"Ah, not bad. At least in there you get a lot of quiet time. I'll tell you onc thing, though: next time, I'll be a lot more careful about having so many guys in my cell. Hell, we were bound to get caught. But it was worth it; that brew was good. It was one of my best."

They chatted for a while, and Shipley was just about to meander over to the barrier and head back in during changeover, when Owen said, "Hey, you hear about that guy with the connections? I think his name's Domino or some wop name like that."

"Ah, you must mean Dominic, and no, I haven't seen him for a couple of days."

"Well, you won't see him for a while now; two pigs showed up at his shop this afternoon and scooped him. The word is that they've charged him with two more murders, and they're holding him for trial. Ain't that a bitch? Christ, he's already in here for life. What the hell more do those assholes want from the poor guy anyway?"

When that news sank in and Shipley realized what it meant to him, he felt as if the whole world had just crashed onto his shoulders, and he sank down onto his knees. It only took a moment or two for the other inmates to stare his way, so, acting as if he'd just tripped, he stood up and gave his knees a wipe. But he felt as if he'd been punched in the gut. He also knew damn well that he didn't have a lot of time before word about Dominic got around and that he'd better get back to his cell during the changeover.

Shipley, who was close to a state of panic, headed for the open barrier to get the hell out of the yard. He knew better than to run—he'd learned that was something one never did in a prison, that or whistle—but he was gulping air as if he'd just finished a marathon. His head felt as if it were on a swivel from looking around every time he heard a noise; each time, in his mind, he was sure it was someone running at him while swinging a big knife. His feet felt as if they were fighting to get through molasses, and he was beginning to think he wouldn't make it back to his cell without passing out or having something worse happen.

He did make it to his range, but just before stepping into his cell, he stopped cold. *Good God, what if some prick's in there waiting for me? Or slips in right behind me?* He looked around wildly but only spotted a few inmates coming and going, and he didn't think any of them belonged to the Crothers bunch. But on the other hand, who knew? So, acting nonchalantly, he stood there as if he were trying to remember something. At the same time, he edged over to his cell door and peeped in, hoping no one would wonder what the hell he was doing. Not seeing anyone, as soon as the doors rattled to give everyone a warning, with his heart in his mouth, he slipped in, and the door slammed shut right behind him. He stood there for a minute or so, waiting and taking deep breaths, and nothing but blessed quietness filled his ears.

With what almost sounded like a sob, he fell onto his bed and just lay there trying to get his breathing and emotions back to normal, or at least what was normal for him. Once he calmed down, he tried to think of different ways to get out of the mess he was in, but he couldn't come up with anything.

After several minutes, a thought struck him like a ton of bricks: *Good God, I was out there without my knife! Christ, what if one of those idiots had jumped me? I would've been screwed!* That line of thinking was mostly bravado on his part. He knew if he was jumped, it would be by three or more guys, and he knew they'd be a lot better armed than he was with his sharpened five-inch piece of Plexiglas with a razor blade glued onto the end of it. But that pretend knife did make him feel tougher—not a lot safer but tougher.

Shipley stayed in his cell for the rest of the evening. Each time the cell door opened for a changeover, he'd leap up and stand next to it with his shank stuck out in front of him, praying that no one would rush in at him. No one did, at least not yet.

A few days crawled by, and Shipley, even though he was a nervous wreck, with little choice, continued his regular routine. He went to work, made sure he got his meals and even went to a common room a few times. He still figured a common room was his safest spot. *Jeez, how could anyone get at me in here? There're always two armed guards in the control with a clear view of all of us.* He didn't realize things like that could and did happen. Whenever an attack did happen, the action went down quickly.

Another week slowly crept by, and Shipley, who was even more paranoid and nervous, managed to carry on. But he flinched at every loud noise—and there was a lot of noise in a prison—and a few times, he even spun around when he was sure he heard someone sneaking up behind him. He realized that the other inmates were starting to give him the look and that a few of them thought he was going off the deep end—and maybe he was. But there was nothing he could do about it; he couldn't help but twitch and sometimes even jump at every little sound.

More time passed, and Shipley, despite jumping at every little noise, staring at everyone with a suspicious glare and losing some weight, was still alive and kind of proud of that fact. One morning, on his way down for breakfast, an inmate he didn't really know sidled up to him and, with a glare, quietly asked, "Hey, Shipley, where's my carton, asshole?"

Shipley jerked around. "Carton? What carton? What the hell you talking about? I don't know you."

"You should. I'm the sucker who snuck that saw out for you. And now I want that carton you owe me."

"Jesus, man, I thought you knew. The broad who was bringing my stuff in got knocked off by the pigs on her way in for the visit. I'm working on another way to get the loot in. Christ, it should only take another week or so. God, another week won't hurt." Shipley didn't think his little white lie would make things any worse. He just hoped the idiot would swallow it.

"OK, man. I'll buy that shit for one more week, and then the price doubles. If I'm not paid off, it's your neck. I don't screw around, you know."

"I'll have it. No problem. Just relax, for Christ's sake."

The conversation ended Shipley's need for breakfast. He immediately spun around and cautiously made his way back to his cell. *Jesus Christ,* he thought, *that goddamned Jacob didn't tell me he was charging me two cartons for his little part with the saw. He said the three cartons were for the con stealing it. That prick. He's like all the rest of them, just out for himself; he should join up with that asshole Crothers.*

The conversation put even more pressure on Shipley, and he certainly didn't need that. If he hadn't been at his wits' end before, he was now. *God, I can't watch everyone. I'm going to end up getting shanked and all because Jennifer wouldn't do her part. God, she sure screwed me. Christ, Dominic screwed me, Jen screwed me, Crothers and his idiots want me dead and this other asshole wants a carton of smokes or my head. Hell, all I wanted was out of here. It wasn't my fault that old idiot fell over and hit his head.*

Now Shipley's mind was really screwed up. He made it into his cell, flopped onto his bed and just stared at the ceiling. He didn't move until the cell door opened for workup, but he had no intention of going into the servery to work. In his mind's eye, he could see all the knives floating around in the area and could visualize someone grabbing one and ramming it into his back or slashing his throat open.

It only took 20 minutes or so for his door to slam open, and once Shipley stopped shaking, he saw that it was his boss, who wanted to find out why he wasn't in the servery working. With a shake of his head, he mumbled that he was sick and was going to stay in his cell, and he rolled over and pulled his pillow over his head. Once the cell door closed with its usual bang, Shipley suffered his usual twitching. Then he settled down, and his mind started its swirling around. Within a minute or so, he calmed down and started drifting off to dreamland.

* * *

Richards was making his way down to the shop area to have a chat with the head instructor. Staff had been searching the cells in J unit and discovered a steel shiv hidden inside a mattress. The knife was so well made that Bill knew damn well it had come out of the machine shop, and staff couldn't figure out how in hell the inmate had gotten it made, let alone smuggled it out of the shop. The knife was a thing of beauty and was so well made that it could have been sold downtown in a store. The problem was that there sure as hell weren't any stores selling knives in the prison. Now staff had to find out how the con had managed to make it and then smuggle it out to the unit.

Richards was busy trying to think of how to approach the instructor about such a delicate subject without pissing him off, when he noticed inmate Johnston coming toward him. Richards saw that Johnston spotted him at about the same time and also noticed Johnston take a quick look around to see if anyone else was in the area. They both slowed down a little until they reached each other, and Richards couldn't help thinking, *Oh Christ, what's going on now?*

Johnston looked at Richards and, in a low voice, said, "This'll only be a minute, but you gotta know something's gonna happen in the unit pretty soon. Not sure what—I'm not part of the in crowd—but it involves that Shipley guy and the Crothers bunch. But this time, there's also some other turkey who has it in for Shipley because of something that involves smokes and the servery. Whatever it is, Shipley's in some pretty deep shit."

"Jesus, man, this sounds serious. Any way you can get more information to me?"

"I doubt it. I gotta watch my back, you know, and I don't really wanna get mixed up in this bullshit. Just wanna do my own time and get the hell out of this place. I'll give it a try, but just so you know, there's no way I'm risking my fucking neck over some stupid idiot who ain't got two cents' worth of brains in—"

"That's fine, and it's all I can ask. But you watch yourself in there; it must be getting hairy."

After that short conversation, they both went on their way. The news gave Richards a little more to think about. He tossed different scenarios around in his head as he headed for the shop but realized he could visualize scenarios all day long and likely not come up with the correct one. And even if he did, he wouldn't know it until the incident went down. But if nothing else, it raised his level of concern a few notches. *Hell, maybe I should've stayed in A unit. That place was a little boring, but it was sure a hell of a lot easier than this dammed J unit.*

Richards reached U corridor, and the officer posted to the area opened the machine shop door. In Bill went. He spotted the head instructor and headed over to him. Jerry looked up and, seeing Richards walking toward him, stood up and strolled over toward Richards. Bill said, "Hey, Jerry, got a couple minutes? I need a little information, and I hope you can help me out."

"Sure. Come on up to the office, and we'll grab a coffee."

"I won't say no to that; sounds great."

There were only a couple of desks in the room. They each got a coffee and settled down at one of them. "What's up, Bill? Hope it's not too serious."

"Nope, not really. Just trying to stop something from happening again—that is, if we can. Anyway, one of your workers, a con named Evens, got caught with a really well-made knife hidden in his cell, and he's now—"

"Aw crap, not another one. Sorry for interrupting, Bill, but your guys also found one just last month from this shop. Christ, I don't know how it's happening. I've been double-checking and making sure the guys do a proper frisk before each inmate leaves. But it seems like someone's not doing his frigging job, or the cons have figured out another way of getting the damn things out of the shop. That must be the answer. Jesus, the inmates would all refuse to work here if they had to be strip-searched every time they leave the shop. There's gotta be another way the cons are doing it."

"That's kind of my way of thinking too, Jerry. Oh, and I was going to mention that Evens is now residing in the hole. Anyway, this is all kind of new to me, but I was wondering if some night, the IPSO could maybe stick a few cameras up in the area until we figure this mess out."

"You got me, Bill. That's sort of security's bivouac; hell, I wouldn't have a clue about doing it or even if it's legal. Just make sure you let me know about it if they go ahead and put them in."

"To be honest, I'm not up on something like this either. I just never ran into it before. I'll get in touch with the powers that be to see what the hell they say about it. For all I know, they may say no way in hell it can be done. Or they might say, 'Sure, it's done all the time.' I guess we'll just have to wait and see. Anyway, I just wanted to run this by you and see if you might have another idea. I do know this camera thing is way above my pay grade. At any rate, I'd better be getting to my unit. Thanks for the coffee; it hit the spot. I'll talk to you later, and you have fun in here."

"OK, Bill. See you later. Just let me know how it goes, eh?"

Bill gave Jerry a wave and headed out of the shop. On his way back to the unit, he thought, *Jeez, cameras may just do the trick. There's sure no way it can't be done; we've done it before, and it's legal. I just don't know if Jordon's got the cameras. I have to see him anyway about the latest news from Johnston. Christ, we're lucky that con's willing to talk to me.*

Richards made it back to the unit, had a chat with the two officers and found out that nothing unusual had happened while he was gone. So he just sat there for a while and thought about the conversation he'd had with Johnston. He realized the situation could be serious and could have dire repercussions for him if it wasn't handled properly. *Jesus*, he thought, *here I am, worrying about covering my ass, and people could end up injured or dead. What in hell's happening to me? It seems like my priorities are kind of screwed up.*

Once he jotted down the gist of his conversation, he made sure he put the notes into his pocket and then phoned Jordon in the preventive security office. He gave Jordon a brief idea of what Johnston had told him, and they arranged a time to meet in the IPSO's office. They both thought it would be better if Bill waited until his relief showed up; then he could just stop in on his way home, and no one would be the wiser.

Bill and his staff completed the balance of their shift without anything out of the ordinary happening. They did have to listen to the usual complaints about the mistreatment of inmates, and naturally, Richards had to listen to the range representative rant about how he was going to lay a complaint about the needless assault of Pezzio and how the staff had torn the cells apart during the search. Richards let him carry on for a while and then finally, once he'd had enough, said in a low and, he hoped, menacing voice, "That's just about enough of the mouth. You either get the hell out of the office right now, or you're going to the fucking hole. Hell, we'll even be nice and put you in a cell right beside Pezzio, and you two can tell each other how tough you are."

Richards realized a lot of the rep's carrying on was a show for the other inmates, but he also figured he'd done enough listening and knew he was on the verge of blowing up. He knew that wouldn't be a wise idea, especially with the present tension in the place. At any rate, the range rep stormed out, and the staff sat and rehashed the events of the shift while waiting for their relief to show up.

Once Bill's relief came into the unit office, Bill gave him a quick rundown on the day shift's events and then took off for home. He was almost at the gate, when he remembered the preventive security officer was waiting in his office for him. With a not-too-nice comment directed at himself and a shake of his head, he turned around and headed back inside.

He reached the IPSO's office, knocked, entered and plopped down in front of the desk, and they had their little chat. Once Bill had filled Jordon in on everything, they both realized the situation, not just with Shipley but in the whole unit, was becoming serious.

"Christ," Jordon muttered to Bill once they'd gone over everything, "I wish we could just scoop up Crothers and that gang of idiots of his and ship them out to the special handling unit. The trouble with doing that—and we both know it—is that there'd be complaints right up to Ottawa, and those goddamned do-gooders would be on us like a ton of bricks."

"Yep, I know just what you're saying, but sometimes I think it'd be worth it. I'll tell you another thing that I'm getting really concerned about. I'm worried Johnston is talking to me too often, and the other inmates may be noticing it. I may be getting a little paranoid, but I really don't wanna see him get hurt or worse. I'm not sure why he's been feeding me all this info, and I know it's lucky for us that he's doing it. But you know, I'm really getting concerned that we're going to find him tits up in a corner one of these days."

"I know what you're saying, Bill. But it's his choice, and he's been around long enough to know what he's doing. The best I can suggest is for you to tell him to be careful and maybe see if you can arrange some other place to meet or something. But be careful; we don't wanna lose him.

"At any rate, you're doing a good job, and I have an appointment with the deputy and warden to discuss this whole mess. I'm not sure what they're gonna do, but it's their decision, and I must admit that makes me kind of happy. This is one of those 'Damned if you do, and damned if you don't' things. But I'm with you; I just hope no one gets hurt. But all we can do is do what we can and let the chips fall where they may, eh?"

That was the end of the discussion. Bill had to get going. As it was, he was late in getting away, and Bill and his wife had made arrangements to go out for dinner and take in a movie. *God, it's going to be a nice evening. No kids, I'll forget about work, a couple of drinks and hopefully a good night's sleep.*

He was looking forward to the night out. There hadn't been many lately, not since their oldest, dusty and disheveled, rushed into the house one day after school and excitedly informed them that he'd been asked to join the school's hockey team. Then, a few days later, the youngest boy insisted on joining a team. That gave them two youngsters going into organized sports.

Bill and Shirley sat there looking at each other with a bit of a stunned expression while the youngest told them of his plans. Once Bill recovered, with a big smile, he gave the boy a hug and said, "Way to go, Jimmy. We're proud of you."

Actually, they had just finished a conversation about how tough money issues had become since they'd decided Bill should cut back on overtime. But Shirley still didn't want him to start back doing heavy overtime. "We'll just cut back a little more here and there, and I'm sure we'll be OK. Just a little perseverance should do it. Eh, hon?"

"I agree, babe. I really don't wanna get back into that old groove if I don't have to. We'll just take it easy and see how it goes. If it does get too tight, I can always work a few extra shifts. I've done it before, and I can sure do it again."

After they paid for the uniforms, the memberships and whatnot for their boys, Bill happily realized he likely wouldn't have to do more than a few overtime shifts a month—not all that bad, he figured. Things were still a bit tight, but it was nice to be home with Shirley and be able to attend most of their boys' games.

A couple of months later, Bill was due to take their car in for its regular servicing. He'd been a little worried for a while now about the poor old thing. The mileage was creeping up pretty high, and he'd been hearing strange noises escaping from it every once in a while. So, on one of his days off, with his fingers crossed, he drove in to get it serviced.

Bill parked the car and walked into the service area. Spotting Norm, who usually was on the desk, he headed over and said, "Hey, Norm, how you doing? I'm in for the usual service that you guys insist on."

"Glad to see you, Bill. You going to wait for it, or do you want a lift home?"

"Nah. Just going to hang around and wait." Bill handed the keys over and, having decided to look around, headed out to the car lot. *Boy,* he thought, *there sure are a lot of nice cars around here.* He looked at a few and then went back in and sat down to do a bit of reading while waiting for his car. It didn't take long, and Norm gave him a wave that his car was ready. Bill waved back and headed for the counter.

Norm handed him the bill and the work order. Bill paid what owed, and on his way out to the car, he glanced down at the work order and noticed a few comments. He took a few minutes to sit in the car and read the notes before heading home. Apparently, the car was in need of some work, and it was highly recommended that the repairs be done fairly quickly. Then he did a double take at the cost of the required repairs. *Holy shit, what the hell are we going to do about this mess?* he thought.

Based on the cost of getting the car fixed, Bill thought they might have to invest in a new or newer vehicle. One way or another, though, he knew he would be back doing extra overtime again. There was no doubt in his mind that he and Shirley were going to be having another discussion about finances.

And there were a few discussions over several days. They decided that financially, it would be better to just buy a new car, and within a couple of weeks they were the proud owners of a brand-new vehicle, which Bill loved with a passion.

He realized that amid his changing units, dealing with the problems that had been ongoing in J and thinking about money all the time, he had likely been a tad cranky—well, maybe a bit more than a tad. He also realized that since he was going to be working more overtime again, he'd have to make a special effort to be a little more pleasant. *But boy, that was a beautiful car!*

Bill and Shirley ended the night out and were a little later in getting to bed than normal. They'd had more than a couple of drinks. Bill had not forgotten about work, but all in all, it had been a nice ending to a rough day, and he couldn't help thinking, *Ain't life grand?*

He gave a lot of credit to his wife. He realized that sometimes he was crabby, but she was great at putting up with him during those times. He'd been injured a couple of times, they had two kids and who didn't have money problems? Shirley always covered his back, and other than the odd argument, she was a loving wife.

He often reflected on the time when he'd first met Shirley. He had decided after much vacillation to attend a friend's wedding, and that had been when he was introduced to Shirley. They'd really hit it off. Who would have ever thought the next wedding he attended would be his and Shirley's?

Life worked in mysterious ways. There were many times when he thanked whoever was up there looking out for them for doing a good job.

Of course, Bill didn't know it yet, but he was going to wish he'd taken the following week off.

Chapter 12

By the time morning rolled around, Shipley had calmed down a little. Once he rolled out of bed and stood up, he realized he had to keep to his regular routine, or at least as close to it as possible. He'd just finished getting his clothes on, when his cell door slammed open. Once his heart slowed down and he could breathe again, he realized it was time to get to the servery and start his day.

With a great deal of trepidation, trying to watch everything going on around him, he managed to get the day in. When the four o'clock count was due, there he was in his cell, alive and not even injured. He felt proud of himself. During the count, he thought about the position he was in, but he knew he had to eat, so he decided to get his supper meal and eat in a common room, still foolishly believing it was the safest place to be. But who knew? Maybe he was right.

He finished his meal, dropped his tray off at the servery and scurried back to his cell with no problems. He decided he wouldn't push his luck and would stay in his cell for a couple of nights. Heck, he had everything he needed. He had water and a toilet, and he had pop, chips and smokes from the canteen. He could even stare at the outside world through his window. He didn't mind that the only things he could see were the lonely tower, the fence and its coils of razor wire and the mobile patrol vehicles driving around. Heck, he was safe!

Vern Thibedeau

He stayed in for a couple of days, but he knew that eventually, he had to get out to the yard for some fresh air. He'd noticed he was spending most of his cell time staring out the window and thinking about his early life and all the problems he'd had. He didn't miss his old man; in fact, he hoped he'd never see him again. But he did miss his sister. *Jesus, I wish I knew where in hell she was or at least knew if she was alive. Out of my whole screwed-up family, she's the only one I got along with. Now I don't even know if she's alive. Goddamn it to hell!* Once again, Shipley could feel that his eyes were a little damp.

After a few days of working in the servery and staying in his cell during the evenings, he was going a little stir-crazy. Eventually, after a lot of thought, he decided to head for the gym.

He chose the gym rather than the yard because it was a much smaller area, and because of the size, the guards had a better view of the inmates. He could walk around a little but still stay kind of close to the gun cage for protection. He was well aware that the officer behind the glass was armed with a rifle and a revolver. His hoped that if anyone came at him, the screw would spot the problem and, if necessary, fire a round off. It was similar to his line of thought regarding the common room. He didn't realize it was more wishful thinking than anything else. He also chose the last changeover to head down, because it usually wasn't as busy, or at least he hoped it wouldn't be.

With his little knife and a great deal of trepidation and hesitation, he left his cell and headed for the gym. He tried to keep an eye on everyone around him and made a conscious effort not to keep checking for his weapon. He felt it was causing a large bulge in his jacket, but in reality, it was insignificant. It wouldn't be much help anyway if something ever did happen.

He made it to the gym, and except for some twitching and flinching on his part, not a thing happened. It felt good to be out of his cell and walking around. It took him several minutes to relax, and even when he did, he kept checking the gun cage to make sure the guard was awake and doing his job. He appeared to be; at least he was awake and looking around while he drank coffee or whatever out of a thermos.

Shipley and an inmate named Wilson, who was new to the range, spotted each other at the same time and, with a nod, started walking beside each other and chatting. During their stroll around the gym, Shipley kept glancing at the gun cage, and Wilson finally asked him if something was going on. Shipley said, "Aw no. Just looking around and trying to spot if anything's going down. But it sure does seem quiet."

Shipley and Wilson didn't get involved with lifting weights or shooting a basketball around; they just walked and chatted. Wilson, being new to the unit, was full of questions and was starting to drive Shipley a little nuts. In fact, when the call came to clear the gym and head back for the last count, he was kind of happy.

Most of the inmates—and there were several dozens of them still in the gym—started heading for the exit at the same time. As usual, a few hung back, and the guard had to get on the speaker and remind them that if they were late for the count, it would be a frosty Friday in hell before they'd be allowed back into the gym. The reminder got them all moving out and caused even more of a human crush at the barrier.

Shipley, as usual, tried to hang back so he wouldn't get jammed up in the crowd, but it didn't work this time. With all the hollering, laughing, cursing, pushing and shoving, he couldn't even keep an eye on who was around him. Within a couple of seconds, he was giving himself hell for not staying in his cell. He was becoming nervous—actually, scared. He kept trying to look around to see who was crowding him, but there was so much pushing and shoving it was impossible to spot any individual inmate. All he could do was try to ignore it all and just go with the flow. And he almost made it.

He was only a step or two from the gym barrier, when someone's foot got tangled up with his, and he felt someone's shoulder give him a hit. Then came what he thought was a kick in the side of his head. Later, he remembered seeing the concrete floor rushing up toward him. He also recalled a flash of light, and that was about it. But lucky for Shipley, he never felt a thing.

*　*　*

Jeff Woodall was standing in a corridor, supervising the inmates leaving the gym. He caught the unusual movement out of the corner of his eye, and at first, he wasn't sure what was going on. Naturally, his first thought was that an inmate was either getting stabbed or being stomped on.

Once he moved closer to the incident, he spotted an inmate lying on the floor and not moving—a sight that reinforced his line of thought. He immediately noticed the other inmates didn't seem concerned and just kept stepping over him and moving toward N area. It also struck him that none of the inmates in the vicinity appeared to be in an extra rush to get the hell away. Jeff's intuition kicked in and told him it wasn't an assault; however, he knew he could be wrong. Like everyone else in that business, he'd been wrong more than once during his career.

He grabbed his radio, told S control he had an inmate down and asked them to close the gym barrier. Then he yelled at the inmates to clear the area and get to their units. Using the radio, he explained to N control what'd happened and said that an inmate coming toward them may have assaulted a con at the gym barrier. His next radio call was to Raymond, the officer posted to the institutional hospital. Jeff informed him that the nurse and a stretcher were required and that the barrier would be opened as soon as all the inmates were clear.

Jeff knew the sergeant in charge of the institution would've been listening to all the radio calls and would be down shortly. That couldn't happen too quickly as far as he was concerned.

It only took a few minutes to clear the inmates from the area so that S control could open the hospital barrier. The nurse; Raymond, who was pushing a stretcher; and Jeff reached the inmate, who was sprawled out on the floor, at about the same time. The nurse immediately checked his pulse and breathing. She also did a quick perusal for any stab wounds, and when she didn't find any, she told the staff she was fairly sure he was just knocked out. But she also told them they had to get him into the hospital for a more thorough check. The sergeant arrived while they were loading the inmate onto the stretcher, and the nurse repeated everything for his benefit.

"Well," he said, "at least that's a positive. I hope he doesn't have to go downtown to the hospital, but if he does, could you try to hold off till morning? But if he does have to go, I'll get an escort together to take him down. I'm just concerned that'd leave us kind of short-staffed."

"I'll see what I can do. If he does have to go, I'll let you know as soon as I can."

Off they hurried to the hospital with the inmate. Jeff and Raymond pushed the stretcher as quickly as possible, and the nurse rushed right behind them. As soon as they were clear of the barrier, S control slammed it closed, opened the gym barrier and told the dozen or so inmates who were left to get up to N area.

* * *

While all that was going on, the staff in N area rushed the inmates into the units and told them to get into their cells. The staff weren't all that concerned. After all, the area around the gym and S control was secure, and there was no staff member in danger. They also knew that as soon as the inmate was removed, the rest of the inmates would be up from the gym, and they could get the count in and go home. And that was exactly what happened, at least as far as the inmates getting up from the gym and being rushed into their units.

While the staff were rushing the inmates into their units, Richards thought, *Christ, I hope that's not one of J unit's cons down there. If it is, I'll end up here for an extra hour or so. Jeez, just what I need—having to phone Shirley to tell her I'm going to be late again. Christ, wouldn't that be just wonderful?*

He was about to learn that he was going to have to phone Shirley and that he was going to be a lot more than an hour late in getting home.

N area had just cleared the last inmate into the units, when the radio call came through: "This is J control. We have a major problem in here. The inmates are refusing to go in on 1K. They've wired the range barrier closed and are in the process of hanging a blanket up over the barrier; we soon won't be able to see down the range. All other ranges are secured, with inmates locked in the cells. Other than 1K, the unit is secured."

Richards, who was standing beside an officer who had a radio on his belt, heard the call. He looked toward his staff and said, "Oh Christ! Let's get in there, but watch yourselves in case they're not all locked up. Goddamn it to hell."

J unit staff and a couple of other officers rushed into the unit to see what the hell was going on. Richards strode past the office and around to 1K. Sure enough, he couldn't really see what was going on on the range, because of the blanket the inmates had hung over the barrier. But everyone, including God, could sure hear them!

This was standard procedure for inmates. Every time something happened on a range, whether it was a smash-up or they were just refusing to go into their cells, they hung up a blanket or something similar. Naturally, that made the staff nervous. They weren't able to see down the range well and never knew what was going on.

Also, during every incident, the noise would start—banging, hollering, screaming and whatever else the inmates could do to make noise. Eventually, it would be so loud the staff would hardly be able hear themselves think, let alone talk to one another. On top of that, staff, once they eventually made it back onto the range, never knew what they might find.

Sometimes these incidents were a cover for an escape attempt, and sometimes the inmates just wanted to give staff a hard time because they were pissed off about something. Often, the reason was to attack another inmate. It could be they thought a guy was a rat, or someone might have been in debt to one of the heavies and faced payback. Unfortunately, often, someone would end up being raped by someone or something, or staff could even find someone dead.

Staff knew that what they found might not be pleasant. Several staff, at one time or another, had found out that it was unbelievable what inmates could do to one another.

Richards just stood there for a minute or so, trying to assess the problem, and then, without warning anyone and almost giving the staff a heart attack, he cupped his hands around his mouth and screamed, "Jenkins! You get your ass up here, and tell us what the hell's going on!" Jenkins was the range rep, so usually, any communication in that type of situation would start with him.

After a few minutes, Jenkins made his way up to the blanket and yelled, "What the hell do you want, Richards? Just screw off and leave us alone."

"You know damn well that's not happening, Jenkins. What the hell brought all this on? Christ, we can usually talk these problems over and settle them without all this crap."

By that time, Sergeant Patrick had arrived, and he heard the last comment from Jenkins. "Jenkins, this is Patrick. I don't know what's going on, but I'd advise you to tell the rest of them to get the hell into their cells before I have to deploy the emergency team. Christ, no one wants that."

"I'll tell you the same thing I told your asshole buddy: just fuck off."

Patrick and Richards walked away from the range so they'd be able to hear each other, and then Patrick asked Richards, "Any idea what in hell brought this on?"

"Nope, no idea at all. I'm concerned about a couple inmates who live on the range, though. One is Shipley, who apparently owes something to that Crothers bunch, and the other is a con by the name of Johnston. Between you and me, Johnston's been feeding us some pretty good info. But a couple of days ago, when I was talking to preventive security, I told him I was worried the other cons may be onto him." Richards spoke quietly. He didn't want anyone, staff or con, to overhear.

"Well, at least you don't have to worry about Shipley. He's the idiot who was injured coming out of the gym, and he's in our hospital. As far as the nurse can tell, he's OK, likely just knocked out for a couple of minutes, and it seems like it was an accident. But if they're onto the other one, he could be in real trouble. And from my perspective, that throws a different light onto the subject. I'll get back up front and tell the team to suit up because they'll likely be going in, and I don't wanna waste any time. Be sure you make a note about Johnston in your report, and if he has an informant's number, be sure you use it.

"Oh, one other thing. Do you think you have enough staff? If not, I can always bring Raymond up from the hospital. There's not much to do down there, and if needed, the nurse could contact you to send him back down."

"Oh no, we're fine here. I have plenty of staff—actually, too many. You might as well just leave him there."

With a bit of a questioning look on his face, Patrick replied, "OK, I'm outta here; talk to you later. If there are any changes, let me know right away." With that, away went the sergeant, likely as much to get away from the noise as anything else.

Vern Thibedeau

There wasn't much for Richards to do. The inmates on 1K certainly didn't want to chat with him, and he had staff walking the other ranges to make sure that everything was OK and that the inmates were locked in their cells. That was about it. He just stood around listening to the racket for a while and then went back to the office.

He'd just made it back, when he received a radio call to let him know they had a couple of extra staff in the control. He already had extra staff walking the ranges, so that was about all he had to do, except to sit and make a few notes and, of course, listen to all the screaming and banging and hope things would work out for the best.

Within a few minutes, the officer in charge of the emergency team popped in for a few minutes to talk to Richards and take a quick look around. "We don't have enough guys for two teams, Bill, so I guess we'll only be able to make an entry from the front of the range. I'd really prefer to enter at both ends, but there's just not enough time. Once we do our entry and get things straightened out a bit, I'll let you know how it's going. When everything's more or less under control, I'll give you the word, and you and a few of your guys can come in behind us to check on the cons. Up till then, we'll just make sure they're secure and see if any of them need a nurse or an ambulance. Just don't come in until I give you the word. That sound about right to you?"

"Sounds good to me, Steve. I don't have a clue about what brought this on, so it may be a set-up for something; you guys watch yourselves in there. Oh yeah, one other thing: I don't know if Patrick mentioned it or not, but I'm sort of concerned about Johnston. He sleeps in twenty-three and may be—"

"He did mention it. That's the main reason we're going in with only one team."

"OK, Steve, see you guys shortly. Good luck."

With that, Steve headed up front to get suited up and to explain the plan, such as it was, to the team.

Once the staff finished checking the other ranges and reported back to the office, Bill filled them in on what was going to happen. Then, looking at one of his guys and pointing a finger at him, he said, "Once the team goes in, you stay in the office to monitor the phone." Then, looking toward the other three officers, he continued with his instructions. "When I receive the go-ahead from the team, you three follow me onto the range. From then on, we'll be playing it by ear and hoping for the best."

Then Bill turned his attention back to Jerry, the officer who had to remain in the office. "You'll likely have a lot of company in here with you, but you make damn sure you stay next to that phone. If we need a nurse, an ambulance or whatever, I'll let you know by radio, and then you phone the sergeant and make damn sure he hears the radio call. He may wanna come down and check for himself, but in any case, it's not up to us to notify those people. We'll just let the powers that be worry about that end of it; that's why they get the big bucks. We'll likely be busy anyway."

The staff spent the next 10 minutes or so, which felt like a couple of hours, just standing around talking and pacing up and down. They also had to listen to the racket and the odd scream coming out of 1K and hope to hell no one on the range was being beaten up or worse.

In a reasonably short time, which still felt like a couple of hours to the staff, they heard the unit barrier open. As soon as they heard the barrier, they all looked at one another with a sense relief but also with another spike of adrenaline because they knew it would be the emergency team on its way in. Mixed in was a feeling of apprehension. The staff knew they would soon be on the range, and every one of them dreaded what they might find.

Richards headed out of the office to check with Steve and make sure nothing had changed. He also wanted to ensure that Steve knew nothing had changed on his end and that the guys in the control were aware of the plan. As he strode toward the barrier, he watched the team hustling in and thought, *Good God. Every time I see them suited up with their shields, sticks, vests and all that other crap, I get nervous. Thank God we're on the same side. Those cons are nuts to cause all this. They know damn well the team'll be in and will likely gas them. Oh well. Maybe the idiots are into pain.*

Richards met the team about halfway into the unit and had a few words with Steve before the leader pulled his helmet down. In answer to Bill's question, he replied, "Yep, no changes, Bill. I'll let you know by radio when I want you to come in. I imagine I'll be a little too busy to be thinking about fancy radio calls, so I'll just say, 'Come on in, Bill.' That sound good with you?"

"Yep, sounds OK. Go give 'em hell, but watch yourselves."

With that, Steve pulled his helmet down, and the team headed toward 1k.

The idea was for the team to quietly approach the barrier, cut the wire tying it shut and wave to the control, and then, while they were pulling the blanket down, the control would open the barrier. Then they would head in. Also, just in case, everyone in the unit had a gas mask handy. If gas was used, it would be fired as soon as they stepped onto the range. In any case, they were likely going to toss a flash-bang grenade down the range in the hope of disorienting the inmates. At least that was the plan.

The unit staff prayed the gas wouldn't be needed. No one enjoyed working in the aftereffects of that stuff, and over time, the gas masks became uncomfortable.

Richards and his three officers stood back from the barrier while the team cut the wire and started tearing the blanket down. They knew that if they needed any help, there were all kinds of staff pacing around in the unit, raring to go in. But they'd been told to stay back unless called upon. In that type of situation, there was such a thing as too many people getting in the way, but it felt nice to know they were there if needed.

Suddenly, the blanket was ripped down, and just before the team started onto the range, Richards and his guys plugged their ears and looked away. If a grenade was used, the four of them wouldn't be much help if they were disoriented, couldn't see and didn't know if they were coming or going.

Out of the corner of his eye, Bill watched the team start down the range, and then he jerked his head around and closed his eyes. He was lucky he did, because within a split second of his closing his eyes, *bang!* Even with his eyes closed, there was a flash of light. Bill thought, *God, I hope they don't have to use that damn gas!*

The team, with the shield man in front and nightsticks in the up position, charged down the range in formation. Thankfully, Richards spotted several inmates running into their cells even as they screamed warnings and dire threats of what was to come. He tried to keep track of the inmates who'd been on the range, but with all the commotion, he spotted only a few and soon gave up.

Bill didn't think it could get any noisier, but with the team banging on their shields and the inmates screaming their threats, it became a hell of a lot noisier. The range also seemed to get hotter and, for some weird reason, dustier.

Bill and his three guys waited at the end of the range, almost prancing in their eagerness to get onto the range to help.

Approximately five inmates remained on the range. Bill figured they must have wanted to prove how tough and hard they were. The team rushed them and, one at a time, forced each one up against the wall with a shield. A couple of the team would then grab the inmate, put him into a come-along hold, march him to an empty cell, toss him in and radio the control to close the applicable cell.

Bill tried to keep track of the cell numbers that the team wanted closed, knowing that each cell would now have an inmate in it who might not belong there. But it didn't take long to lose count. With all the wrestling, yelling and orders to the control to close the doors, Bill soon gave up. He figured he'd just wait until he couldn't see any inmates on the range and all the cell doors were closed; that would mean they were all locked up. At least he hoped that was what it would mean.

Once the team were about halfway down the range, Steve radioed Bill to start checking the cells. Bill acknowledged the call, looked at his three guys and hollered, "Let's go! Stay close to me, and watch so we don't catch up to the team. First, we have to make sure each inmate in the cell is OK and doesn't require medical attention. At the same time, John, list the con's name and the cell he's in, so we can sort them out once we're done making sure they're alive and kicking."

Bill started at cell number one. He looked into the cell, saw the inmate sitting on the bed, radioed the control to open it and told the inmate to stand up and keep his mouth shut until he was asked to say something. John wrote the inmate's name down and noted he was in the proper cell, and after Bill asked the inmate if he needed medical attention, John wrote down that the inmate said he was OK and didn't require anything.

Vern Thibedeau

While that was going on, a couple of team members grabbed the last inmate, put a come-along on him and started marching him to a cell. The three of them took about two steps, and Bill saw the inmate, for some silly reason, start to resist. Bill noticed one of the officers tighten up on the hold, and suddenly, the inmate started walking on his toes and screaming, "OK, for Christ's sake, I'm going in!"

The inmate was screaming so loudly Bill could hear him above all the other racket going on. Apparently, the other inmates could also hear him, because their screaming died down for about two seconds. But of course, after that slight pause, the threats against the staff and their families and the screeching about all the mayhem they were going to cause started right up again.

Once that last inmate was pushed into a cell and the team were on their way out, Steve, who'd stayed down at a cell, gave a yell: "Bill, get down here to twenty-three! That con you're worried about may need some medical attention—and don't take too long getting down here!"

"On the way, Steve."

With a "Let's get going, guys," they headed down to Johnston's cell on the run. As soon as Bill looked through the window, he knew there was a problem. Johnston was kneeling on the floor with his upper body bent over the bed. Even through the cell door, Bill could hear him moaning, but there wasn't any movement at all. Bill radioed the control to open 23, and with a quick look around the cell, he rushed over to Johnston.

He didn't spot the blood until he'd almost reached the inmate, and then, when he bent down to get a better look, he saw a pool of blood on the floor and then saw more blood dripping off the bed. Johnston looked like he was in rough shape.

Bill took a couple of seconds to see if he was breathing, and then he thumbed the radio. "I need the nurse down in twenty-three right now. It looks like we have a stabbing!"

Bill had hoped there wouldn't be any serious injuries. He knew that any time a disturbance like this happened, complaints flew in to the do-gooders, but if an inmate was injured, either by staff or by another inmate, the complaints appeared to double. The investigators, when they came in, seemed to think staff should know where each and every inmate had been at every moment of time during the disturbance, and of course, it appeared as if the staff were always the bad guys.

Bill, who'd stepped in the pool of blood and felt a little nauseous, squatted down beside Johnston and informed him that the nurse was on her way down. "Jeez, man, did you see who did this to you?" Bill grabbed a towel and pressed it against Johnston's side, where it appeared he'd suffered a stab wound. At the same time, the other guys lifted Johnston up and laid him on the bed.

"Oh yeah, I saw the pricks; couldn't miss 'em. They came right up to me, and one grabbed my arms while the other stuck a shiv into my side." With a loud groan, he continued. "God, it hurts like hell! It was that fucking Ronald who grabbed me and Jones who stabbed me. While he was sticking me, the son of a bitch said, 'Crothers says to say hi to you, you fucking rat.' Christ, if your guys hadn't come in when they did, I'd be dead now!"

"You're gonna be OK. The nurse is here, and she's one of our best." With that bit of encouragement, Bill stepped back so the nurse could take over.

She gave a quick look at Johnston's injuries, saw the amount of blood on the floor and the bed and, looking at Bill, said, "Radio the sergeant, and tell him we need an ambulance right now and an escort to the downtown hospital!"

Bill passed the unwelcome news to Patrick and informed him it was definitely a stabbing. Then he continued the radio call by saying, "I also have some other news. We'd better have a chat as soon as you're finished with your phone calls."

"OK, I'll get down as soon as I can."

By then, there were several staff on the range, and Bill ordered a couple of them to give the nurse a hand. He looked at John and the other two officers and waved them out onto the range. Once the four of them were out of the cell, Bill walked down the range to get away from all the staff, and then he turned toward them.

In almost a whisper, he started with his instructions. "Listen, guys, this could be very important. I imagine you heard what Johnston said to me." Once Bill received affirmative nods from them, he continued. "I want you to write down exactly what Johnston said to me and include the time and circumstances of the situation. This may be our opportunity to get rid of that bastard Crothers and a couple of his goons. But listen up. Don't say a word about this to anyone. If you have to talk about it, get somewhere where there's just the three of you, and make damn sure you can't be overheard. Christ, I don't want this screwed up!"

The three guys looked at Bill and said they understood and would be careful.

With that acknowledgment, Bill, in a much louder voice, said, "OK, guys, there's plenty of help here. You take off up front, and do your thing. If anyone questions why you're up there, tell them to give me a call in the unit."

Just as Bill turned to head back to Johnston's cell, a stretcher, pushed by an orderly, passed him on the way down. Bill followed it and watched as Johnston was loaded onto it, and then he followed it back up the range until the nurse, the orderly and Johnston were gone.

With some relief, he knew Johnston was still alive because of his groaning and because the nurse kept talking to him as they headed for the hospital. Bill was thankful for that because the stabbing was already starting to eat at him a little. He couldn't help feeling partly to blame for the mess Johnston was in. Then Bill turned around and headed back down the range again.

He left instructions for the staff to finish checking the inmates and to ensure each one was in his proper cell. "And don't worry," he said, "about any whining regarding missing their meds or anything else. Just sort them out one at a time and make sure it's the right cell, and just throw them in if you have to. And tell them to keep their fucking mouths shut, or they'll be in the hole." With that, Bill headed to the office.

As soon as Richards reached the office, he contacted the sergeant and suggested the team stay suited up until they'd had their little chat. "I don't know for sure, but you may want them to put two or three inmates into seg."

"OK, Bill. I'll pass the word along, and I should be down to see you in a few minutes. Things getting all sorted out on the range?"

"Yep. Almost back to normal, at least whatever normal is around here."

While Bill waited for the sergeant to show up, he sorted out everything he knew about the problems with Crothers. Crothers had been moved to E unit a while back, so he had to phone over there to find out which cell he was in. He made the call and, speaking to the corporal, asked which cell Crothers slept in.

"Oh, he's in 2F13. What's up, Bill? Anything I should know about?"

"Yes, there is. We're almost back to normal here in J unit, but the good news in this screw-up is that we may have enough to lock that prick up. If we do, the team'll be in shortly to take him to the hole. So keep your fingers crossed."

"Jesus. I hope you're not pulling my leg, Bill. If we could get rid of that asshole, it would make a lot of staff happy. Hell, even several cons would like to see him gone."

"Hope it all works out. Someone'll give you a phone call before the team shows up. You know, I almost hope the idiot puts up a fight and gets the shit kicked out of him. Oh, one other thing: you'd better keep this on the QT just in case it doesn't work out for us, but I'm sure it will." With that hopeful statement, Bill hung up.

While he waited, he jotted down what Johnston had told him and noted the cell numbers where Crothers, Ronald and Jones lived. Once that was accomplished, all he could really do was sit and wait for Patrick and hope to hell he would lock the three of them up. *God, this must be enough to get them into the hole and, with luck, maybe even transferred out.*

Finally, Patrick made it to the unit, and it only took Bill five minutes or so to fill him in on the situation. The sergeant looked at Bill with his usual harried look and said, "I would imagine your guys have put everything on paper?"

"Yep, they're up front finishing it now, and they're almost done." With an expectant look, Bill added, "Do you think it's enough to get all three into the hole?"

"Oh, I would think so. Between you and me, the warden's been hoping for a reason to lock Crothers and, hopefully, a few of his idiots up. This should do the trick. In any case, I'm going to get the team to do it right now, and with any luck, we'll get them transferred into the special handling unit." With that, the sergeant got on his radio and told Steve to get his team together and come back to the unit.

The team must have been just sitting and waiting for the call, because it only took a couple of minutes for them to reach the unit. Bill gave Patrick a bit of a surprised look, and with a grin, Patrick said, "I was hoping and kind of expecting to get enough info to lock that goof up. I think you've fulfilled the wish of a lot of people around here."

Patrick gave the team their instructions and told them to go to E unit to grab Crothers first and then go back to J for the other two. "I would imagine once they know Crothers is locked up, they won't put up much of an argument. But one way or another, I want them in the hole."

With those orders, the team happily headed for E unit. Owen looked at Richards and, with a grin, said, "Wanna come along? I think they can manage here without you for a little while."

Bill jumped off his chair and said, "Oh God, do I ever!"

So Owen and Richards followed the team over to E unit. Owen, Bill and the corporal of the unit followed the team up to 2F. The three of them waited at the head of the range while the team headed for F13.

*   *   *

As soon as the team reached the cell, Steve gave a wave to the control, signaling them to open the door. Steve and two team members crowded into the cell before the door was even fully open. One team member in the cell with Steve had the shield, and the other had the can of mace. Before Crothers had an opportunity to say anything, Steve yelled, "Crothers, one way or another, your ass is going to the hole! Now, turn the hell around, and get your hands behind you."

"You pigs go fuck yourselves! I'm not go—"

Before Crothers could finish his statement, Steve gave a two-worded command: "Mace him!"

Tom was only too happy to carry out the order. He aimed the canister at Crothers, pressed the button and watched the stream contact Crothers on the forehead, just above the eyes—a perfect shot! Within moments, Steve ordered the shield man to do his thing. While the shield was being used to push Crothers up against the wall and Crothers was fighting to try to get around it, Steve and another officer rushed him to force him down so they could apply the handcuffs.

Just as Steve reached Crothers, the inmate managed to free one arm and took a swing at Steve, hitting him in the chest area. Steve let out a whoosh, and his first thought was that he had been stabbed. Within a moment, he knew he'd only been punched, but it had been one hell of a punch. *Jesus*, he thought, *thank Christ I'm wearing a vest!*

As Tom latched on to Crothers's arm, he threw a quick glance and a question toward Steve: "You OK?"

"Yep, I'm good. Just get him down!"

By that time, all five members had rushed Crothers. With a lot of grunting, yelling, a few fists thrown and some arm twisting, they managed to force him down onto the floor. Eventually, even with Crothers fighting, kicking and trying to roll around and with tears streaming out of his eyes, they managed to roll him onto his stomach and secure him with the plastic tie-cuffs.

Steve looked down at him and couldn't help saying, "You stupid idiot. You knew you were going to the hole—why in hell act like a fool? All you managed to do was get yourself maced and gain a few bruises, and you can bet your ass I'm charging you with assault."

"Aw, screw the whole lot of you assholes!" Crothers yelled while trying to catch his breath and wipe his nose and eyes, which was difficult to do with his hands cuffed behind his back. By that time, the staff had him bent over almost kissing the floor while they hustled him out of his cell. Once out of the cell, Steve waved to the control to secure it, and they headed off the range.

Steve couldn't help looking down at Crothers while the two officers held his arms as they shuffled him down the range and saying, "Ah, quit your crying, you big, tough con. Boy, your eyes look kind of sore. Jeez, they must be with all the crying you're doing. Christ Almighty, grow up, and act like a man, for God's sake!"

* * *

The three officers waiting at the end of the range couldn't see any of the action. They heard only the command "Mace him," some scuffling, yells and Crothers letting out what sounded like a loud sob. Then, in a short time, out came Crothers, held by two team members. Crothers was bent over with his hands behind his back, and with all the tears streaming down his cheeks, he seemed to be crying. He certainly didn't look like a big, tough guy at the moment. In fact, Richards heard one of the team members say to Crothers, "Well, not such a big, tough guy now, are you, you asshole?" Not surprisingly, he didn't receive any comment from Crothers.

Seeing Crothers in that position, Owen, Richards and the corporal looked at one another with happy smiles on their faces.

When the team reached Owen, Steve, between puffs, exclaimed, "Well, we got him! I'll be laying an assault charge on him; he actually had time to punch me in the chest. We'll take him down to the hole and throw him into a very cold shower. As you can tell, we had to use the mace. But we'll be back up to J in twenty minutes or so. But all in all, it went pretty good."

Patrick and Richards followed the team out to N area and headed into J unit while Crothers made his way, with some help, to segregation. While Owen walked around to the office, Bill took the stairs up to the control to let the staff know what was going to happen in a short time. That bit of information seemed to make their day, especially once they were informed about Crothers being maced and put into the hole. Once that little job was finished, Bill went around to the office, and everyone sat around chatting while waiting for the team to show up.

Everything went as planned. It had already been decided, because of the possibility of problems and because it was normal routine when placing more than one inmate into segregation, that each inmate would be escorted one at a time to the segregation area. The team entered the unit and marched down to each individual cell. The inmate was informed that he was going to the hole, and it was up to him how he went. He could choose the easy way or the hard way. Each one was also told that the staff didn't really give a damn which way he picked to go, as long as he realized his ass was going to be in the hole within a short time.

Each inmate was also informed that mace would be used if there was any resistance and that Crothers had been maced and was already in lock-up. Then each inmate was individually escorted to the hole. Other than the usual threats and noise, which were mostly bravado on the inmates' part, within 30 minutes, they were both residing in segregation. No mace had to be used. So much for being a hero and standing up for a buddy. Surprisingly, the other inmates didn't make a sound. Maybe they were happy.

As soon as the last inmate left the unit and was on his way to the hole, Owen looked at Richards and said, "Well, that's a good night's work. And now I think we'd better get the hell home; it's been a long one. Oh, one other thing before I take off. This thing with Paul Raymond—is there something I should be aware of? It isn't very often that someone turns down extra help in the middle of an incident. If there is something going on, I'd really appreciate being told about it."

"Ah, it's really no big deal. It's just that some of us don't like the way he works. When there's something going on, he's not a great deal of help. He sort of stands back until staff get the inmate under control, and then he steps in and, acting like a hero, gives the con a lot of lip. If it's an actual fight, he's been known to throw a few unneeded punches. Naturally, quite often, that just gets the con going again. To be honest, it's usually easier if he's not around. Mind you, he's OK on the normal routines; it's pretty well just during situations that he's a pain in the ass."

"OK, thanks, Bill. That's very good to know. I'm going to go up to finish a few things; would you thank the staff for me and tell them to head out? And thanks again; that was well done. I'll see you tomorrow afternoon."

Richards did just that. However, before he left, as soon as he had a moment, he phoned Shirley. He knew she was likely sitting on pins and needles waiting for him, so he let her know that everything was back to normal and that he would be home shortly. He had phoned earlier to explain that they were having a problem and that he'd likely be late in getting home. He'd also made sure to tell her not to worry, because it was no big deal, and there was no danger. But he knew his little speech hadn't eased her mind much.

Bill did one other thing before leaving the institution for home. Because it would only take a few minutes, he decided to walk down to the hospital to see how everything was going.

He walked in through the hospital barrier, spotted the officer leaning back with his feet up on the desk and gave him a wave. As he walked over to him, he saw a pocket book lying upside down on the desk and knew damn well he had been sitting there reading. "Hey, Raymond, everything all settled down in here?"

"Oh yeah, finally. Boy, it's been a busy night, but I must admit I'm glad I was here and not in the unit."

"Don't blame you a bit. I was just wondering how Johnston was doing and if he got away OK."

"Aw, he seemed OK. There's no doubt he's alive; you could tell by all the noise he was making." Paul grinned. "God, you'd think he'd been stabbed or something. Seriously, though, the nurse is pretty sure he's going to be OK. And the ambulance was here in no time at all, so we got him out really fast, and that's always a good thing. The nurse did say it's lucky you guys got to him when you did, though. Much longer, and he would've bled out."

"Yeah, that's good to hear. Oh, while I'm down here, how's that Shipley doing? He awake yet?"

"Aw yeah. He's fine. Woke up after a few minutes and knows where he is, so other than a bit of a headache, he's OK."

"Good enough. Thanks for the news. I'm gonna take off home. See you around, Paul."

Once he had that bit of information, Bill felt a little better. He didn't even feel quite as tired. But as he walked out, he couldn't help thinking, *Well, Raymond, I'm also kind of glad you were down here instead of in the unit. You are more or less useless when there's a problem.*

That was it for Bill. Suddenly, he was anxious to get home and see Shirley. He knew the kids would be sleeping, but he'd see them in the morning. Feeling relieved, he took off for the parking lot. As he walked out, he couldn't help but think, *Boy, everyone got to go home, and we're another day closer to retirement!*

Chapter 13

Once they reached the gym and had Shipley loaded onto the stretcher, Jeff and Raymond, with the nurse right behind them, quickly exited the gym corridor and had him in the hospital within a minute or so. Upon reaching the hospital, under the nurse's direction, they pushed the stretcher directly into the examination room. After they roughly lifted Shipley onto a bed, Jeff told Raymond to put cuffs on him because he had to get up to N area to give them a hand with whatever was going on in J unit. Raymond cuffed Shipley to the bed, and Jeff strongly suggested the cuffs stay on until the nurse was finished with him and he was locked in a cell.

Raymond looked at Jeff and said, "Ah, you don't have to worry about that. He's a hell of a lot bigger than me, and I've no intention of getting into a fight with him. I just hope he doesn't have to go downtown."

By that time, the nurse had finished checking Shipley, and she looked at both staff and said, "I don't think we have to worry about that. He'll be staying here overnight so I can keep an eye on him, but I'm pretty sure he'll be OK. I just hope nothing happens in J unit."

Of course, things were going to happen in J unit, and she didn't realize she was soon going to be much busier, attending to Johnston's injuries.

After hearing the nurse's comment, with Shipley cuffed, Jeff looked at Raymond and said, "All's good here. Just keep the cuffs on the con.

I'm taking off for N area. Any problems, contact N control." With that bit of direction, Jeff took off.

*　*　*

After several minutes, Shipley woke up with a start and didn't have a clue where he was, how he'd gotten there or what'd happened. He opened his eyes, and once he knew he wasn't in his cell, he tried to sit up. When he realized he couldn't use one hand, he looked down and saw that it was cuffed to a bed. Suddenly, he remembered coming out of the gym, and that was it. The only thing he knew was that he had a blinding headache.

Just then, the nurse walked in to check on him. "Oh, you're awake. Good for you. I'll bet you have a really bad headache; how would you like a couple of pain pills?" She approached the bed to see how he was doing.

"My God, you're right about the sore head. Where am I, and what the hell happened?"

The nurse took a couple of minutes to tell Shipley what she knew and then headed out to get him a couple of pills. On the way to the meds room, she told Raymond that Shipley was awake and that she was getting some meds for him.

Paul looked up from the desk, and as he stood up, he said, "OK. I'll go in and have a chat with him. I don't imagine he has a clue about what's going on."

"You're right about that; he didn't even know he was in the hospital. I'm going to keep him for the night and then send him back to his unit in the morning."

With that, Raymond headed in to see Shipley, and the nurse continued on to the meds room.

As soon as Paul walked into the examination room, Shipley looked up at him and asked, "What the hell's going on? What am I doing in here?"

Raymond explained as best as he could that Shipley had gotten his head thumped and that staff were pretty sure it had been an accident. "But," he said, "we're having problems on your range in J unit, so even if the nurse said she could release you, we'd be keeping your ass in here until we get things settled down. So maybe it's just as well you hit your head. At least you're not involved with the shit on the range, and if gas has to be used, it won't affect us here in the hospital."

Shipley questioned Raymond about 1K and asked what'd started it. He also wanted to know if anyone was hurt.

"As far as I know, the cons are just refusing to go in, and no one's been injured, at least not yet. But the team's getting suited up to head in, so keep your fingers crossed. But before it's over, I imagine a few of your buddies'll end up in the hole. Anyway, once I know what's going on and I get a minute or so, I'll fill you in. Got any idea what could have set this screw-up off?"

"Nah. No idea at all. It's probably just the usual shit. I ain't got a clue."

Of course, once Shipley found out what was going on, he desperately hoped staff would lock the Crothers bunch up. As an added bonus, it would be nice if Jacob and his buddy went in with them.

Once Paul left to go back to the office, Shipley just lay back in the bed, happy as hell that he wasn't in the unit and only had a sore head. Once the pills the nurse gave him kicked in, he managed to drift off into a hazy sleep. He stayed asleep until a hell of a racket coming from the hospital entrance jerked him awake. He heard yelling, and then the nurse, with a strident voice, said, "Oh God, this could be bad! Into the examination room! Has anyone called for an ambulance?"

Someone shouted a reply: "Yep! It's on the way. Be here any minute; someone's at the entrance, waiting to let them in through the sally port!"

Shipley was wide awake now. He looked toward the doorway just as several staff pushed a stretcher into the room. The nurse was running beside it, holding a cloth to the side of an inmate lying on it. The inmate was covered with blood, moaning and giving out the odd yelp.

Shipley got a quick glance at the inmate and thought, *Jesus Christ, that's Johnston. God, he lives just up from me. What the hell happened to him?*

Shipley heard the nurse say in a calm voice, "Help me get his shirt off. I've got to get some compression on the wound, or he'll bleed out!"

After that, staff crowded around the stretcher, and Shipley couldn't see much of anything. But he could hear the moans, which were much louder than the instructions the nurse was handing out.

Within a short time—Shipley wasn't too sure how long—three paramedics rushed into the room, pushing a gurney. Johnston was transferred onto it, and the paramedics did whatever it was they did. Then, followed by two staff, they pushed the stretcher and Johnston out of the area. Afterward, other than the nurse cleaning up the blood, everything quieted down, and he drifted back off into his dazed sleep.

Shipley was released from the hospital after lunch the next day and told to go back to his cell. He was given instructions not to go to work for a few days, and if his headache became any worse, he was to report back to the hospital. Shipley didn't want to go back to the hospital; after all, the memories weren't pleasant. But as he was walking back to the unit, he thought, *Hell, if I can go back down and get some free pills, why shouldn't I? If I don't wanna use them, I could trade them for some smokes.*

Once Shipley made it back to the unit, he stopped at the office and checked in with the corporal. He wanted to make sure they knew he was back and that he didn't have to go to work for a few days.

"Glad you're back, Shipley," said the corporal. "I understand you ran into a barrier coming out of the gym last night, eh? It's just as well you weren't in this nuthouse anyway; it was a real screw-up. You doing OK?"

"Oh yeah. Hell of a headache, but that's about it. Nurse said to go get some pills if it gets worse. Not supposed to go to work for a few days. Any changes on the range?"

"Your buddies'll fill you in, but we put a couple of assholes into the hole, and Johnston's in the downtown hospital. He was stabbed, but the word is that he's gonna be OK."

With a "Glad to hear it; he's a good guy," Shipley walked around to the common room to have a chat with a couple of inmates from his range whom he'd spotted sitting around having coffee.

Shipley strolled into the common room as if nothing had happened, poured a coffee and, as he sat down at the table, said, "Hey, how you doing?"

Both guys looked at him, and one replied, "Aw, not too bad once all this shit settles down. Where the hell you been? You missed all the fun."

Shipley, thinking it'd be a good chance to let them know how tough he was and knowing it was an outright lie, replied, "Aw, some asshole got behind me while we were leaving the gym last night and rammed me into a barrier. Spent the whole night in the hospital. I'll tell you this, though, and you can take it to the fucking bank: when I get him, he's gonna have a shank up his ass. I'm getting sick of all this bullshit."

"Don't blame you. Did you hear about Donald and Myers from the range getting locked up? The pigs say they shanked Johnston—what a load of crap. They even locked Crothers from E unit up. Donald—or maybe it was Myers—told the screws that Crothers ordered them to do the shanking. What a bunch they are; pigs never change."

Hearing that bit of news floored Shipley. *Holy hell, Crothers and two of his goons are locked up. I don't think any of them are left in this unit. Jeez, I'm home free.*

The other inmate at the table joined the conversation by sarcastically saying, "Sorry to burst your bubble pal, but I think the screws got it right for a change. I didn't get involved with all the bullshit, but I was standing at my door, watching everyone running around like goddamned idiots. Then I spotted those two guys heading for Johnston's cell, which is right next to mine, and I could tell they meant business. I'm not stupid, and as soon as I spotted one reaching under his jacket as they ran into the cell, I ducked back into mine; I didn't wanna see a damned thing. But I'll tell you, I could hear the yelling, fighting and banging and then Johnston, even though it sounded muffled, let out a hell of a scream. I'm guessing they must've covered his mouth with a hand or pillow or something. I'll tell you all something else too. I've been around, but that scream scared the shit out of me. I would've bet anything that the poor guy had bit the bullet. At any rate, there's no doubt what those assholes did. And you know that guy Johnston didn't seem like a bad dude. Hope to hell he's OK."

"Ah, I don't know, but there's talk going around that he's a rat. If he is, I think it looks good on the fucker. There's nothing I hate more than—"

"Ah bullshit. He's not a rat. And even if he was, he didn't deserve being shanked. Maybe a bit of a beating or being run off the range but not shanked, for Christ's sake."

For several minutes, the three of them sat around and discussed the problem and the effect it would likely have on the routine of the unit, especially on the range. Then the little meeting broke up when Shipley told them his head was getting worse, so he was going to his cell to try to get some sleep. With a "See you later, guys," he headed for his cell.

Shipley was about halfway down the range, when all of a sudden, a sense of euphoria struck him. *My God, I'm gonna be OK after all! I'm alive, and I'm gonna stay alive. I feel like I could dance! Hope those assholes stay locked up forever.*

Shipley slept. He even forgot all about owing Jacob and his buddy for the saw. But eventually, all good things had to come to an end.

After a few hours, Shipley woke up. He felt refreshed, with no headache, and once he remembered his great news, he still felt like dancing. But he just lay there luxuriating in the great feeling, which he was unaccustomed to. Even as he lay there staring at the four walls, the barred window and the sold steel door with its little window, he felt almost like a free man.

Suddenly, jarring him out of his dreamland, the speakers gave out their usual squeal, followed by a voice giving the inmates some new instructions.

"Attention, 1K inmates. The range is on lockdown, and each cell is going to be searched. The evening meal of sandwiches and coffee will be delivered to your cell. When your turn comes to be searched, your door will be opened, you will step out with nothing in your hands and you will be patted down and escorted to a common room. Once staff has completed searching your cell, you will be escorted back and locked in. You will not argue or cause any problems, or you will be locked up in segregation. As soon as the search is completed, the range will be back on normal routine."

As soon as the announcement was completed, the usual yelling, banging and threats started up. That was expected, and no one thought anything would come of it. Naturally, the inmates were pissed off. To them, such a search was a direct violation of their God-given right to privacy. However, the only ones really concerned were the inmates who had contraband hidden in their cells.

Several inmates, because there was nothing they could do, just hoped the guards wouldn't find what they had hidden away. The ones with homemade brew stashed away immediately jumped up and started tearfully pouring it down the toilets and flushing it away. The ones holding drugs or an excessive amount of medication had to decide whether to flush the stuff or keep it hidden and hope it wasn't found. Drugs were expensive, and if they were holding for one of the heavies and lost them, one way or another, they had to come good for the cost of the stuff.

The staff always kind of chuckled as they listened to the toilets being flushed when that type of situation popped up. It was kind of neat to have the cons flush the brew away instead of having to lug it out, take samples, write up the charges and then listen to the inmates whine and snivel about being picked on.

At first, Shipley tensed up at the announcement. Then he remembered he didn't have his little shiv in the cell; he'd lost it a couple days before. He didn't even have the saw that had been part of his great escape plan. He hadn't been able to pay for it, so it hadn't been given to him. At the time, he had been upset with Jacob and felt like whacking him on his stupid head. Now he couldn't have been happier. *Hell, let them search all night and day if they want. Who cares? Certainly not me. I hope Jacob or that other goof gets caught with it. That'd really be great!*

Shipley flopped back down onto his bed and listened to the noise, which was quickly becoming a murmur. He reflected a bit on his life and felt happy as hell.

Within a short time, Shipley's door was kicked, and he was told to get up and grab his supper. His sandwich and coffee were passed through the door opening, and then the opening was slammed shut again. He finished his meal, such as it was, and figured he had a lot of time before the search party reached his area, so he just curled up on the bed and watched television. *Jeez*, he thought, *life is just too damn tough.*

It was difficult to imagine that a short time ago, Shipley hadn't thought he'd be alive for much longer. Apparently, difficult things in life could change quickly.

While Shipley lounged in his cell, watching television, every once in a while, he could hear a few cell doors opening and staff telling the inmates to go to the common room to relax for a while. He knew they were frisked before being allowed to leave the area and that they were escorted to the common room. He also realized the staff were in the empty cells searching for anything they could find, and the cells would likely be in a hell of a mess by the time the inmates were allowed back into them. It struck him that he was lucky he'd lost his little shank. *Christ, if the screws'd found that, I'd be in the hole for sure. Jesus, I'm glad Jacob's buddy wouldn't give us the saw until we paid him. God, there's no place to hide that thing!*

Shipley watched TV and listened to the cell doors opening and closing, guards giving orders and inmates arguing, and he knew it would soon be his turn. Once again, he thought, *Thank God I don't have anything that would get me in trouble.*

He listened as the guys just down from him were taken out, frisked and escorted away, and he knew he would be in the next bunch to have his cell torn apart. Sure enough, within 20 minutes or so, he heard the inmates being escorted back. He could hear comments being thrown back and forth and was a little surprised to hear his neighbour yell to another inmate, "Hey, Joe, I got a letter from my honey! Boy, even when we're being screwed over by these bastards, the mail must go through. Ain't life just frigging grand?"

Then Shipley's door slammed open. As soon as the door opened, he stepped out and put his arms up to be frisked. At the same time, he glanced around and saw there were four inmates being searched and knew they'd soon be on their way to the common room.

While Shipley was standing there being searched, he couldn't stop contemplating how his life had changed. He still felt so good he was almost high. He felt as if he were another foot taller. Once he had been frisked and was escorted to the common room, he held his head high and strutted down the range. This was a new feeling for Shipley. He felt invincible. He couldn't get over it; all this just because a few jerks had gotten locked up.

Once in the common room, they just sat, watched TV and hoped the guards didn't make too much of a mess in the cells. But they were aware that the cells would likely be torn up. Shipley could visualize his bedding, clothing and personal effects being thrown all over the cell. He just hoped they didn't damage the television.

During the wait, there wasn't much for them to do, so they just sat and looked at one another and chatted about what had gone on. One of them said he'd heard the guards took one guy to the hole. "Not sure what he had, but the fuckers grabbed him, said something about a saw or some fucking thing and marched him down the range. Guess we'll find out more later on. Hope the buggers don't make too much of a mess, though. I've been through this a couple times, and it's not pretty. They're just a bunch of pricks, and they enjoy doing this; it's just their way to get back at us."

Holy Christ, that's great! God, maybe Jacob and his buddy are both in the hole along with Crothers and his bunch. Christ, this is wonderful; maybe there is a God. Jesus Christ, things are getting better and better! Shipley could almost feel himself grow another inch or so.

Within a short time, just minutes before they had to go back to their cells, a staff member walked in with a few letters to hand out. Shipley couldn't believe it; with envious looks from his fellow inmates, he received two of them. *Holy hell, I go for ages with no mail, and then I get two at once!* Suddenly, with his heart thumping, he couldn't wait to get back to his cell so he could relax and read the letters in private.

On his way back, he kept reflecting on all his great news. *A saw? Christ, I hope that's the saw that jerk-off is trying to make me pay for. God, that'd be great. Hope they keep him in the hole forever.*

He made it to his cell, stepped in and looked around. *Hell, they didn't make much of a mess at all,* he thought. His clothes had been shoved around, and his bed was a mess because the mattress had been flipped over, but all in all, it wasn't much worse than the way he'd left it. He didn't mind admitting that he wasn't the neatest person around the place.

As soon as the cell door slammed shut, he flopped onto the bed without even turning the television on. He tossed one letter onto the desk and opened the other one, which was from his mom, and started to read. Apparently, his mom and Tom were still happy. She was working part-time at her job, but the hours had been cut. Tom had had a part-time job for a short while, but he had run into some difficulties with his boss. Tom had told her the boss, who was very young, kept bugging him to do things that weren't part of his job. On top of that, the boss had always informed Tom that he wasn't doing the work properly. Finally, Tom had had enough and told him to stick his job.

Vern Thibedeau

They were debating remortgaging the house to get out of debt. She wrote that they'd looked at the figures and spoken to some guy who recommended going ahead with the plan to remortgage. His mom said they thought it was the only way to get out of the debt that had built up.

Ah Christ, Shipley thought, *the only reason you are back in debt is because of that sponging Tom. Jeez, Mom, you didn't owe hardly a cent to anyone until he got his hooks into you; even the house is, or was, paid off. God, I'd like to have a few words with him before you sign for all that money.* It never entered Shipley's head that Tom could actually have been in love with his mother.

Shipley realized he could never tell his mother that Tom was just after her money. As naive and self-centred as he was, he knew all he could do was write a letter to her to suggest that she wait for a while before going back into debt. He even thought he might suggest that she and Tom come in for a visit. *Especially that fucking Tom. I'd really like a few words with him. I'd make damn sure he remembered that I'd be out of here eventually, and if he screwed my mom over, he'd disappear very quickly.*

Shipley knew it was unlikely his mother would be in to visit him. In the few letters she had sent him, she never once had suggested coming in. He also knew Tom would never step foot into the prison for a visit. But Shipley, who was starting to feel hard and tough now that his circumstances appeared to be changing for the better, felt he would like to have a discussion with old Tom.

He knew the other letter was from Jen. He was a little hesitant about opening it, but at the same time, he was eager to hear from her. The last few letters had made him think she was pulling away from him. She seemed distant. He knew she was happy to be back with her parents in that large house. The house, along with the huge yard, gave Timmy a lot of room to run around and play in. He knew all this because Jen had mentioned it several times in her letters. That was part of the reason he was hesitant about reading the latest letter—that and the concern about what was going to come next.

With his fingers shaking a little, he managed to rip open the envelope and pull out the two sheets of paper. He only had to read the first few words, and he knew. There was no "Dear Mac" or "Hi, love" or "God, I miss you, Mac," just "Mac." That was all it took; he knew.

Jen tried to keep the letter friendly. Once again, she explained how much she and Timmy enjoyed living at her parents' place. Then she continued on for a while about how there was a lot less stress about money and several other things. But then it got down to the nitty-gritty. She had met someone else.

Apparently, he was a wonderful guy; even her parents were impressed by him. *Holy hell*, Shipley thought. *Boy, that's sure saying something*. The letter continued on, telling him how well Ray and Timmy got along. Jen explained that they had become acquainted at the store where she worked, because Ray was the manager. Jen wrote that even though it was still early, there was talk of a wedding. Jen said that Timmy was still his son, and he had every right to see him. She also insisted she and Ray would never try to stop Mac from visiting him, no matter where they were living.

At the end of the two pages, Jen was nice enough to sign the letter. But once again, there was no "Love you" or "I miss you, Mac" or "I'll write again shortly, hon." It was just signed, "Jen."

Shipley read the letter three of four times before it really sank in that Jen was telling him they were through. *God, how can she do this to me? Doesn't she realize how much I need her? Christ, I'll never get that money in to me now.*

Shipley turned the television on and just stayed on his bed, half watching the TV, while he thought of all the good times he and Jen had shared. He sort of forgot about the arguing they used to do over money, over her being tired from working and then looking after Timmy once she got home and over the fact that he seemed to be getting lazier and doing less to help around the apartment.

Then his mind drifted to Rita and how they'd met. *God, I'm glad I went to that group meeting. If Owen hadn't talked me into going, I wouldn't have met Rita. She might not be as slim or as beautiful as Jen, but she is a little younger, and with that long blonde hair, she is a turn-on. And boy, with the way she always wants to sit really close to me and is always putting her hand on my arm, she must like me. And besides, looks don't really matter, because the only women I see in this place are a nurse behind a mesh window when I can get some meds and, once in a while, an office worker heading somewhere. God, the only other women I see are in uniform, and they look at me as if they can't wait to whack me over the head with a nightstick.*

Three or four months prior to Shipley getting his head rapped on the gym barrier, Owen had finished another batch of brew and invited Shipley into his cell for a couple of drinks. By then, Shipley had to pay for his drinks, but it wasn't expensive, and he didn't mind. While they were chugging back the booze and telling each other how tough they were, Owen started telling Shipley about a group he had joined. He explained that they came in once a week and told him how great it was to talk to people, especially women, who didn't work in the pen.

That news grabbed Shipley's attention. "Women? I never really thought about women coming in with those idiot groups."

"Well, sure," Owen replied. "Hell, I didn't realize you weren't up on these groups. The one I joined has mostly younger people in it, and most of them are girls. And believe me, some are fucking beautiful—just sexy as hell. Mind you, almost any girl becomes beautiful after a guy has spent time in this nuthouse. Hell, there're outsiders who come in for different religious groups, including the Salvation Army. There's even an AA group that comes in two or three times a week."

Patrick continued explaining how his group worked and what it tried to accomplish. "You should think about coming down with me next week. Just get in to see your case management puke, and tell him you wanna join. But make damn sure you tell him you want the group we're talking about. It has a lot of university students who are taking some idiot course on how to save society, and some of them really have their heads way up in the clouds. Christ, they'll talk about anything.

"You must remember Atkinson, who lived just down from you and got out last month? Anyway, he had the phone number of one of the chicks in the group, and as soon as he got out, they hooked up. He's having a hell of a time. Lucky for him, her parents even have money. Christ, he really lucked in. I can't wait to get his next letter. Boy, I'll tell you, they are interesting!"

That all sounded great to Shipley, and the next day, even with his hangover, he managed to get an appointment to see his case management officer. The CMO had him cleared for that particular group within a day, and he and his buddy Owen headed down for the next group session.

Owen was right; several girls were there. Most of them seemed excited about being in a big, rough, tough prison and hanging out with all the tough cons. There were a few male students in the group, but they didn't earn nearly the attention the females did. To Shipley, the women all looked beautiful; even a couple who were a little older didn't look all that bad. He couldn't help thinking that maybe when a guy was locked up for a while, all females became beautiful. And Shipley, including court time, had been locked up for well over a year.

One of the older girls reminded him a little of his sister, Connie. At least he hoped that was what his sister looked like. He hadn't seen or heard from Connie for years, and he could only hope she was living a normal life and not on the street, hooking or doing drugs, or, like him, in prison, doing time.

He often thought of his sister and the life they had shared. It had been about 10 years or so since he'd seen or even heard from her. He remembered they used to fight and argue a lot, but he also recalled how she had helped him out of several tight scrapes. There had been times when there wasn't a lot to eat, and she had pretended she was full and given him the rest of her meal.

He remembered the last time he saw her. It was in the evening, and according to his recollection, it was hot that night. He was sitting on the front porch, watching traffic whiz by and dreaming of making lots of money, when Connie sat down beside him. That was a little unusual because she was usually off somewhere and didn't have all that much time to sit around and chat with him. They didn't talk about anything unusual, just the normal "Hey, how you doing? Everything going OK?" But just before she got up to go out somewhere, she gave him a hug and said that things were bound to get better; she even said she loved him. Then she got up, walked down the steps and headed up the sidewalk, and just before going around the corner and disappearing, she turned and waved to him.

Once he left home and witnessed how most other people lived, he came to realize their life had been far from normal. But he also knew that if his father hadn't left, it likely would have been a hell of a lot worse. He no longer blamed his sister for leaving him.

Just then, the cell doors slammed open to inform the inmates that they were back to the normal routine, and his contemplation of life suddenly halted.

Shipley looked at his watch and realized this would be his only chance to get out of his cell before the nightly lock-up, so he decided to head out and take a stroll to the gym. He didn't do much; he just walked around, said hi to a few guys and hoped his headache would let up. In less than an hour, he was back in his cell for the night.

Chapter 14

Several days after Shipley had his head rapped on the gym barrier, he had a wonderful idea. He had visited the institutional hospital a couple of times, and even though he didn't need them, he'd managed to wheedle several pain pills from the nurse. But the last time he had returned for more, he had been told in no uncertain terms that it was the last time he was getting any. *Christ*, he thought, *there go my free smokes. Damn it to hell.*

But then, one evening, the wonderful idea suddenly struck him. *I'm going to go down to the hospital in the morning and tell them my head's been pounding something terrible. God, there must be something wrong with me. Holy shit, I should've thought of this a few days ago. Even if I don't get some real pills, I should at least get an escort downtown to the hospital.* And that was what he did.

The next morning, he told the unit corporal about the great headache he had and said he was going to go to the hospital on sick parade. He made his way to the hospital, went up to the officer on the desk and said, "Hey, boss, I gotta see the nurse. My head's been pounding all goddamned night; must be from when I hit my head on the gym barrier."

"Oh, all right," he grumbled. "Go sit down in the waiting room, and I'll let them know you're here."

It took 20 minutes or so before Shipley finally heard his name being called. He looked up and saw the nurse waving at him from the door. He followed the nurse into an examination room and was told to sit in a chair; the doctor would be in shortly. So there Shipley sat, happily holding his head as if he were in a great deal of pain and waiting for the doctor. The doctor came in, asked him several questions and, while leaving the room, told him to stay put, as he'd be right back. The doctor made it back in a few minutes, handed Shipley several pills with instructions on how and when to take them and then said, "Don't really know why you're still getting headaches; they should have stopped within a day or so. I'm thinking we may have to take a closer look and see what we can find. Anyway, that's it for now. You be careful with those pills; they're pretty strong."

With a "Thanks, Doc. Hope I'm OK," he headed out of the hospital and back toward his cell block. *Jesus, these will be worth a lot of smokes. Christ, a closer look? I hope he meant a trip downtown to the hospital. Holy shit, would that ever be great!*

It didn't take Shipley long to happily trade his pills for several packs of smokes. By this time, he was getting several regular customers, but he realized his little business wasn't going to last much longer.

The next morning, Shipley, as usual, reported to the servery and started work. He had been there for only a couple of hours, when the unit corporal hollered at him to come up to the office. He did as he was told and walked in, saying, "Here I am. What's up, boss?"

"You're to go down to your cell. Leave your green pants on, take off that red polo shirt and put a green institutional shirt on, and then wait for the escort officer to pick you up. He's taking you out to the downtown hospital. Apparently, they're going to check you for those headaches you've been getting. Hope you're not screwing around, because they may have to remove part of your brain. It'd be a shame to do that for nothing, eh? Oh, you'd better take your issued jacket; it's chilly out there."

The part about removing his brain gave Shipley a bit of a shakeup, but when he looked at the corporal, he realized there was a grin on his face, which eased his mind somewhat.

Shipley hurried to his cell, and when the door opened, he stepped in and headed over to grab a green issue shirt but then hesitated. *Hell, if I'm putting on a jacket, they won't know what the hell I have on underneath it. Screw them; I'm gonna wear my red shirt. If they spot it, all I'll have to do is come back and change into a green one. Shit, I'll just say I forgot to change shirts. Who the hell's to know the difference anyway?*

He grabbed his jacket, put in on and zipped it up. Then his cell door opened, and he heard someone holler, "Hey, Shipley, get your ass down here! We have to get going."

Shipley stepped out onto the range, headed toward the control and spotted Raymond, who had been working in the hospital when he hit his head, standing there waiting for him. *Aw hell,* he thought, *why'd I have to get that damned jerk? Oh well. Maybe he won't spot my shirt.*

When he was about halfway down the range, he heard someone say to Raymond, "You make sure you keep a close eye on him. He's been in some mix-ups in the unit, and he's one hell of a big one."

"Ah, don't worry. I've been around him, and he knows better than to cause a problem with me." Once Shipley reached the head of the range, Raymond gave him a look and said, "Let's go, Shipley. We have to move it, or we'll be late."

Raymond, with Shipley in tow, headed out of the unit and toward the dock area. As soon as the corporal witnessed Raymond strutting along in front of the inmate, he was on the verge of calling him back and having a chat with him. Didn't Raymond realize that walking in front of, rather than behind, an inmate was a no-no? But then he thought, *Ah, what the hell? He does know better, and I'm getting sick of reminding him of security issues. Besides, nothing'll happen; Christ, there's staff all over the place. So to hell with him.*

Just before reaching the outside barrier, Raymond told Shipley to hold on and turn around. "I have to put the cuffs and leg irons on you before we get outside. Just turn around and kneel on that bench, and I'll put the leg irons on first." Once that was accomplished, Raymond instructed Shipley to stand up and put his hands out, and on went the cuffs. Then they headed for the exit.

Once they were out in the fresh air, Shipley spotted a prison vehicle sitting there with the motor running and a driver behind the wheel, reading a book. Raymond opened the rear door and told Shipley to get in, and then he went around and got in behind the driver. Once they were all in and settled, they headed for the sally port. Once they arrived, they pulled in through the first gate and stopped. The officer came out and checked the staff and the vehicle to ensure everything was kosher, and upon his signaling the tower officer, the massive chain-link outer gate with the coil of razor wire along the top slid open. Suddenly, they were out of the prison and entering the civilized world.

Shipley sat there and gawked at the wondrous scenery. The two-lane highway stretched out before them and then disappeared around a curve. He stared at the trees on the side as they flashed by and the huge blue lake to the right, which had ducks swimming around and diving into the water. *My God*, he thought, *this is just goddamn beautiful; who would've ever thought? And it's so close to that hellhole that's just off the road.*

Shipley looked over to Raymond and said, "This is wonderful. Everything looks great; even the air smells better. Boy, it'd be great to never step foot into that crazy pen again!"

Raymond didn't look over toward Shipley but glanced up front toward the driver and asked, "What's that old saying, Dave? Oh yeah, now I remember: if you can't do the time, don't do the crime."

Shipley just gave Raymond a dirty look and went back to admiring the scenery, and for the rest of the ride, he never spoke another word. Within a couple of minutes, a thought struck him: *Jesus, that idiot didn't even frisk me, let alone give me a strip search. Holy hell, I could've been carrying my shank, and he'd never know it—at least he wouldn't know until I stuck it into his stupid throat. Christ, I could do that and then wrap my cuffs around the driver's throat and force him to drive me wherever I wanted to go. Oh shit, I wish I'd known all this. The jerk doesn't even realize I didn't change into a green shirt. What a lazy, stupid asshole. And they call us cons lazy.*

Shipley didn't admit to himself, and never would, that he'd never in this lifetime have the intestinal fortitude to try anything even close to what he was daydreaming about. But it did give him a sense of power to think about it.

After a half hour or so, they arrived at the hospital, and Shipley couldn't help staring; it seemed huge to him. He couldn't remember ever being in a hospital in his lifetime, although he imagined he'd been born in one. But with his family life, who really knew? Probably just his mother, and he had never asked her about it.

Once they were parked and Raymond had opened the door so Shipley could get out, Dave looked over at Raymond and said, "I'm just gonna stay here with the vehicle and keep an eye on it; I don't think you really need me in that damned place."

"Yeah, OK. I'll let you know on the radio when we're on the way out, and you can pull back over here to pick us up."

"Yep. Will do. See you in a while. Have fun."

With that, Raymond and Shipley, moving rather slowly due to Shipley's leg irons, made their way to the hospital entrance. An attendant at the front desk directed them to a waiting room, and there the two of them sat and waited. When an officer was escorting an inmate, there was usually a separate room for them to sit and wait in. Heaven forbid regular citizens had to mingle with convicted felons.

Within a few minutes, they both started to feel the warmth and were quickly on the verge of sweating. Raymond stood up and removed his jacket and then threw it onto the chair beside him. Looking toward Shipley, he asked, "Do you wanna take your jacket off? If you do, now's the time."

"Yep, think I will. Christ, it's cooking in here." At that moment, it suddenly struck Shipley that Raymond, when he'd applied the restraint equipment, had put the keys in his jacket pocket. It was the first he'd ever noticed something like that; the other screws always hooked them onto a secure snap-on gadget attached to their belt. *Well, what do you know?* he thought. *And there's his jacket, just lying there on the chair, waiting for somebody to grab it.*

"OK, stick your arms out. Once the cuffs are off, pull your jacket off, and hold your arms out again. And don't screw around; remember, you still have leg irons on, and as you've found out, they are a little difficult to run around in." Shipley did as he was told, and as soon as the jacket was off, Raymond stared at him and exclaimed, "What the hell you doing with that shirt on? You were told to put a green issue on for the escort. God, I've a good mind to put an offence report in on you."

"Aw Christ, I forgot. I went in my cell to get ready and just never thought of it. But listen, I've been trying to get a job in the gym; if you charge me, I'll never get it. I can't see it being a big deal. You and me are the only ones who know about it, and I'm not going to yap to anyone."

Raymond, as he reapplied the cuffs, put the keys back into his jacket pocket and, throwing the jacket back onto the chair, replied, "Well, it's too late to do anything about it now. Just don't do any screwing around, or we'll head right back to the joint."

Shipley didn't reply but knew damn well he was full of shit. *Stupid idiot. Sure, rat me out, and you'll be in more trouble than me. Christ, you didn't search me and didn't spot my shirt, and wouldn't they like to know that you keep the keys in your stupid jacket pocket and then leave the thing on a chair? Fucking idiot jerk-off.*

Within 20 minutes or so, a nurse stuck her head in and hurriedly said, "Hey, guys, your turn is up. Just follow me, and I'll take you to the examination room."

They followed her down a couple of corridors, made a turn or two and then entered a room with a bed and a weird-looking machine hanging down from the ceiling. The nurse said, "Make yourselves at home, guys; it may be a bit of a wait." With a glance toward Raymond, she added, "There're a couple of chairs over there if you want to use one." Then, with a stern look toward Shipley, she said, "You might as well get comfortable on the bed while you wait." With that, she was gone.

Raymond looked around, tossed his jacket over a chair and sat down.

There they waited, one sitting on a chair and one lying on a bed, staring at the ceiling.

Shipley, while looking around, noticed Raymond's jacket thrown over a chair and recalled seeing a door at the end of the corridor marked with a large red Exit sign. *Hell, we're on the ground floor. That door must head right out onto the street! Christ, ain't that something? So close!*

After 10 minutes or so, Raymond started to get edgy. Shipley noticed him shifting around in the chair, standing up a couple of times and then pacing around. Then he threw a look toward Shipley. "Look, I'm going out into the hall to look around. I may even slip down to where I noticed a coffee machine; it's just down at the end of the hall, so it'll only take a minute or so. If I find it, would you like a coffee?"

"God, I'd love one. Good luck." Shipley knew damn well there was no coffee machine at the end of the hall. *Sure as hell, that prick is going somewhere for a smoke*, he thought. Shipley watched him walk out without his jacket and turn left, which was the direction opposite the exit he'd spotted before entering the room. Suddenly, Shipley got excited. He waited for a few minutes and then slipped off the bed and shuffled over to the door. He eased his head out into the corridor, looked both ways and saw no one. Then he glanced at Raymond's jacket and thought, *Oh my God, it can't be this easy. Jesus Christ, should I try it? Ah, what the hell? Why not? What can they do—put me in jail if I get caught?*

Hesitantly, he eased over toward the uniform jacket while constantly glancing around. He reached the jacket, and sliding his hand into the pocket, he felt the key ring. In a rush, he pulled it out and, feeling as if he were going to puke, squatted down and unlocked each leg iron. *Holy God, I'm gonna do it! I can't quit now; Jesus, all my planning, and now this just falls into my lap! I'm as good as gone. Will that asshole ever have some explaining to do! Looks good on the goof.*

He was too excited, or maybe too scared, to even think about trying to remove the cuffs, so he shoved the keys into his pocket, jumped over to the bed and pushed the leg irons under the pillow. While he was shoving them under the pillow, in his excitement, he couldn't help thinking that they would be a big surprise for whoever found them. Then he grabbed his jacket and threw it over his wrists to hide the handcuffs. He silently eased over to the door, tentatively stuck his head out and, seeing no one, stepped out into the corridor and pulled the door shut behind him. He quickly and quietly, but almost dancing and feeling like singing, headed for the big, glowing red Exit sign.

Shipley didn't do much thinking. He had his red civvy-looking shirt on, which hopefully would help him pass for an innocent civilian, but he didn't even know where he was. He had no money and no way of getting any. He wouldn't be able to get on a bus, couldn't call a cab and would have a tough time hitchhiking. But he was too excited to think of any of that silly stuff. He'd always been sort of a do-it-and-worry-about-things-later type of guy. Sometimes things worked out for the best.

Shipley was about a dozen strides from pushing the exit bar that would open the door to his freedom. He couldn't believe his luck; in fact, he had a difficult time not breaking into a run or singing. He couldn't have been happier. *Jesus H. Christ, locked up all this time because some old idiot hit his head when he fell over, and here I am, practically free again. God, life is grand!*

Shipley kept going. He took one more step and was just about to swing his cuffed hands out to push the door open and be free, when *bang!* A heavy hand wrapped around his shoulder, and he felt it tighten up enough to start hurting. With a gut-wrenching sense of crushing defeat, his happiness suddenly evaporated, replaced by a sense of apprehension. Shipley's shoulder was starting to verge on numbness, when a deep, gravelly voice demanded, "Where the hell you think you're going there, boy?"

Shipley managed to turn his head enough to see a person in a white shirt who was a heck of a lot larger than he was. The insignia on his shirt said, "Hospital Security."

"Oh hell," he shakily replied, "you scared the shit out of me. I'm just heading out for a smoke. Got tired of waiting in the room for that nurse to come back and figured I might as well wait out here and have a fag."

"Don't try to bullshit a bullshitter, boy. I worked in the pen long enough to spot a con when I see one. What room you in, and where the hell's your escort?"

Shipley was too devastated to say much, so he just pointed back down the hall. The two of them, with the security guard firmly clutching Shipley's shoulder, headed down the corridor toward Shipley's room. As soon as they entered it, they spotted Raymond standing beside the bed, holding a set of leg irons in his hands, looking around with a frantic expression on his face.

The huge hospital security guy looked at Raymond and, in a wise-assed voice, asked, "Hey, you looking for this turkey?"

"Yep, am I ever. Where the Christ was he?"

"Oh, he was down the corridor, about to push the exit door open and take off on you. Where the hell were you anyway?"

"Give me a couple minutes to get these leg irons back on the idiot and do a quick frisk. And how about after that, we'll step out and have a chat, eh?"

Raymond, with a relieved expression on his face, looked at Shipley and said, "Get your face up against the wall, and lean into it, boy."

Shipley did as instructed and received a thorough search. Raymond found his keys in one of Shipley's back pockets and quickly and quietly slid them into his own pocket, hoping the hospital guard didn't notice.

Shipley ended up back in bed with the leg irons on. The irons were a little tighter than they should've been, but at the moment, he didn't think he should bring the subject up by complaining; he figured he was in enough trouble as it was. He watched the two uniforms head out to the corridor.

On his way out, Raymond looked back at Shipley and, in a voice that left no room for compromise, said, "We're right outside the door, boy. Don't you even think of getting off that bed."

Once the door was closed, the two officers just stood looking at each other for a few seconds, and then the hospital security guard began the conversation by introducing himself. "My name's Cliff Hewitt. I worked at the pen for several years and then got the hell out. You're damned lucky I spotted that turkey when I did and realized he was a con. About two more steps, and he would've been long gone—and probably your job along with him."

"Christ, I know. I owe you a big one. Jeez, I just slipped out for a minute to try to find some coffee."

"Where the hell's your partner? There must be two of you."

"Aw hell, the driver stayed out with the vehicle. Said he had to check something out but never did come in. Kind of left me screwed. You don't have to make a report about this, do you?"

"Well, I should. But I'll do my best to skip it. I don't really think it will be a problem, but hell, you never know."

They chatted for a few more minutes, and then Cliff ended the conversation by saying, "Well, I'd better get going. Few more rounds to do, and I have to check in with my partner. Good luck with everything, and I'll see you later." With a wave, Hewitt took off.

Raymond turned, entered the room and stood there for a moment, frowning at Shipley. "You're a real piece of work, ain't you? Did you really think you could just walk out and be gone?"

"Jesus, boss, I wasn't going to take off. I just wanted a smoke, for God's sake."

"Bullshit. You're a screw-up, and you damned well know it. Christ, you'll likely end up in a supermax for a year or so—and it will look good on you."

Vern Thibedeau

"I'm telling you. I wasn't trying to take off, and I don't think there's any way to prove I was. Granted, I had to use your keys because of the leg irons, but I was gonna put 'em back on. I'm not really sure who'd be in more trouble—you or me. That's kind of an interesting question. Guess we won't know the answer until the hearing, eh?" Shipley wasn't sure where his brashness erupted from, but he did know he was scared witless.

"You sure you weren't trying to get away? I really don't wanna see you screwed up if you're being up front with me. If you really were just heading out for a smoke, I'll maybe let it go this time. But I'll tell you, boy, if you ever try that on me again, you'll wish ta hell you'd never laid eyes on me."

Just then, a nurse and technician entered the room, and with a "Let's get this over with," they went about their business.

Everything went as planned, and there were no more interruptions. Within 20 minutes or so, the nurse and technician completed their work. They then told Raymond they were going out to check the pictures to make sure they'd turned out OK and would be back shortly. Then they were gone.

It didn't take long, and as promised, they were back. The technician told Shipley that as far as he could tell, everything looked fine. "The doctor will check these over to make sure and then send the results to the institution. And then your doctor will likely have a chat with you within a week or so."

With a look toward Raymond, the nurse said, "You guys may as well take off. We'll let the institutional hospital know how everything went."

Raymond and Shipley headed for the front, and Raymond radioed the driver to pick them up. Raymond gave Shipley a look and said, "OK, I've thought it over, and we'll just forget about our little episode. I really don't wanna screw you over just for a smoke."

Oh yeah, sure. You just don't wanna get yourself into a jackpot, you asshole. You must think I'm as stupid as you are.

Back to Mountainview they headed. Not a word was spoken by Raymond or Shipley. Dave, the driver, tried to start a conversation a couple of times, but when there was no reply, he finally gave up and also kept his mouth shut.

*   *   *

Once they were back in the institution, Raymond removed the restraint equipment, took Shipley down to the hospital and turned him over to the nurse. He handed her the paperwork and explained what the x-ray technician had told him, and with a frown thrown toward Shipley, he turned and headed back to begin his other duties.

But the episode at the downtown hospital never left Raymond's mind. He was concerned that it might come back to bite him in the ass.

He vacillated for a couple of days about whether to submit a report or just let it slide and hope for the best. But he wasn't stupid and realized that since he hadn't reported the incident immediately upon their return, it was too late to do it now. So he just kept quiet, hoped everyone else stayed silent and kept his fingers crossed. He didn't even mention the incident to his wife, knowing she wouldn't have been all that interested anyway—that was, unless he lost his job. Then there would be hell to pay.

Unfortunately, he was going to find out that keeping his fingers crossed wouldn't be much help.

He kept going over the episode in his mind and kept wishing he'd never left that damned hospital room. *God, why in hell did I think I needed a smoke and coffee that badly? Jesus, sometimes I'm just stupid. Christ, I could get fired over that stupid con screwing around.*

Chapter 15

Three days after the incident of Shipley's escort, Lockhart, the staff sergeant, phoned Jordon McDonald's office. Once Jordon answered, Lockhart said, "I've received a report regarding an escort to the downtown hospital that took place a couple of days ago. I think you'd better come up to my office so we can go over it."

Within a few minutes, Jordon, the preventive security officer, entered the staff's office, sat down and said, "What's up, Ray?"

Lockhart handed him a copy of a fax. "Give that a quick read, and then we'll chat about it."

Once Jordon finished reading the fax, he glanced up at Ray with a questioning look and waited.

"Not sure what the hell to do about this. But I'm gonna have to have another chat with that Raymond. Before I do that, however, I want you to go down and interview this Shipley to see what the hell he says about the issue. The fax was sent from the hospital, and the security guy involved worked for us for several years, so I imagine he'd know what the hell was going on. I really doubt there's enough to get Shipley into court with an attempted escape charge, but we should have an official hearing with Raymond. But if we don't, at the very least, I'm gonna bury this guy in the tower squad for a while. Christ, I'm scared to have him around inmates anymore. Lord only knows what he's done or what he may do next."

The staff sergeant and the preventive security officer discussed the problem for a short while. Then McDonald, while getting up and heading for the door, finished the conversation by saying, "I'll head down to see what I can find out. I'll get back to you as soon as I have any info."

McDonald went straight down to the unit, walked into the office and told the corporal that he was going into the spare office and to send Shipley in to see him. "See if you can get him down as soon as possible. I'm just gonna grab a coffee and head on in."

McDonald picked up a coffee from the servery and got settled in the office, and within a minute or so, a nervous Shipley walked in.

"Just grab that chair and sit. I'm going to talk to you about that incident when you tried to take off the other day. And I don't want any bullshit!" As soon as Shipley entered the office, McDonald could tell he was exceptionally nervous, so he made the last comment forcibly, and he was rewarded by Shipley visibly giving a jerk.

"Well, ah, what do you mean 'tried to take off'?" the con stammered.

Within moments, he broke down and told McDonald the whole story. He didn't even try to make himself the innocent party. He just explained that the keys had been left in Raymond's pocket, Raymond had left the room and he had removed his leg irons. But he reiterated that he had just been going out for a smoke. "Christ, if I'd planned on taking off, I would've taken those stupid cuffs off, and I would've been running!"

Shipley wasn't completely stupid; he was pretty sure he couldn't be charged with an attempted escape. He figured the worst he could get was an institutional charge and maybe locked up in disassociation for a few days. *What the hell? I'm locked up anyway. That goof Raymond will be in more trouble than me. Looks good on the prick.*

"What the hell you talking about? Keys left in the pocket? Whose pocket and what pocket? You've lost me here."

"Well, Raymond's pocket. That's where the keys were. He always leaves them there. Jeez, I only wanted to go out for a smoke, for Christ's sake. It felt like I'd been sitting in that damned hospital for hours."

McDonald listened to the rest of Shipley's story, had him repeat parts of it and then said, "You get back to whatever in hell it is you were doing. I have to go up front so the powers that be can figure out what they're going to do about this."

Shipley left the office, and McDonald sat there for a few minutes, trying to digest what he'd been told. He couldn't help but wonder if the story was completely true, but then he thought, *Jeez, Shipley was pretty scared, so maybe it is all true. Holy God, no staff member could be that stupid or that lazy! Or could he?* He was beginning to wonder if they would be able to charge Shipley with attempted escape. He had the feeling a prosecutor wouldn't even take it to court. McDonald gave his head a bit of a shake and figured he'd best get up to Lockhart's office to fill him in.

McDonald went straight up to the office and gave the door a knock, and upon hearing, "Come on in," he stepped inside, looked at Lockhart and, as he sat down, said, "Jesus Christ, you're not going to believe this. But I really think Shipley told me the truth; he was too shaken up to lie." After that opening, McDonald filled Lockhart in on the rest of the story.

Once McDonald was finished, they just sat there looking at each other while Lockhart attempted to absorb what he'd been told. "You're sure that's what he told you? You didn't get the story mixed up somehow?"

"Nope. Sorry, but that's it. I went back and forth over it several times, and that's the whole story."

The two of them discussed the problem, came up with different solutions and threw each one out. "Ah hell," Lockhart finally exclaimed, "I'm going to get that idiot Raymond up here to see what he has to say! I don't know what the hell to do. But I think you're right; we'd never get Shipley into court on this one. Likely just be a waste of time and money. Probably just a minor charge and some OP for a while, and that's about it. Anyway, that idiot is working the evening shift tonight. I'm going to have to hang around for a while, and he and I'll be having a chat. Thanks for the report. I'll let you know how it goes."

*   *   *

Raymond, after having two days off, started a week of evening shifts in E unit. He reported in to the sergeant taking roll call and headed down to start his shift. *Damn units anyway. Don't know why they couldn't just leave me in the hospital. At least in there, there're hardly any cons. Hell, there's not even a corporal hanging over your shoulder, yapping at you all the time about one thing or another. But by God, this is the third day since the escort with that damned goof, and I haven't heard a word yet; I just might be OK. I'm sure I would've been up front by now if it was gonna hit the shit fan.*

Raymond and the other guys posted to the unit got busy with the afternoon routine, and once the inmates returned from work, they completed the count. When it was certified correct, so they supervised the supper meal, started the recreation period for the inmates and then settled down in the unit office to have coffee and do some chatting.

They'd only been sitting for a few minutes, when the phone got their attention with its ringing. Roberts, the corporal in charge, who was sitting at the desk, picked it up and said, "E unit. Roberts here." He sat listening for a minute or so. "Sure, boss. He'll be right up."

Roberts put the receiver back and looked over toward Raymond, who was sitting a little ways away from the desk. Raymond and his partner were both looking toward Roberts, wondering what the phone call was about. Roberts, while glancing in Raymond's direction, said, "Hey, Paul, the staff sergeant wants to see you up in his office for a few minutes. I guess you might just as well head up now."

Raymond immediately had a pretty good idea what the call was about. "Aw shit. He didn't happen to say what he wanted me for, did he?"

"Nope, just that he wanted to see you. Just head up, and when you're done, come on back down. We've got a couple cells we have to toss."

Paul gulped the last of his coffee down, stood up and, with a "See you all shortly," headed out of the unit. *Christ, what the hell does he want? I hope it's not about that escort. God, if it's not cons giving me a hard time, it's my so-called buddies; if it's not them, it's management. Boy, around here, a guy just can't win.*

Once Raymond left the unit office, it only took him a few minutes to get through the barriers and up to the administration area. Naturally, he knew Lockhart was the staff sergeant, but he'd had few dealings with him. *Jeez, I hope this isn't about that thing at the hospital the other day. I'm sure the con wouldn't say anything, but I'm not so sure about that rent-a-cop.*

Vern Thibedeau

Raymond was nervous and couldn't imagine why else the staff sergeant would want to see him. After all, a staff sergeant was pretty high up on the food chain. Raymond reached the office, gave the door a couple of raps and then heard a loud voice say, "Come on in."

Raymond opened the door and saw Lockhart sitting behind his desk. He gave Raymond a stare and, nodding toward a chair, gruffly told him to have a seat.

As soon as Raymond was seated, Lockhart started right in. "You and I have to have a chat, Paul. I imagine you realize our discussion is going to be about the other day when you had Shipley down at the hospital. We received a report from hospital security about what went on, and preventive security has already interviewed Shipley about the situation. And for your information, he was quite forthcoming. The first goddamned thing I want to know is what on earth you were thinking when you stuffed the security keys into your jacket pocket. And as if that wasn't bad enough, you took off and left the keys and your jacket just lying there. Jesus, it's bad enough you put them in your pocket, which, as you know, is a big no-no, but then you just left your jacket lying there? Are you crazy?"

"Hell, I was just going to get a coffee. That's the first time I've ever left keys like that. Jesus, I'm not sure what I was thinking. Actually, my stomach was bothering me, and I had a hell of a headache. I likely shouldn't have come in to work that day. Boy, now I really wish I'd stayed home."

"Well, you're not the only one wishing you'd stayed the hell home. Can you imagine what the deputy warden felt like when he read that report from the hospital? Well, if you can't imagine it, I can tell you he was not a happy camper."

The interview didn't take long, and it ended with Lockhart telling Raymond that he was going to be put on the tower squad until management sorted out what they were going to do. "That's about all we can do at the moment. None of us are sure what the results are going to be." Then, just to shake Raymond up a little more, Lockhart, as Raymond was heading out the door, loudly said to him, "Just in case this gets any bigger, I think you should have a chat with your union rep to make sure he's aware of the situation."

A shaken Raymond quietly pulled the office door closed and started back to the unit. *Christ, at least I'm not fired yet. That damn Shipley—it's all his fault. But towers? Hell, they're not bad; how'd I luck in like that? Christ, some punishment that is. No cons. I have ta keep my eyes open; can't get too engrossed with a book. I also have to make damn sure I don't fall asleep. Jeez, other than all that crap, this'll be great! Hope I can stay there until I retire.*

Raymond didn't know it yet, but Lockhart's advice to keep his eyes open in those towers might have been the most important part of the conversation.

That was how Raymond ended up in the tower overlooking the exercise yard during a major incident that involved Shipley. He also didn't realize he might emerge from the incident as a hero.

At first, Raymond was eager to inform his wife, Charlotte, of the big change. He excitedly thought he might stop on his way down to the unit to give her a phone call and fill her in about it. But then he remembered that things had been a little strained; in fact, things had been very cool between them for the last few months or so, so he changed his mind. *Heck, I might as well wait till I get home and let her know then. I'm pretty sure it won't be a big deal for her.*

Raymond entered the unit, and the only one in view was the corporal sitting at the desk. He looked up at Raymond and, with a questioning look, asked, "Hey, Paul, everything OK?"

Raymond, with a huge smile, filled him in on the change that was going to take place shortly.

"Jeez, Paul, I'm sorry about that. Who'd you piss off?"

"Oh no, I'm looking forward to it. Towers will be a nice change for me."

"Oh, OK. I just didn't think you'd like being stuck up there in one of those things day after day. Christ, half the reason I became a corporal was so I wouldn't have to do towers. I was always bored out of my gourd when I got stuck in one. I guess it's different things for different guys, eh? Anyway, good for you." *I won't say it out loud, Raymond, but it's also really good for us. Don't know if Lockhart realizes it or not, but he sure did all us guys a favour.*

* * *

Vern Thibedeau

Shipley, other than the interview with McDonald, hadn't heard anything about the hospital situation, so he figured he was free and clear. A few weeks slipped by, and nothing much happened. The same routine carried on: counts, meals, the yard and work in the servery each day. That was about it.

But Shipley, who was still fed up with Mountainview and felt he was going nuts, was still diligently searching for a way out of the place. He knew there was no chance of using the food-tray route. Staff were careful about checking the trays on their way out. In fact, inmates had heard talk that a couple of screws had gotten themselves into some serious trouble over that escape, so he threw the idea away. But he was still pissed about it. He realized if he'd moved on his plan a little faster, he would have been the one who got out and not that other turkey.

But Shipley's time in that prison was almost up. Fortunately, or maybe unfortunately, he didn't realize it.

With Crothers and his two idiot buddies locked up, hopefully forever, he felt on top of the world. His demeanour now matched his size. He had always been tall, but now he also walked tall—no more slumping shoulders, darting nervous looks around or checking behind himself all the time. In fact, he'd even noticed his fellow inmates appeared to move out of the way when he was strutting down the range. Heck, he'd even started going to the gym every couple of evenings or so to work out with the weights. Now, besides feeling a hell of a lot better, he was starting to look more like a real tough con.

Another week slipped by. Shipley still felt like a winner. Hell, everything—other than his great escape plan—was working out great. He'd heard Crothers and his two buddies were being moved to a supermax, he was getting along wonderfully with Rita and he had enough credit with the canteen that he didn't really want for anything; hell, all was just tickety-boo with the world.

Chapter 16

Finally, another Tuesday rolled around, and after the count and evening meal, Shipley and Owen, who was now his buddy, eagerly headed for the Tuesday night group. Surprisingly, Shipley had found he really enjoyed the sessions, especially when he was sitting beside Rita. He usually did sit beside her, because no one else had the guts to try to take his spot at the table. There were even a couple of times when Rita and Shipley held hands for a second or so. Neither one mentioned it, and they both tried to pretend it had happened by accident, but both knew darn well it hadn't been an accident. Shipley surprised himself by becoming excited just from simply touching hands.

The more often Shipley attended the evening group, the closer he felt to Rita. He also sensed she was feeling the same way toward him. There were even a couple of times when the back of Rita's hand lightly brushed against his groin area. Talk about becoming excited—but was it by accident? Did she realize what she'd done? Did she realize the tremendous effect the simple brushing had on him?

As his feelings for Rita continued to grow, he seldom thought about Jennifer and Timmy. His feelings were mostly sexual, and he could visualize Rita in several wondrous positions, but he wondered if his feelings were beginning to turn into love.

He was also starting to wonder if Rita might be willing to bring in some drugs or money for him. The idea of her lugging something in stuck with him, especially after the hand holding turned into the odd secretive kiss. He realized there was a risk, but he was also positive that it was a small one. He knew that contraband was lugged in fairly often. The thought whirled around in his mind constantly, and he started to believe she might be willing to do it.

He figured it would be a lot easier to smuggle something in through an evening group than during a regular visit. In his mind, the visiting area was observed much more thoroughly than the group sessions ever were. However, he was going to find out that once again, he was wrong. Unfortunately, Rita was the one who would suffer for his misconceptions.

Shipley continued attending the evening group, and he and Rita became friendlier and friendlier; in fact, even though Shipley wasn't aware of it, Rita was telling all her friends on the outside that they were deeply in love. Shipley helped Rita's thinking along that line by informing her of that fact more than once. Shipley knew he felt something; it might not have been a deep, undying love, but it was surely something.

Shipley carefully, over several group sessions, mentioned that it would help him get out of a severe and potentially dangerous problem if she could bring some drugs in for him. Eventually, Rita gave in and told him she could maybe bring some money in if that would help. But she stressed in no uncertain terms that there was no way in hell she was going to touch or get involved with drugs. "I've seen what drugs can do to people, including a couple of my friends, and I swore I would never have anything to do with them."

Rita and Shipley continued to discuss his problems, and finally, during a meeting, they agreed on a date when she would come in with some cash. "My God, Mac," Rita whispered to Shipley while staring into his eyes, "I never thought I would ever get involved with something like this. But if you are sure it's the only way out for you, I've decided to do it. I'll stop at the bank, draw some cash out of my savings account and bring it in at our next meeting."

"God, Rita, that'd be great, and it'll save me some very serious problems. Just tuck it away somewhere, and once we're together down here, slip it over to me. Be sure to act naturally, be careful in passing it over and no one will ever know. Jeez, my love, I can't thank you enough!"

During their conversation, they got closer and closer, and their whispering became a little more animated. It was easy to see that they really wanted to give each other, at the very least, a big hug. Just by looking at Shipley's huge smile, one could tell he was a happy camper.

Unfortunately for both of them but mostly for Rita, the group leader noticed the happy couple and kept an unobtrusive watch on them for the balance of the evening. He had been doing that job long enough to think the two of them might be conspiring together about something. He thought it might be something more than sexual excitement.

At any rate, Shipley's plan was all set. It wasn't all that complicated, but sometimes the simplest plans worked out the best—not all the time but sometimes. Naturally, Shipley was on pins and needles all week, waiting for the next group session and praying the plan would work out.

As usual, the next morning rolled around. Shipley climbed out of bed and spent several minutes staring out his cell window. He spotted one of the mobile patrol vehicles cruising around the outer fence, stared at the one ominous tower in his view, saw the sun shining brightly and thought to himself, *Way to go; another nice day in the nuthouse. Ain't I lucky?* Right then, he made a promise to himself that he would never leave another pet dog locked in a cage. Then, as usual, he prepared himself for another hard day of working in the servery.

It ended up being just another regular day. The three meals were served to the inmates in his cell block, and then, naturally, he had to help clean up after each meal. In between the cleanups, he just hung around the common room, drinking coffee and talking to his fellow workers, or sat in his cell, watching television. It was kind of nice; he did his thing, and no one bothered him, including staff. Time floated by.

His mind was active, though. He'd had his interview with the doctor and had been informed that there were no repercussions from his head injury. The doctor also had said now that everyone was aware of that fact and because he wouldn't be able to get his hands on any more drugs, his headaches would likely magically stop.

Also, now that there would be no more pain pills, he stepped up his plan for the great escape. Shipley had no way of knowing it, but his problems were about to become much more extreme.

At the moment, though, he was excited. The time finally rolled around for his evening group. This was the session when the love of his life was to bring the money in for him. It was difficult for him to kill the hours until it was time to head down for the group, but he managed. He was almost prancing.

Finally, the time rolled around. Shipley and Owen started down. Owen looked over toward Shipley and asked, "What the hell's up with you, Mac? Holy hell, you know you'll be seeing her in a few minutes, for God's sake. Christ, you'd think you were gonna be jumping into bed or something; it's just a regular meeting, you know."

"Oh, I know. I just like to be around her and dream about things. She's a beautiful girl, eh?"

Shipley and his buddy Owen continued chatting about their lives. They entered the meeting room, sat down in their usual spots and waited for the outside participants to show up. Shipley, with Rita's empty chair beside him, managing to contain himself somewhat, looked around at everyone and said hi to a few of them. While looking around, he gave several extra side glances toward the group monitor. Shipley noticed that for some reason, he seemed to be paying extra attention to him.

Finally, the group members, who seemed surprisingly agitated, started coming in. Shipley eagerly stared at the doorway and waited for Rita to walk in and sit down. But Rita didn't show up.

Everyone sat, but the doorway was still empty. Within moments, a staff member stuck his head in and waved to the counsellor, who immediately stood up and headed for the door. The staff member and counsellor stepped out into the hallway and had an animated conversation.

The counsellor eventually turned and came back into the room. Naturally, this situation was unusual and caused everyone to stop chatting and to stare expectantly at the counsellor. One could have heard a pin drop.

The counsellor looked around at everyone and then, with what Shipley thought was a smug look, glanced at him and at Rita's empty chair. "Sorry, folks, but we are going to be one short tonight. Apparently, one of our members tried to bring in contraband and is presently waiting for the police to show up. We will, however, continue on with our evening plans."

Shipley sat there with a sinking feeling and thought, *Oh Christ, what now? Poor Rita. What if she's charged with some stupid crime? It's probably that asshole sitting in front of us looking like an idiot know-it-all. God, I'd like to walk up there and kick him right in the balls. Jesus H. Christ, I just know I'm fucking screwed again.*

* * *

Rita, though she had told Mac she wouldn't bring drugs in for him, had changed her mind. She had a small amount, plus a fair sum of cash, hidden on her person. She pulled into the parking lot, parked her car and just sat there in deep thought. She realized this was her last chance to change her mind. *God, Mac is in such big trouble. If I don't help him get out of it, what else can he do? I've heard of guys getting really hurt or, heaven forbid, even killed. I have to do it for him.*

So, having firmly decided she was going through with her decision but feeling a great deal of apprehension and even fear, she eased out of the car, slammed the door and headed into the penitentiary. While walking in, she looked through the fencing with the razor wire running along the top, stared at the darkened towers and couldn't help thinking that the horrible place looked even more forbidding than usual.

She continued on with the short walk, which seemed a lot longer than usual, and caught up with Joanne, another member of the group. Rita, although she had a difficult time in doing it, chatted with Joanne until they reached the entrance. Just before entering the huge door, Rita hesitated one last time, which earned her a questioning glance from Joanne, and then she took the final step and entered right behind her friend.

Rita and Joanne walked over to a bank of lockers, and as usual, each one placed all her personal belongings in a locker. Then they walked over and joined the rest of their group, who were standing around discussing worldly affairs and patiently waiting.

Vern Thibedeau

While the group were chatting among themselves, an officer approached and asked if they were ready to head down. Several voices replied in the affirmative, and he said, "OK, let's get on our way."

They all headed for the brightly coloured steel-barred corridor barrier. Rita always had thought the nice colours were an attempt to make the area less forbidding. If that was the reason, however, she believed the idea was a miserable failure.

Rita, with a vast sense of relief, turned to follow them, but moments before going through the corridor barrier, she spotted another officer coming out of a room. He approached the group and instructed them to hold on for a minute. He looked toward Rita and said, "Ms. Jessup, would you come with me, please? The rest of you folks can head on down to the group." Then, with a wave of his hand, he signaled for Rita to enter the room he had just exited.

Rita, with her heart in her mouth and feeling sick, did as requested. Once inside the room, the officer closed the door, and Rita saw a female officer standing there and giving her the look.

The male officer looked at Rita and sternly told her, "We know you are in possession of contraband. To make this a lot easier on all of us, I'm officially ordering you to surrender it to me. If you refuse, you will be searched by a female officer, and your refusal will be noted in the report. I also want to inform you that a police officer will be here within a couple of minutes.

"OK, Rita, now that the official part of this is over, I want everyone to relax a little. We are ninety-nine percent sure that you have contraband on your person, and this, as you realize, is very serious. I'm being honest here when I tell you that it will look a lot better if you just hand it over before the police get here. Believe me, no one wants to go through all the crap of strip searches, more charges and all the paperwork and publicity; it's just not worth it, and we'll get the stuff anyway."

Rita, who was in tears and gasping for air, nodded and, turning around, retrieved the contraband and handed it over to the staff. *Oh my God. What am I gonna do? My life is over. I have to phone Mom and Dad, but what'll I say? Oh God, they might not even wanna talk to me. Oh hell, poor Mac. He'll be in big trouble. What'll he do? Oh, why? Why me?* She sobbed to herself.

The officer counted the money, opened the other package and found the drugs. "Jesus, I didn't realize you were bringing drugs in along with the money. My God, Rita, what on earth were you thinking?"

It took a couple of hours, but the reports were filled out, and a sobbing, shaken Rita was read her rights, handcuffed and put into the back of a squad car. She was on her way to the police station.

* * *

There was no more Rita in the evening group. In fact, that evening was also Shipley's last attendance. Luckily, at least for him, no charges were laid against him. There was no proof he was involved; he hadn't received any of the contraband, and Rita, with her undying love for him, refused to tell the authorities who was going to receive the contraband. That was not to say staff didn't know, but knowing and proving were two different things.

Once the evening group was over and everyone was heading back to the ranges, the main topic of discussion among them was the missing Rita. Shipley and Owen were walking by themselves, and with a low voice, Owen looked at Shipley and asked, "Hey, Mac, what the hell was that about Rita not showing up? Were you two up to something?"

A devastated Shipley answered, "Aw Christ. She was going to do me a favour and bring some stuff in. The pigs must have checked her out and found it. I'll tell you, sometimes a guy just can't get a break. What do you think they'll do with her? Will she be in big trouble or just not allowed in anymore?"

"Who the hell knows? It depends a lot on what she was going to bring in and if they want to make an example of her. If it was just money, she may get a break. But if it was drugs, she'll likely be at the police station by now, hoping to get bail. It's really hard to figure out; you just never know."

The conversation carried on until they reached their respective cells, and that was about it for the night. With a manly wave to each other, each entered his own cell and prepared for the night. A sad and shaken Shipley had difficulty in settling down, but eventually, he drifted off into a restless sleep. Once again, he dreamt about those damned vultures flying overhead.

Vern Thibedeau

Owen and Shipley had become friends. In fact, they travelled together to most of their outings, though the only outings they had were the gym, the yard and the common room. But they had, at least in Shipley's mind, become buddies, and Shipley was glad he had someone he could chat with about his problems. Unfortunately, Shipley was going to learn that most inmates didn't really have buddies. Depending on circumstances, usually, friends quickly came and went.

Chapter 17

About a week after Rita's episode, during an eight o'clock changeover, Shipley and Owen were heading to the gym and chatting, or at least Shipley was chatting. They were almost at the end of the range, when Shipley noticed his buddy Owen was exceptionally quiet and didn't seem interested in what he had to say. Finally, Shipley looked over at him and asked, "Hey, Jim, what's up? Christ, you're really quiet. Something going on in your life?"

"Nah, not really. Just a few things I've been tossing back and forth."

On their way to the gym, Shipley had planned to tell Owen about the phone call he'd made to try to contact Rita and the disastrous results. However, Owen turned around and headed back to his cell in such a hurry that he never had a chance.

It had taken Shipley a couple of days after Rita's episode to attempt to reach her by phone. He figured it would take a day or two for her to make bail, but he wanted to know what charges she was facing, and of course, he was concerned about her. Naturally, he also had to know if she was going to be allowed back into the pen. He didn't expect that she would be and had already decided he'd likely have to arrange another method of getting some money in.

Rita had left her phone number with him, so one evening, he thought he'd give it a try. He dialed the number and heard a male voice say, "Hallo?" He then waited while the operator asked if the person would accept charges for a phone call from a federal institution. The gruff voice replied, "Yes, I certainly will, but it will be a short call."

Assuming it was Rita's father, Shipley started the conversation by saying, "Ah, hello, is this Mr. Jessup? Could I speak with Rita, please?"

"Not very damned likely, Shipley. The only reason I took your call is to inform you that you are not to try to contact my daughter or this house again. If you do, there will be serious problems on your end. She has had enough problems because of you. She joined that damned group to try to help you assholes, and all she's received in return are problems with the legal system. From now on, you leave her, and us, the hell alone. If I hear from you again, I'm gonna speak to my brother, you asshole!"

Shipley figured that was the end of the one-way conversation, because all he heard after that was a dial tone.

Before Shipley could tell his buddy about the phone call to Rita, Owen turned and left him standing there and headed back to his cell.

* * *

Of course, Owen couldn't tell Shipley that he'd been crowded into a corner by a couple of heavies a few nights ago. It was a quick conversation, and Owen hardly had an opportunity to open his mouth. In fact, the first words ominously whispered to him were "Keep your big mouth shut, and just listen up, asshole."

The instructions were whispered into his ear by an oversized, tattooed brute who smelled as if he hadn't had a shower or brushed his teeth in a week. But the really scary part was that he was holding a shank. He pressed Owen into a corner and pretended he was talking to him, so no one would take note of what was really going on. At the same time, he held the sharp point of the knife against Patrick's chest while hiding what he was doing with his huge body. The smaller of the two assailants, who was still a great deal larger than Owen and was also covering up what he was doing, grabbed one of Patrick arms and bent his wrist in a direction in which a wrist wasn't intended to go.

Owen had the impression these guys were experts in this type of thing.

Both heavies did an excellent job of hiding what was going on. Several inmates walked past on their way off the range and didn't notice a thing. However, even if they had spotted the trouble, they would've carried on as if nothing usual were happening. Inmates didn't want to get involved with other people's problems, and that type of problem wasn't all that unusual.

There wasn't much Owen could do about his predicament except stand there terrified and hope to hell he lived through whatever was going to happen. He figured if he managed to punch the big guy in the throat or somewhere else just as damaging, the other one would still have his wrist bent back, and Owen didn't doubt for a second that he was also armed. He also realized that even if he managed to escape and make it to a control post without too much damage to his body, he would have to go into protection. If he did that, the staff would find out he had been gambling and would likely charge him. Plus, he'd be tarred with the hated title of rat.

All those thoughts flashed through his mind within a millisecond or so, and he was too terrified to do anything about his situation anyway. He figured he was going to be killed and knew there wasn't a damn thing he could do about it.

"Listen up, punk. You gambled and lost once too often, and now you owe us, asshole. Have you forgotten about it, or were you just wishing we'd smile and tell you to forget it? Well, we're not gonna forget it. You owe us big time, and it's time you paid up, boy. And if you don't, you're going to get your fucking throat laid wide open and your nuts stuffed into your mouth. I actually really think that would be kinda cute."

As that was whispered hotly into his ear, the knife was pushed a little harder into his left chest area, hard enough to draw a little blood, which gave Owen more reason to think his life was about to end.

"Jesus, guys, I told you I have the money coming in. It's just taking longer than I thought it would. Christ, easy with that goddamned knife. If you do me in, I won't be able to pay you back!"

"We ain't dumping you yet, asshole; in fact, we're gonna give you a break. I sure as hell don't agree with this, but we've been told you're gonna do a favour for a crew out on the street, and then your debt vanishes. But you'd better not screw us around." With a sneering smile that lacked a few teeth, he continued. "And don't forget, goof, that I'd rather stick a shank up your ass!"

"Jesus, man, take it easy with that shiv. Whatever you want, Christ, I'll do it. Just let up on that knife. Christ, it hurts like hell!"

"Shut up and listen, asshole. Here's what you're gonna do. And you've been given a week to get the job done. You're buddies with that asshole Shipley, eh?"

"Oh God, not buddies. We just hang out a bit."

"Shut your stupid mouth, and listen up; we ain't got all day, you know. Your buddy has pissed some big people off. By this time next week, he'd better be tits up. I'll tell you right now: some turkey's gonna be. And if Shipley's still walking around, you're the one who's going down. Understand what I'm saying, shithead?"

"Oh Christ, yeah, I do. Why him? What'd he ever do? Jesus, he don't even know nobody."

"Not your concern, goof. Just do your job like we told you, and you'll live a little longer, punk."

With that bit of encouragement and a little extra push on the knife for emphasis, Patrick's two buddies backed off a little. They glanced around, and with another dirty look thrown his way, they mixed in with a few other inmates and headed off the range.

For a few minutes, Owen was shaking too badly to do anything, let alone walk. He just stood there looking around, trying to calm down and get his breath back and suffering weird looks from a few of his fellow inmates. Once he felt he could walk without his knees banging together, he turned around and, almost running, retreated back to his cell. He knew that his chest was bleeding a little and that he should get a towel or something to put pressure on the cut. He also knew damn well he couldn't go to the hospital and have the nurse check it. That would have raised some serious questions he couldn't answer.

Owen staggered into his cell and, while ripping his shirt off, noted that the cut on his chest had stopped bleeding. He was thankful for that at least. He tossed the shirt into a corner and stood there flexing his wrist in an attempt to regain some feeling in it. He knew he would have to give the shirt a quick wash before someone spotted the blood and started asking questions. He also decided it would be a good time to finish the little bit of brew he still had hidden away. *Jesus, I'd better finish it or dump it. If the screws happen to toss my cell and find it, I'll be locked up again. Christ, then those pukes would think I got locked up on purpose and come after me when I got out. Jesus, what a mess!* After he shakily poured a mug of brew and downed it, he started to calm down a little and thought he'd better wash the blood off himself. Once that little job was completed, he sat on the bed and tried to think.

Oh Christ. What the hell do I do now? God, I shouldn't have played cards with those assholes. I knew what they were like, but I was so sure I'd win. Oh God, why? It's about the stupidest thing I've ever done. Mac has never screwed me over; in fact, he's done me some favours. But God, Mac, I don't have a choice. I'm so sorry, but friends or not, it ain't my fault; there's just nothing I can do about it!

Owen, while those thoughts and others continued to whirl around in his mind, started to get worked up again. But not knowing what else to do, he just sat on his bed, looking wildly around, as if he expected someone or something to jump out and grab him around the throat.

It took him several more minutes to settle down again and stop shaking. Once he more or less accomplished that, he continued to sit on his bed and thought more calmly about his dilemma and what he was going to do about it. It never entered his mind that he could go to staff and explain his and Shipley's problems. His first thought was that he had to pick a time and place and figure out how he could get it done and then how to get away with it. Right off the bat, he figured his best bet was to try to do it in the yard.

Owen believed in the old adage "Preservation of life is much more important than friendship," especially when the life was his own.

A couple of days passed, and Owen, except for going to work, mostly stayed in his cell. The few times when he was coming or going and spotted his buddy Shipley, he just gave him a wave or, if they bumped into each other, a "Hey, Mac, how you doing?" He had a lot of planning to do.

He managed to get his hands on an oversized spike from the carpenter shop. It needed a lot of work done to it, but he had the time. It had to be honed down to a needlelike point, and he managed to sharpen one side of it so that it was also a small knife. On top of that, it also had to have a couple of pieces of wood measured to a certain size and taped around one end to form a handle. Taping, besides making a good hand grip, was also a neat way to frustrate the cops if they tried to get fingerprints. Within a few days or so, the weapon was ready. He now was in possession of a homemade ice pick. It wasn't fancy, but it would be deadly when used properly.

His next problem was to find a safe hiding place for the thing. He already had a spot picked out, so there it sat, waiting to be used. Most importantly, he also had to pick an opportune time to do Mac in. After all, he didn't want to get caught. The best bet usually was a busy time with a lot of inmates shuffling around but hopefully no staff, at least none in sight. He had been around long enough to know that his safest bet would be during a disturbance on the range, but he also realized he couldn't count on something like that, because it was unlikely to happen. He also knew damned well that he didn't have the power to get something like that started up.

Now that he had his mind made up that he was actually going to do the job and had the weapon hidden away, his biggest problem was figuring out when his opportunity would come along. One evening, after much planning and discarding, an idea suddenly popped into his tired mind. *Hell, in three weeks or so, we're having that silly-assed noon barbecue in the exercise yard. Christ, most of us always turn out for it. Just what I need! Trouble is, I'll have to convince those assholes to wait an extra two weeks. The dumb bunch of idiots shouldn't complain. At least I hope they won't, or I'm screwed!*

Once Owen had decided when, how and where he was going to get his buddy Shipley, he had to talk that huge thug into giving him an extra week or so to carry out his orders. It still had not entered his mind to refuse or to go running to the hole.

It took him almost two days to get close to Slug. That was the name Owen had given to that particular heavy in his mind. Never would he have called the heavy his assigned nickname out loud; Owen did like to live.

Once he finally worked up enough nerve to talk to Slug, yard was cancelled due to rain and fog. Unfortunately, that meant a stressed-out Owen was going to have to go through the nerve-racking procedure all over again at the next yard-up.

That was standard procedure. Anytime the tower staff couldn't see the complete exercise yard, yard-up was cancelled. *Jeez*, he thought, *fog would be great when I do my thing. The screws in the towers wouldn't be able to see it go down.* However, he also knew he would never be that lucky.

So he figured he'd have to wait until the next day. The only place Owen wanted to chat with Slug was in the yard. He figured that out there, the discussion wouldn't be as noticeable—at least he hoped it wouldn't be.

The next evening, after supper, he headed for the yard. It was a great day, with no fog and still lots of sun and summer heat. Owen stepped into the exercise yard, blinked a couple of times in the bright sunlight and, within a few minutes, spotted Slug walking around with a couple of his buddies, including the wrist-twister. Owen headed in their direction, and once he was within earshot, remembering not to call him Slug out loud, while still a fair distance away, he quietly and not overly forcibly said, "Hello. Got a minute to chat?" Owen knew a person didn't walk up to those guys from behind, tap them on the shoulder and say, "Hey, I wanna talk at you!" That wouldn't have been a smart thing to do on his part, and Owen was not a complete idiot.

The group heard his timid hello and turned around, and once Slug saw who it was, he waved him forward. "What the hell you want, punk? I gave you your orders the other day; just do what you're told, will you?"

"Oh, I'm gonna. I have a plan all set to go, but I'll need about another two weeks. Christ, just two extra weeks. I've picked the time and the place, and I have a shank all set, but please, I just need an extra two weeks, for God's sake!"

"Aw, for Christ's sake. You punks really piss me off. A simple job like this, and you're all fucking teary. Christ. 'Please! Please, two more weeks!' You got it, but listen here, boy. It'd better be worth it. Now, get your ass outta here!"

"OK, I'm gone. Thanks for the two weeks." Owen headed back to his range. *Oh yeah, big, tough guy, eh, Slug? At least you are when all your buddies are around.* But after the little chat, Owen felt safe enough to resume his daily showers.

Chapter 18

Several weeks before Owen found himself in his mess, Shipley received a letter. He was excited because it was the first one he'd received in three or four weeks. He clutched it in his hand until his reached his cell, thinking, *Jeez, it's pretty damn thin, and no return address. Christ, that's kind of weird; I wonder who the hell it's from.*

As soon as Shipley entered his cell, he made himself comfortable at his little desk. He hurriedly opened his letter and roughly pulled the one sheet of paper out. It started out with "Mr. Shipley." He immediately glanced down to the bottom and saw that it was signed, "Mrs. Connie Shipley-Patterson."

It took him a second of thinking, and then he almost went into shock when it struck him: *Oh my God. This must be from my sister. Holy hell!* It didn't take him long to read it. After he reread the *Mr. Shipley* part, he continued reading the rest of the short note.

Mr. Shipley,

My married name is Connie Patterson. My name before I was married was Connie Shipley. I am looking for my brother, whom I haven't heard from in several years. His name is Mac Shipley. Our parents' names are Sharon and Ronald. Our last address was 68 James Street in the town of Ryerson.

If you are not the person I am looking for, please let me know at the following address. If this is you, Mac, please write, and I'll reply as soon as I hear from you.

Shipley finished the note and reread it three times. He couldn't move or even think. Once it sank in that the letter writer was really his sister, tears came and wouldn't stop for several minutes. He kept saying to himself, *Oh my God, it's really her. Oh my God, it is!*

Shipley, despite his size and his newfound toughness, was still an emotional person. The letter had rocked him both emotionally and physically. He didn't think he'd ever been so worked up in his life, not even when he'd been sentenced to his eight and a half years.

It didn't take him long to grab his writing pad and start formulating a reply. *Jesus, I have so much to write about. Where in hell do I start? Married! I wonder if Connie has any kids. It's been years. How did she find me in this hellhole? She must have finally gotten in touch with Mom, but I didn't think she would ever do that. Oh God. I have to shut up and write!*

He finally completed his letter. It took him quite a while. In fact, he had to rewrite it several times. Once it was completed, he stuffed it into an envelope, addressed the envelope and shoved it into the mail slot during the next changeover. *Damn, it'll take at least a week to get to her. I probably won't hear anything back for at least two or maybe even three weeks. How in hell am I ever going to be able to wait that long?*

But there was nothing he could do about it, so he continued on with his life, such as it was. He spent much more time in the gym, working out and trying to calm down. Despite knowing the reply would take at least another two weeks, he couldn't help but expect that it would be there each and every day.

But Shipley was busy, at least for the type of environment he was in. He was still determined to get out of Mountainview, or, as he referred to it, the nuthouse. He had formulated about half a plan. Part of his problem was that he was still working in the servery, and to activate his plan, he had to obtain a job in the recreational department. That was part of the reason for his going to the gym; he was now going five or six times a week. He figured if he got to know the staff and they got to know him and if he made sure they realized he wanted to work in recreation, he might eventually land a job in the area. He figured once he was there, it should only take him a few weeks or, at most, a couple of months to finish his plan, and he'd be gone.

A couple of days after Shipley mailed the letter to his sister, he was heading to the gym for his regular evening workout. Just as he cleared the range, he spotted his buddy Owen. "Hey, Jim. How the hell you doing? I hardly ever see you anymore. Jesus, you must be busy." Then, in a much lower voice, as they drew closer, he continued. "Hell, you'd think you were planning a getaway or something."

Owen gave a little jerk and replied, "Oh, hi, Mac. Nah, just hanging around, trying to stay out of trouble. You know how it is. Just the usual bullshit. Nothing big time. You hanging in OK? Where you headed?"

"Aw, nothing new. Just heading for the gym for a little workout. You going there?"

"Nah. Gonna try the yard and see how things are out there."

"Yeah, good idea. Maybe I'll head out with you and do my workout at the next changeover."

"Sure, Mac, sounds good. We haven't done anything like that for a long time. Maybe later we can head back to my cell; I still have some brew left." Then Owen stopped dead as if he'd suddenly remembered something and said, "Oh Christ, Mac, I just remembered. I have to get back to my cell before the screws lock up. I'll catch you later, buddy."

Once Owen turned around and rushed back toward his cell, Shipley decided to carry on to the gym to complete his workout after all. *Hell, I wonder what the heck's up with Jim. He sure doesn't seem to be himself lately.* Then his memory slipped back to Bentley, who had done himself in. *Christ, I hope Jim's OK. Aw, I'm sure if something big was up, he'd talk to me about it. God, I don't want another friend hanging himself. Christ, one's enough!*

Shipley continued on to the gym and completed his workout, not knowing that he would have been better off if his chum had checked out by suicide.

A couple of days after Owen abruptly left him at the range entrance, Shipley was leaving his cell to go out to the yard to do some walking around. Owen and his change in behaviour were still on his mind, almost as much as getting in contact with his sister. *Jeez, what the hell could be eating at Jim? Nothing's changed around here except those assholes getting sent to the supermax, and that's a good thing for all of us. I'm gonna have to get him to sit down with a coffee one of these days to see if there's anything I can do.*

Shipley stepped out of his cell and, because he was thinking of Owen and Bentley, almost bumped into Goodwin. Goodwin, whose nickname was God or Goddamn, lived three cells up range from Shipley, and even though they were not great friends, they got along with each other well.

"Oh hell, God. Sorry. I almost ran you down. Heading to the yard?"

"Nah. Gonna do the gym thing. Haven't been down yet this week. Gotta get back at it. You heading there?"

"Nope," Shipley nonchalantly replied. "On my way to the yard. Everything going OK with you?"

"Not really. Did the screws toss your cell yesterday?"

"Nah, don't think so. Pretty sure I'd notice that."

"Buggers did mine. Bastards found my pail of brew I bought off your buddy Owen. They dumped it down the toilet and said they were gonna write up a report about it. Damn bunch of goofs!"

"Hell, God. That ain't bad. Other than losing your brew, all you'll likely get is some OP for a couple of days. Shit, that ain't a big deal."

They continued on toward the recreational area while updating each other on any news. Then Godwyn looked toward Shipley and asked, "Hey, Mac, you notice a change with Jim? When I picked up my booze the other night, he seemed like a different guy. He's just not himself."

"Yeah, he does seem different. Likely problems at home. Guess there's not much we can do about it."

They reached the gym barrier, and Godwyn, with a wave and a "See you later" directed toward Shipley, headed in to tackle the weights.

Shipley kept going, and as he entered the yard, he took his usual scan of the area and spotted someone who looked familiar. *I wonder who the hell that guy is. He sure looks like someone I know. Christ, if I didn't know better, I'd think it's old Dominic. But it can't be; he's still in a lock-up somewhere, waiting for his trial on those other murder charges.*

Vern Thibedeau

The person had his back to Shipley and was still a fair distance away, so Shipley moved a little quicker to catch up. He caught up and, while he was still a few feet away, gave out a quiet "Hey, Joe, is that you?"

Hearing the question, the stranger quickly spun around and looked toward Shipley.

It was Dominic! But Shipley immediately noticed that he didn't seem like the same guy at all. Dominic looked several years older and seemed frail.

"Jesus Christ, it is you, Joe! What the hell you doing back here? Thought you were standing trial or something. Is it over already? Doesn't seem to've been all that long."

Dominic greeted Shipley with a big smile and a handshake that almost turned into a manly hug. "Christ, it's great to see you, Mac. I figured that one way or another, you'd be outta here by now. Yep, I'm back here again. After all that screwing around, they just sat on the charges. Not sure why; guess there wasn't enough evidence to get a conviction. Anyway, they shipped me back here to my old homestead. Kind of a strange thing when you think about it. I got convicted for a murder I didn't do, and they can't get enough evidence on me for the two killings I did do. I'll tell you, Mac, things are sure screwed up around these places. Hell, what's up with you? You look like a new man; you have a changeover or something? Jeez, how's your girl and that young one of yours doing? And I would guess you've decided to hang around here until they transfer you out, eh?"

"Nah, just looking after myself a little better and going to the gym once in a while. Haven't heard from Jen for ages. Don't know what the hell's going on with either one of them; just hope they're doing OK. Also, don't know if you heard about it or not, but Crothers and his creeps are locked up, and that has sure helped. Not sweating nearly as much as I used to. God, it's great to see you, Joe!"

Dominic gave a little laugh before replying, "Hey, slow down a little, Mac. I did hear about Crothers; in fact, that goof and his buddies were in lock-up for a while where I was being held. I'm not sure of the outcome with them, because one day they were just gone. I'll tell you one thing, though: they didn't look very tough while they were in that place. So what's up? You decide to hang around until you get a transfer to a medium?"

"Hell no. Still checking things out. Gonna start work in the rec department shortly, and once I get in there and get a little cash, I should be gone in a very short time. Hell, I've even started going to one of those evening groups, and I'm sure glad I did. They come in one night a week, and I've met a girl. Her name's Rita Jessup, and she's one sweet chick. Believe it or not, I think she's fallen in love with me." Then, with a smirk and a chuckle, Shipley added, "Besides her good looks, she must be one smart broad; she sure knows how to pick a guy." He didn't want to tell Dominic the story about her getting caught while trying to lug drugs and money in for him. He figured he'd tell Dominic the story some other day. However, that decision might have been an error on his part.

"Jessup. I know that name. She from around here? Has she mentioned any of her family members' names? Aw, forget it; can't be who I'm thinking about. I'm sure none of their family would be coming into this place without some judge ordering it after a trial."

"Nah, I'm sure she ain't involved with anything like that. But what the hell's up with you, Joe? If you don't mind me saying, you look like hell—and that's being nice about it. Your eye looks like someone punched you or something. You doing OK?"

"Yep, I do have some problems, though. 'Member me telling you about that crew out on the street that I did some jobs for? I think I also mentioned that they were having a little war with that other outfit." Once Shipley acknowledged that he remembered the discussion, Dominic continued. "As far as the eye goes, an idiot from that other crew who was locked up with me thought he'd make a name for himself. He did that all right. The bugger gave me a black eye, but from what I've heard, he'll never walk again. In fact, they've started calling him Wheelchair Teddy. I was lucky, though; the goof picked a quiet spot to play hero, so no one was around. Once I was done with him, it took another ten minutes or so before he was found. I actually thought he was dead." With a little laugh, Dominic added, "Poor screws worked for days trying to find out who did that nasty thing to the poor fool."

"Christ, Joe, remind me never to piss you off. So your crew is still having problems, eh? Hope it works out for you."

"Well, looks like my side lost. I guess they found a couple more bodies, and from what I was told, they didn't go very nicely. I'll tell you, Mac, there are sure different ways of dying. I've also heard through the grapevine that there's a contract out on me. I'm beginning to think I picked the wrong side this time."

Shipley and Dominic continued to stroll around the yard, chatting. Shipley filled Dominic in on all the news, including the letter he'd received from his sister. He didn't have to tell Dominic how excited he was about it; Dominic could tell by his animated state. Dominic also told Shipley that he was on 2G in E unit, and that was why it had taken them so long to run into each other.

The longer they walked and chatted, the more concerned Shipley became. He didn't want to get involved with Dominic's problems. He was starting to think poor old Joe had some serious enemies, and he sure as hell didn't want to get in between them. He started nervously glancing around and couldn't help imagining several cons coming at them. He envisioned himself going down along with Dominic.

Finally, just before changeover, he looked at Dominic and said, "Well, I'd better get back in, Joe. I'm supposed to meet up with Jim, and we're heading into his cell for a couple drinks. Listen, Joe, if you need a hand with anything, get a hold of me, and I'll help any way I can."

"Sounds good, Mac; I appreciate the offer. But I'm beginning to think I should get into lock-up before something bad happens."

"Aw God, Joe. Christ, that'd be rough, but I have to run. See you next time, buddy." With that, Shipley headed inside, leaving Dominic standing there alone, staring at Shipley's back and shaking his head.

Jesus Christ, has Joe ever got problems. I'm gonna have to keep an eye out and stay the hell away from wherever he's hanging around. It's sure none of my business. On his way back in, Shipley had planned to go into the gym, but being a little concerned about Dominic spotting him in there working out, he decided to just go back to his cell and watch television.

But that didn't work out too well. He couldn't help thinking about the problems poor old Joe had. *My God, Joe looks like an old man. How in hell could that happen so fast? Jesus, I hope he doesn't have to go into protection. God, what a way to do time. Christ, living with a bunch of fucking skinners. Joe can't do that; it'd kill him, for God's sake. Jesus, I do like the guy, but I don't want anyone to think we're buddies. I've enough problems of my own.*

Shipley had no way of knowing it, but his problems were about to become much worse. But eventually, he drifted off into a dream-filled sleep, and once again, those vultures started flying around.

The next day, Shipley checked for mail after he left his illustrious servery job, and he picked up a letter from his mother. Once he made it back to his cell, he opened it up and started to read. It was filled with the usual stuff: life was hard money-wise, Tom had a lead on another job and on and on. He realized he wouldn't read anything about his mom being in contact with Connie. Before disappearing from his life, Connie had stated emphatically that she wanted nothing to do with her mother and certainly nothing to do with their so-called father. She had also told Shipley in no uncertain terms that she didn't care if their father died. In fact, she'd said death would look good on him, especially if it took him a long time to die.

Connie never had told her brother why she felt that way, but a few years after she had walked out of his life and he had grown up a little more, he'd thought he understood what had likely gone on. That threw more guilty feelings onto his shoulders. He had the impression their mother was aware of whatever had gone on but never had done anything about it.

That evening, Shipley was on his way to the gym and heard someone behind him call his name. He turned around, and there was Dominic, hustling to catch up. "Oh, hi, Joe. Didn't see you back there. What's up, bud?"

"Remember you mentioned that girl you met in the group? I think you said her name's Rita," Dominic said.

"Sure. Rita Jessup. Why? What's going on?"

"She run into a problem the other night on her way in to the group?"

Shipley took a look around before replying, "Yeah. The screws said she was lugging stuff in or something like that. From what I understand, the goofs took her away in a squad car."

"That's about what I heard. I also found out she is part of that family I told you about. Her father isn't involved, though; he's a regular stiff and works at a normal job. But apparently, her father's brother is the one who runs the outfit. The word is out that he is really pissed about his niece getting screwed up. It also seems to be common knowledge that she was bringing the stuff in for you."

"Well, yeah, she was. But I thought she was just bringing money in. Christ, I didn't know anything about the drugs. But there ain't nothing I can do for her."

Dominic gave a look at Shipley and replied, "You're right about that, but the word is that her uncle blames you for her mess. Jesus Christ, Mac, it's not like he's a big-time gangbanger, but he does swing a lot of weight around the city. Christ, man, some of his crew're even in here doing time. I haven't found out how much weight he does have or who works for him in here, but until I do, you'd best watch your back."

"Christ. Back to the same old problem, and it's not even my fault. Fuck, I'm getting sick of this shit!"

Shipley and Dominic walked around and chatted about different things for a while, and then Shipley decided to go in to watch television and have a coffee.

On his way back to his cell block, he kept a closer watch on his back and on everything going on around him. But he didn't think this was even close to the mess he'd been in during his problems with the Crothers gang. He also had a lot more confidence now and was in much better shape than he had been. But even so, he couldn't help thinking he'd better start carrying a weapon of some kind around with him again.

He might have been confident, but he was no fool, or so he thought.

Chapter 19

It was the start of another evening shift, and Tom Jamison tiredly climbed the staircase that led into E unit's control. When he popped his head up through the hatch, he saw that his partner, Faraday, had beat him in and had relieved the two day-shift guys. "Hey partner, you beat me in. All set for another thrilling night, eh?"

"Yep, really lookin' forward to it. If I fall asleep, make sure you wake me up in time to go home."

Tom replied with a little laugh, "Oh sure, Jim, as long as you do the same for me, big guy."

Both officers had several years' experience and immediately got busy checking the equipment, including their weapons. Tom also contacted the corporal in the unit office to let him know they were both in and all set for their shift.

Allen Jenkins was the corporal and was not happy about working the evening shift. He'd just finished his day shift, found out there was no relief and told the sergeant he could work the extra shift if he needed him to. It wasn't something he really wanted to do, but he figured the extra money would come in handy, so he thought to himself, *Ah, what the hell?* That was, until he phoned his wife to let her know he was going to do a double shift. He found out his wife had made plans for them to go next door for dinner. He wasn't a happy camper, and he knew damned well that his wife wasn't impressed either. At any rate, he informed the control that there was nothing unusual going on and told them to just stick to the regular routine.

A short reply came from the control: "You got it, Al. Let's just keep it that way and get outta here on time." They didn't know it, of course, but that was wishful thinking on their part.

The regular routine started. Within an hour or so, the inmates started returning from work, the control staff locked them into their cells and floor staff, after receiving the OK from the control, started down the ranges to do the count. They counted the inmates, filled in their count pads and returned to the unit office so Allen could total the unit count and take it up to the sergeant. Once the institutional count was finalized, the inmates were released from their cells so they could pick up their supper meal. That started the usual evening routine.

The routine continued without change. After the supper meal, which some called "the last meal," the first recreational period began. Then the first changeover happened, and recreation continued. So far, it was just another boring evening.

Shortly before the 8:00 p.m. count, Tom looked over to Jim and asked, "Hey, Jim, you notice anything unusual so far? I'm not sure what the hell's up, but I got a feeling that something isn't quite right. Likely just another one of those silly-assed hunches—at least I hope that's what it is anyway."

"Dunno, Tom, but I was just gonna ask you the same thing. Don't know what it is, but I got a feeling something ain't kosher. Think I'll call Allen to let him know something may be going on. He may even have an idea what the hell it is."

Jim phoned Allen in the office. Phoning was a lot easier than trying to talk through a gun port and still keep the conversation confidential. But Al had no more of an idea than Jim or Tom did. "Just keep your eyes open up there, and if you spot anything at all, let me know. But I'll mention it to the guys when we go out to N area to bring the cons in for the count."

About 10 minutes later, Allen looked at the two officers assigned to the unit and said, "I guess we might as well head out to N area; they'll be on the way back for the count shortly." On the way out of the unit, Allen, in a quiet voice, explained the control officers' concerns and instructed them to keep an extra eye out during their walks and during inmate movement.

While the staff from the other units were standing around N area, waiting for the inmates to start coming up from the gym and yard, Allen wandered over to each corporal and explained the concern his control officers had. He received a nod from each one and a "If something goes down and you need a hand, give a holler, and we'll get some people over to you."

In short order, the inmates started back to the units. Staff, especially E unit staff, kept a close watch, but no one spotted anything unusual. Once they received notice from the yard and gym that the inmates were all in, the unit barriers were closed, and then it was just a matter of waiting for an all-clear from the unit controls, signaling that the inmates were in their cells.

Once again, Allen noted how quickly three or four hundred inmates could move along when they wanted to. He also realized they could poke along and take an unusual amount of time whenever it suited their needs. But with that particular count, the inmates usually moved fairly quickly. As a rule, they wanted to get the count in and get back to whatever they were doing for recreation.

Tom and Jim both stood in the control, watching the inmates file into the unit and go to their ranges. Most of them went right into their cells, but as usual, several poked around on each range, talking, laughing and hollering at one another. Jim couldn't help looking over at Tom and, not for the first time, saying, "Jesus Christ. They're just like a bunch of fifteen-year-olds, for God's sake."

"Hell, that's true enough. But dangerous fifteen-year-olds."

Tom was watching 2G range and noticed four or five inmates standing around at the far end, having what appeared to be an intense conversation. He also noted that the inmates kept throwing glances toward the control, as if they were concerned they would be noticed. Of course, that was the main reason they were noticed.

"Hey, Jim, give me a second or so to move over to F range, and then take a quick look down 2G and let me know if you think something's going on." With that, Tom eased over and started to keep an eye on F range.

Jim slowly shuffled over to get a clear view down 2G, and within moments, he looked over to Tom and said, "Yep. I'd bet anything the pricks are up to no good. I hope it's just planning on a drug buy or something; I really wanna get the hell out of here on time tonight. Have to come back in the morning."

"Well, they're not doing bugger-all now. In fact, they're finally heading into their cells. I'm gonna let Al and the guys know they can come in and get the count done. I'm also going to let them know what we saw, just in case something does pop up."

"Yeah, OK, better safe than sorry, eh?"

That was the start of the 8:00 count. The inmates were locked in their cells, the staff walked the ranges and each inmate was counted. Once that job was completed, they went into the office to total the unit count, and then Jenkins headed up to the sergeant's office with the count.

While he was gone, there wasn't a lot to do, so the staff took time to eat some of their lunch, have coffee and, of course, chat about their day. Jim also made sure the unit officers knew about the impromptu meeting on 2G.

Within a short time, the control staff were told that the count was correct and asked to notify the inmates that it was time for gym. As soon as the staff left the unit for N area, Tom used the speaker system to let the inmates know it was gym-up, and Jim opened the cells to release the inmates. Tom and Jim had already discussed what they felt could be a potential problem on 2G, and even though they didn't have a clue what it could be, they agreed to keep a closer-than-usual watch on that particular range.

The cell doors opened with the usual bang, and inmates, with their usual teenage hooting and hollering, left their cells. They continued their pushing and laughing while starting toward the control centre to exit the unit and head to the gym, group, the common room or wherever they planned on going.

Most of the inmates headed out as soon as the cell doors opened; however, Jim and Tom immediately noticed four or five inmates hanging around the back end of the range. They were acting as if nothing unusual were happening, as if they were just having a conversation. But it was unusual, and both staff started paying them a lot of attention. The inmates threw the odd glance toward the control centre, which, naturally, was another giveaway.

Jim was just reaching for the microphone to instruct the inmates to either return to their cells or get the hell off range, when another inmate, who didn't appear to realize there were still several milling around the area, stepped out of his cell. With a sudden awakening, Tom and Jim realized the inmates had been waiting for the guy who had just stepped onto the range. The inmates immediately surrounded him, and he almost disappeared from their view.

At first, both officers had the impression that the inmates were happy to see the guy. It even flashed through Jim's mind that maybe it was the guy's birthday, or they were congratulating him for earning a parole or some silly thing. But several hours later, once the incident was resolved, Jim, who didn't want to sound like a completely innocent idiot, never mentioned to anyone, except his wife, what his initial thought had been.

The inmates surrounded the one inmate, and for the first few moments, it appeared they were just slapping him on the back, shoving him back and forth a little and even hugging him. The officers were shocked when they spotted a spray of blood spurt out of the crowd, and they heard a high-pitched scream that quickly turned into a gurgle. A millisecond before hearing the scream, Tom spotted the flash of a reflection off something, which he immediately figured was a knife. It suddenly struck them both that what they had thought were slaps on the back actually had been punches or maybe even knife thrusts.

Tom grabbed the microphone and yelled for all inmates still on the range to return to their cells. At the same time, he pushed the button to slam the range barrier closed. He figured that at the very least, they would have the guilty inmates locked on the range and not hiding out at the gym or somewhere else. While Tom was locking the range barrier, Jim pulled up a rifle and hollered out through the gun port that they were to immediately stop, or he was going to shoot. The inmates either didn't hear his threat or didn't think he would carry it out, because they ignored him and kept up the attack. Jim fired a round off, which just about deafened both Jim and Tom and almost caused Tom to piss himself.

Vern Thibedeau

The noise of the rifle could be heard all the way out to N area. For a second or so upon hearing the shot go off, the staff froze and just stood there staring at one another. The N area corporal was the first to reach a phone, and as he was dialing E control, Al Jenkins grabbed a radio and, with an excited voice, asked, "E unit, what the hell's going on? You guys OK?"

"We're OK. There's been a stabbing. Jim had to fire a round off. No one hit. Blood all over the place. Need the nurse now! Better also send for an ambulance. Give us a couple of minutes to get the cons locked up. Will let you know when you can get in here. Oh Christ, what a fucking mess! Gotta go. We're busy!" With that announcement, Tom dropped the radio and, using the microphone, yelled, "Listen up, assholes! This is your last chance to get the hell into your cells. The next shot will be into one of you fuckers still on the range!"

With that announcement, Jim stuck the barrel of the rifle out of the gun port, and even though it didn't require it, he manually jacked another round up into the chamber. He prayed the noise would be enough to get the last few inmates into their cells. And it worked! Within moments, the only one left on the range was the injured inmate, who was curled up on the floor, not making a sound and not even twitching. There was an abundance of blood all over the place.

Just as he slammed the last cell door closed, Tom looked at Jim and hoarsely said, "Jesus Christ, how can one person leak that much blood?"

Jim, as he grabbed for the radio, replied, "You got me." Then, into the radio, Jim said, "E control to all staff. E unit is secure; get in here, and sort this mess out!"

When the last cell door slammed closed, Tom opened the unit barrier for the staff piling into the unit. Mixed in with the correctional staff were a nurse and one of her helpers. They rushed up to 2G, and as soon as they reached the range and she saw the amount of blood, Tom heard the nurse say, "Aw hell, I doubt there's anything I'll be able to do for him."

Once Corporal Jenkins heard her speak those words, he yelled to the staff about to rush onto the range, "Everyone just stop right where you are! This is a crime scene, and we can't screw it up!" Pointing to one of the officers, Allen continued with his instructions. "Dave, you come down with me. Just watch where the hell you step; be sure not to step in any of the blood. We'll go down with the nurse to see if there's anything we can do to help. The rest of you just stay here unless I call for you." At the same time, Al was thinking, *Thank Christ the cons went in; at least we won't need the response team to put them in.*

As Allen and Dave made their way down the range with the nurse and her assistant, Allen heard Dave muttering to himself, "Oh my God. Oh my God, this can't be."

Al realized the smell of blood and the foul odour of someone who had emptied his bowels were getting to Dave, and he thought, *Christ, I may have picked the wrong guy to give me a hand.* With a glance toward Dave and with a lowered voice, Allen said, "Listen, Dave, just take deep breaths through your mouth. If you feel like you have ta puke, make sure you get off the range or at least off to the side."

Dave, with a sickly smile and a dazed look, swallowing like crazy, gave Al a nod that he'd be OK.

They were only halfway down the range, when Jenkins spotted two homemade knives that had been tossed and were lying on the floor. They were both covered with blood, but even so, one of them was glinting from an overhead light. After glancing at that knife, which almost looked as if it had come from a store, Allen was sure it was the one that had done the most damage. He also noticed that both knives had taped handles. As soon as he spotted the weapons, knowing there was little chance of fingerprints, he yelled out, "Christ, make sure you don't touch those knives lying on the floor!"

Just before he reached the inmate, the quietness on the range suddenly struck Jenkins. There was no screaming, cursing or banging on cell doors, just the horrible smell. In his experience, which covered more years than he cared to remember, the silence was highly unusual. He knew the reason for the oppressive quiet was because an inmate had been taken down by one of his own. He knew if the staff had been taking an inmate to segregation or trying to gain control of one of their buddies, the noise would have been unbelievable. However, a few questions were being screamed by inmates through their doors, such as, "Who the hell is down? Is he alive? Are the pricks helping him?" The questions were being yelled by inmates who couldn't see what was going on. Once an inmate who lived in a cell across from the incident yelled out a short explanation, everything became more or less quiet once again.

Once they reached the curled-up inmate, the nurse, knowing it was a useless endeavour, followed protocol, bent over the inmate, checked his pulse and listened for a heartbeat. As expected, she found neither. Once again, looking at Allen, she just shook her head. Al, even with the blood smeared over the inmate's face, the tongue hanging out and the back of his throat visible, could tell it was Dominic. *Aw hell, he just got back here, and he wasn't a bad con. I can think of several others I'd rather see lying there with their throats cut. Damn it to hell.*

Allen, glancing toward Dave to make sure he was surviving and receiving a nod in return, cleared his throat, thumbed his radio and called for the sergeant. He received an immediate response stating that the sergeant would be there momentarily. Jenkins acknowledged the reply and explained the situation. He also informed the sergeant that there was no doubt it was a murder, and they'd need the police and the coroner. Then, glancing toward the head of the range, Jenkins, thankfully, spotted Owen, the sergeant on duty. In the back of his mind, Jenkins noted that Owen was being careful not to step into any blood as he hurried toward them.

Patrick reached the group, and after taking a look around, while staring at the body, he told the nurse that since there was no doubt the inmate was dead and that it was a murder, the body had to stay where it was. He also informed Jenkins that the police and the meat wagon would be on the scene shortly and that all inmates would have to remain in their cells until the police completed their investigation. "Having said that," he added, "I really don't see why we can't cover the poor guy with a sheet or something. I'll make sure the cops are informed that they don't have a lot of time to get their pictures, measurements and whatnot. Hey, Al, do your control guys have any idea who the hell caused all this shit?"

"I'm gonna have my floor guys go up to relieve them, and we should know very shortly." With that, Jenkins got on the radio and informed his staff of the change of plans.

By then, the nurse and her helper had left the range and were on their way back to the hospital. Owen and Jenkins headed off, but on the way to the office, the sergeant instructed two staff to remain at the head of the range to ensure the area stayed clear. "You guys stay here. I don't care if it's the warden; no one—and I mean no one—gets down there until the police get on the scene. Do I make myself clear?"

As soon as the instructions were acknowledged, Owen and Jenkins continued to the office.

Once in the office, Jim and Tom, who had been relieved from the control, said they knew the names of the four inmates who had been involved in the stabbing. As soon as Allen heard that news, he looked toward one of the extra officers and said, "Ron, get the cell numbers of those inmates, grab the duct keys, get down the range and shut the water off for each one of those cells—and get it done now!" Once Ron took off, Al explained to the staff that turning the water off might make it more difficult for the inmates to clean the blood off themselves and their clothing. "At least we can hope it'll help."

Once Jenkins was finished talking to the staff, Owen, looking toward Jim and Tom, said, "You guys sit at that desk and start writing." With a glance toward Allen, he continued. "I'm gonna wait up front for the police to get here, but I don't doubt they'll want us to take those four idiots to the hole and isolate them." Then, with a "See you guys later," he was gone.

Most of the extra staff who had rushed into E unit to help headed back to their own posts. The E unit staff, plus a couple more spares who stayed to help out, just sat and watched Jim and Tom fill out their reports. Every once in a while, one would start a conversation about something, but the chatting never took hold, and most of the time, they just sat there looking around. A stranger walking into the unit office could never have guessed how active their thoughts were. Each one was going over in his own mind how they had reacted to the incident and wondered if there was more they could have done or done differently.

Eventually, Jenkins gave his head a little shake, looked toward one of the guys who had stayed behind and said, "Hey, George, would you go up to 2G and relieve the guys who are there? Tell 'em to come down and grab a coffee. You stay around the front of the range, and make sure no one—and I mean no one—goes down to look around. I can't emphasize it enough: no one is allowed down. With any luck, the cops'll be here soon and get their job done, and we can get back to our routine."

George said, "Sure. No problem," and headed out. The rest of the staff continued to sit around, drink coffee and not say or do much of anything.

In short order, Jenkins, hearing the unit barrier open and people talking as they entered the unit, left the office and walked out to the corridor. He spotted Owen coming in with four strangers he knew would be police officers and thought, *Christ, it's about time. Must've been in a shop having a coffee break or something.*

Patrick gave a wave toward Jenkins, and the little group followed Jenkins into the unit office. The four strangers identified themselves and looked toward Allen, and he filled them in as best as he could on what had happened. Then Allen and the staff waited to see how the police wanted to handle their end of the job.

The officer who seemed to be in charge said, "This seems pretty straightforward. Jake and I'll interview the control officers; John and Ed'll go on the range, do their measuring and take pictures. After that, we'll meet back here to talk things over. Once that's done and the coroner declares the death and gets the body out, I think we'll have to segregate those four until the prosecutors get a chance to read the file. Whenever they're finished doing that, they'll decide what they wanna do and let us know. But when we do go down to lock the buggers up, we'll have to go in and grab their clothes, and John will scrape their fingernails. While that's being done, we'll also have to check them over for any injuries. And then, with any luck, we'll get the hell out of your hair. Anyone else have any other ideas?" The officer looked at everyone, and when he received a few head shakes, he said, "Well, guess we might as well get at it then. John, you and Ed head down and do your thing. Jack, you take one officer into that first office, and I'll grab the second one. If we get done first, we'll go on the range to give John and Ed a hand."

Neither the interviewing nor the picture taking and measuring took long, and in short order, everyone was back in the unit office. They'd just made it back, when the coroner and a couple of helpers showed up with a gurney. They were escorted to the body, the coroner declared him deceased, the body was placed on the gurney and away they went.

The police officer looked at Jenkins and said, "Well, I guess the only thing left to get done is to lock them up. You guys are the experts at this end of it, so we'll just follow along. The only thing is, John and Ed have to go into each cell before the con is taken away."

Jenkins and three of his staff, with the police following along, headed for the first cell. Once they reached the cell, Jenkins got on his radio and told the control, "Open 2G18." As the cell door started to open, Jenkins told the inmate, "You get back against the wall, and get your hands up right fucking now. One way or another, you're on your way to the hole. How you go is up to you, but rest assured you're gonna go."

Without a word, the inmate did as instructed. He removed his clothing when told, had his body checked for any injuries and allowed his fingernails to be scraped. Then he climbed into a set of coveralls and, once handcuffed, was escorted to segregation. That was the way it went for the next two inmates as well.

But the last inmate thought he was a tough guy, and when ordered to back up to the wall, he took a fighting stance and made a couple of rude comments. However, as soon as the can of mace was raised and pointed at him, he changed his mind and stuck his arms up. Unfortunately, he wasn't quite fast enough, and he received a short burst of mace. It wasn't much but enough to bring tears and cause him to gasp for air.

Other than that little episode, staff didn't even receive any comments from the inmates going to segregation or from the inmates who remained in their cells. It was kind of a nice change.

Once the job was completed, everyone returned to the unit office. The police officer who had been doing most of the talking thanked the staff and said, "We're going back to the station to write our report up and submit it to the bosses. Someone will let you know what's going on as soon as they make a decision. But I would imagine that at least three of them and likely all four will be charged and go to trial. The place is all yours, guys. Good luck." With that, they gathered up their gear and headed out of the unit.

By that time, it was after midnight, and one way or another, staff had informed their families that they'd be late in getting home. Allen's wife, for one, wasn't happy about it, but she was happy that no staff had been injured. She did inform Allen that they were going next door for supper when he finished his next shift. "So please don't work another double," she said.

When the problem had first started, the inmates had been notified via the speaker system that recreation had been cancelled for the night and that everyone had to remain in his cell. That notification had brought forth some unwelcome remarks, but as usual, that was expected.

All in all, the problem was resolved, and there were no staff injuries, at least no physical injuries, and they were only a couple of hours later than usual in getting home—that was, the staff who went straight home and didn't stop for a beer or two.

Chapter 20

As was his usual practice, Shipley was at the gym for his daily workout. The last few days had been more or less normal. He'd faced no repercussions from Rita getting caught, and he was learning his way around his new job in recreation. Everything seemed to be floating along.

He was still working on his plan to get the hell out of Mountainview, but he realized that without help, he wouldn't be able to put his plan into effect. He was being much more careful this time around about whom he approached to give him a hand. He didn't want to get into the mess he'd ended up in the last time. So far, he figured he would only need one person, but it would have to be one of the inmates who worked in the receiving department. He couldn't decide whom to approach, because he didn't really know the inmates working in that area. He certainly didn't want to talk to a rat about his plan and then watch him run to a screw about it. And now, of course, he had another problem. Since Rita had gotten caught, he had to find another way to get some money in to help with his great escape.

He had just finished his workout, when the inmates were informed that it was time for the 8:00 count and told to go back to their unit. With the usual grumbling, they headed out of the gym. Shipley walked with a couple of guys he was fairly friendly with but kept a close look on everything going on around him. Nothing out of the ordinary appeared to be happening, at least not yet.

Shipley and his two buddies reached N area and started into J unit. They were almost into the unit, when Shipley looked over to Godwyn, who was walking beside him, and asked, "Hey, God, you notice anything unusual about the screws?"

"Nah, I don't see nothing. What's up?"

"Oh, I dunno. They just seem to be watching us. Usually, they just stand around and yap with each other. Just seems like something's strange—that's all."

They carried on into the unit, up to their range and into their cells. Shipley grabbed a can of pop and some junk food, turned on his television and collapsed onto his bed. He figured he might as well rest up after his workout and decided he'd go to a common room to have a coffee after the count came in. He figured one of the guys who worked in receiving would likely be in there, and he thought he might be able to sit at a table and have a coffee and a smoke with him. He didn't think it'd hurt to try anyway.

Shipley was lying on his bed, half asleep and listening to the television, when he sensed movement at his cell door. He glanced up, saw a staff member peering in at him and realized they were in the process of taking the count. He also knew that unless one of them screwed up, he'd be in the common room shortly. Finally, his cell door opened, and at the same time, the intercom announced, "Count is in. Gym up."

Shipley and most of the inmates on the range stepped out of their cells and, with a lot of shoving and laughter, started toward the control to exit the unit. Shipley was about halfway down the range and talking with a couple of guys, when the intercom gave out a screech, and a loud voice said, "All inmates return to your cells now!" At the same time, the range barrier slammed shut, locking them all on the range.

The inmates looked at one another, and the laughter and joking around quickly changed to yells and cursing directed at the staff and even at God and his helpers. As usual, the inmates were not in a hurry to follow the orders yelled at them through the intercom.

Rather than heading straight to their cells, they continued to yell, curse and mill around. Then disembodied voice repeated its command with the addition that if the order wasn't carried out, gas was going to be used. The order ended with "Get your asses in there; we don't have time to fuck around!"

That last little bit helped the inmates decide that it might be a good idea to head back into their cells and relax. So with many yelled comments and unpleasant gestures, they returned to their cells, and the doors slammed shut.

Shipley pulled out another can of pop, lay down on his bed and tried to figure out what the hell was going on. He knew it could be almost anything, from a medical problem to an escape. But once he thought it over, he didn't think it was an escape, because the count had come in. But who the hell knew?

Then Shipley had a thought. *Hell, I know both screws working tonight. When I hear the barrier open, it'll be one of them doing a cell check. I'll wait till he gets to my cell and just ask him what the hell's going on. With any luck, he'll fill me in.* So that was what Shipley did: he lay on his bed and listened for the barrier to open.

Within 20 minutes or so, he heard it open. Shipley jumped up, stood at the door and stared out his little window, watching for the guard. He could hear him approaching before he saw him and just hoped it'd be one of the guards he knew from working in the servery.

It was! As soon as the guard doing the cell check came into his view, he recognized Berry Newman. *Well,* he thought to himself, *it's that asshole Newman. I'll be nice and see if he'll tell me what the hell's going on.* Just before Newman was about to glance into his cell, Shipley asked, "Hey, Mr. Newman, can you tell me what the heck's going on? I was gonna go to the gym and do a workout."

"Not really sure, Shipley." That, of course, was a little lie. "All I really know is that E unit is having a serious problem on upper G. Apparently, an inmate's been injured. At any rate, you guys are in here until morning. So you might as well go to bed and get some rest."

"Will do. Thanks for the news, Mr. Newman." *Ah yeah, fat-ass, you know goddamned well what the hell's going on. You just wanna be a big shot and keep it a secret. Christ, now I won't know till morning. Thanks a lot, asshole.*

Vern Thibedeau

With that bit of news and his silent thoughts, Shipley got ready to jump into bed. While he was taking his clothes off, he remembered that Dominic slept on 2G. *Christ, I hope he's not mixed up in whatever the hell's going on. He's got enough problems as it is.*

Shipley watched a little television and read a bit more of his book. But then, because he couldn't really concentrate on any of those things, he turned out his light and drifted off into a troubled sleep. Dominic was on his mind, and he was still concerned about whatever was bothering his chum Owen.

Once again, morning rolled around, and noise on the range woke a tired Shipley. One blessing about working in the recreational department was that he no longer had to get up before everyone else to help get the breakfast meal set up. Now he got up with everyone else and went down to eat; it was great. To top it off, for the first time since being locked up, he didn't mind going in to work. He'd never thought he'd think of work in that manner, but for now at least, all was good.

Shipley rolled out of bed, pulled his pants and shirt on, splashed some water onto his face and, while still trying to wake up, headed out of his cell. Once again, he almost ran Godwyn down. With a shake of his head and a silly grin, he apologized by saying, "Holy Christ, God, we've gotta stop meeting like this."

"That'd be a good idea. Jesus, one of these times you come running out of your den, I'll end up on my ass."

With that greeting, they headed down the range to collect their first meal of the day. "Hey, God, you got any idea what the hell we were locked up for last night? The only thing I could find out from one of screws was that it was in E unit and maybe on 2G."

"Nah, not a clue; must've been pretty big, though. We'll likely find out shortly. Some jerk'll know what the fuck went on."

While rushing down to pick up their breakfast, the inmates questioned one another about what had gone on the night before. It was the subject of the hour. One inmate, with a know-it-all look, said, "Oh, I heard all about it. Some guy called one of the heavies a goof and got himself stabbed for it. Looks good on 'im."

That got him a reply of "Ah, screw off. You don't know any more about it than we do, for Christ's sake."

Shipley and Godwyn were among the first group of inmates to reach the servery area. As the line slowly advanced, the inmates were still firing questions back and forth, but there were no real answers, just several more questions.

Shipley reached the first wicket, and as he reached in to pick up his tray, he asked the inmate worker, "Hey, what the hell went on over in E last night?" Shipley knew the servery workers would've found out all about the episode from the staff while they were preparing the morning meal.

"Ah, some guy named Joe got some people pissed off at him and ended up with a whole bunch of holes in him. Christ, they even tried to cut his head and an arm off! Then they just left him lying there on the range, for Christ's sake."

Just as the servery worker completed his story, which everyone had stopped to listen to, a voice yelled out, "Jesus Christ, Jefferies! I told you that if you're gonna open your big mouth up about it, at least be truthful. Christ, you're just making everyone feel worse, for God's sake! For you guys out there listening, that was just horseshit. One of the inmates in E unit did have a beef with some guys, and just after count last night, they went after him with a couple of knives. Unfortunately, he's dead from stab wounds, but the rest of that story is crap. It was just the usual stab wounds, and there was nothing the hospital could do for him."

Except for a few inmates talking, everyone had quieted down so they could hear what had happened. Once the food officer completed his explanation, it was really quiet, and one could've heard a pin drop. Shipley, recognizing the food steward's voice, knew it was true and just picked his tray up, grabbed a cup of coffee and made his way to one of the common rooms. He walked in with his head down, found an empty table, set his tray on the table, sat down and just stared at his food without eating a bite.

Goodwyn sat down across from him, set his food down and looked at Shipley, who was still just staring at his tray of bacon and eggs. "Jesus, you OK, Mac?"

"Nah, not really," replied Shipley as he fought to keep his eyes dry. "I think they're talking about Dominic getting it last night."

"Aw fuck. I've heard you talking about Joe. He's a buddy of yours, eh?"

"Yeah, he was. We came in on the same bus. He was a hell of a nice guy. The bastards hung two murder raps on him that he didn't do, for God's sake. And then, as if that wasn't enough, they took him back to court and tried to hang another one on him. The pricks couldn't prove that one, though, so they sent him back to this hellhole. We were talking out in the yard the other night, and he was telling me that his crew were in a fight with another gang; I guess the other guys won, and Joe's side lost. I hope to hell the screws got the assholes who did this. Christ, he never hurt nobody!" Shipley spoke the last few sentences with a gravelly voice. Finally, with a shake of his head, he said, "Screw it. I have to get back to my cell and get ready for work." He stood up, left his tray and headed back to his cell. Godwyn, watching him walk away, shook his head, picked both trays up and left the common room.

Once breakfast was finished, workup was called, and everyone reported to work for another usual day in the big house.

That afternoon after work, while heading back to his cell, Shipley stopped to check for mail. And there it was: the expected letter from his long-lost sister! He rushed back to his cell without talking to anyone and even forgot to watch for anything unusual going on around him. He had no more thoughts of his buddy Joe. He made it to his cell, flopped onto his bed and ripped his precious letter open.

The letter started,

> For my long-lost brother, Mac. My God, it was you! I'm so happy to hear that it was you I sent my note to. Thank God. I've been worried sick about you! It's a lucky thing that I bumped into the Howells, who used to live next door to us. And lucky for us, they had an idea what may've happened to you.

It was a lengthy letter. After all, Connie had to fill him in on several years of her life. She was married to a wonderful man and had been for almost eight years now, and they had two children. Connie still hadn't spoken to their mother and had no intention of doing so. She still didn't know if their father was alive or dead and didn't really care one way or another; she just hoped she'd never have to hear from him or see him again. She apologized for not being there for Mac and not doing more for him when she was there. Near the end of the letter, Connie said they had to stay in contact; she didn't want to lose him again. She explained that if it was allowed, she could come for a visit, but she would need a little time to set it up. Apparently, a husband, two children and a part-time job took some organizing. She wrote her phone number down and included the best time for him to phone. She also asked if she could phone the prison to speak to him. Connie certainly was naive about prison life. She ended the letter with "Please, please write, or phone if it's allowed."

Shipley read the letter four or five times before he really understood everything his sister had written. He couldn't understand what the hell she was apologizing for, though. He'd always been when she was around the house and sad when she wasn't. She couldn't have done anything more for him than she had. At least that was the way he figured it anyway.

Shipley was at a loss regarding what to do: write a letter back to Connie right away or phone her at the first opportune time. *Hell, what to do? Christ, I'll do both—phone and then write a letter. God, what's wrong with my head? Just do both, you idiot!*

He decided to wait to write a letter until they had a chat on the phone. The problem with phoning was that according to Connie's schedule, he would have to wait until around noon the next day. *God, I'll have to wait all night and tomorrow morning. Oh well. It's been seven or eight years; guess I can wait another day. God, I'm so glad she's doing good. Holy shit, I'm an uncle twice over. Well, ain't that something? Me, of all people.* Now Shipley's biggest problem was trying to settle down and wait for tomorrow; he didn't even realize staff had come around to take the count, until the call for the supper meal rang out.

Shipley wasn't even sure he wanted to bother eating; however, he did want out of his cell. He needed more room to pace back and forth, so he decided to head out to get his meal. After eating, he went to the gym and had a strenuous workout. Then he went back and had a shower, and once that was completed, he started his pacing again.

He was having a hard time. He felt very up when he was thinking of Connie and the letter, but then he would think of Joe, and his feelings would crash to a new low. His buddy Owen intruded into his thoughts as well; Shipley was concerned about the change in his mannerisms and what the change could lead to. After all, he had noticed a change in Bentley, and he certainly remembered Bentley's suicide.

The last lock-up and count time finally arrived, so Shipley had to do the pacing in his cell. He would sit, read Connie's letter over and think about the phone call he was going to make the next day, and he would become excited. But then he would think of Joe, and his feelings would come crashing down again. When thinking of Joe, he recalled that he hardly ever saw Owen hanging around anymore. Then he started to worry about that again. Then his mind slipped to Rita and how their happiness had ended. He also recalled the information Joe had given him about Rita's uncle, and he wondered if Rita's dad had said anything to him about Rita's predicament. *God, I hope not; I've enough goddamn problems as it is.*

Eventually, it was well past Shipley's usual bedtime. He crawled into bed and just lay there, staring at the ceiling, with all those thoughts drifting in and out. His mind drifted back to his childhood, and he wondered how things could have been different. But when he thought of his father, he didn't think anything he or Connie could have done to change a damned thing.

Eventually, he drifted off into a restless sleep, and those black vultures eased back into view. They seemed to float around up in the dark sky, making their usual squawking noises. But this time, someone was suddenly standing or kneeling there and waving his or her arms at the large black creatures. He couldn't make out who the figure was, because it was dark, and he could only see the back side of the person. But then the vultures, while still making their horrible racket, suddenly floated away. The person gave a backward wave to Shipley and then seemed to melt into the ground.

Shipley drifted into a deeper sleep, and when he woke up the next morning, he felt almost rested.

Chapter 21

Shipley rolled out of bed the next morning, splashed water onto his face, put his clothes on and was about to head out for breakfast. Then, suddenly, he remembered the phone call he had to make. He finished his breakfast, reported for work and excitedly told his boss that he might be late in getting back from lunch. Once he explained why he was going to be late and his boss noted how excited he was, his supervisor said, "Take all the time you need. Good luck with the call, and be sure to let me know how it goes, but I'm sure it'll be great."

The morning slowly floated by. Shipley was too excited to do a lot of chatting or carrying on with his fellow workers, but he did fulfill most of his duties. Finally, it was time for lunch. Shipley and the other inmates headed back to their cells for the count, and once it was in, it was meal time. Shipley didn't feel hungry, as he was too excited, but he headed down to the servery anyway. He decided to eat in a common room, and as soon as he entered, he spotted his buddy Owen sitting at a table, staring down at his food. Shipley was on his way over to join him, but when he noticed Owen glance up and then pretend he hadn't seen him, Shipley decided he'd sit somewhere else. Even though he was excited about his pending phone call, Owen's behaviour bothered him.

He spotted Goodwyn sitting and shoveling food into his mouth with great gusto and decided to join him. "Hey there, God. How you doing?" He sat down and immediately started to fill Goodwin in on the all-important phone call he was going to make shortly.

Goodwyn listened to him with a great deal of patience. Once Shipley wound down a little, Goodwyn replied, "That's great news, Mac. I can't even imagine what you must be feeling. If you think of it, give her my best." With that, they grabbed their trays and headed back to their cells.

Shipley couldn't sit and relax, so he just paced around and around in his small cell, and then he stood staring out the window at the lonely tower, the wire fence and the mobile patrol doing its circling. All he could think of was how much he missed his sister, which, of course, caused him to dwell on their past life. Finally, workup was called, the cell doors opened and Shipley, almost running, headed for the phones. Unfortunately, there were only two of them, and he wasn't the first to make it down to grab one. So he stood waiting his turn, almost vibrating, standing first on one foot and then switching to the other one. Finally, his turn came, and he pulled Connie's phone number out and started dialing.

He listened intently while the operator made her usual speech about accepting charges from a federal institution, and then he heard, "Oh God, yes, I will!" Even though it had been several years, he immediately recognized Connie's voice.

The all-important conversation started. "Oh, Connie," Shipley said with a catch in his throat, "I can't tell you how great it was to get your letter. God, you sound beautiful. Two kids. My God, who would've ever thought we'd be talking like this, with you at home and me in prison?"

The conversation carried on for a long time. After all, they had a number of years to catch up on. Of course, Shipley's robbery was one of the first things Connie wanted to know about. He filled her in and concluded by saying, "I didn't mean to hurt anyone. I was desperate for money, and at the time, that seemed to be the easiest way of getting some. I feel so sorry for that elderly guy who fell down. I certainly didn't mean to do that to him."

Connie told Mac about her life and how happy she was that everything was perfect for her. Her children were perfect, their house was perfect and her husband was a wonderful guy. "I'll tell you, Mac, when we were young and living at home, I never, even in my dreams, believed life could be so wonderful!"

Eventually, though, they had to call an end to their conversation. After all, there were only two phones, and the line to use them was getting longer. There were a few rude comments from the back of the line about hogging phones. But it was a wonderful conversation. Shipley was now generally caught up on almost everything that had gone on in Connie's life. *Jesus Christ, I wish my life had turned out as well as Connie's. I'm so glad she's OK; would've been nice if she could've come back and taken me with her, though. God, does she ever sound happy; I'm so fucking glad for her. At least one of us is doing OK.*

They had a complicated chore in arranging a date and time for Connie to come for a visit. She thought it would take about four hours to drive to the prison, and that was the easiest part. Connie figured the best way was to take an extra day off in conjunction with her regular days off. She figured that would give her three or maybe even four days. With that much time, Connie planned on getting a hotel room and staying overnight. "That way," she said, "we can have two or maybe even two and a half days to visit. This'll be so good, Mac; God, I've been so worried about you."

They finally decided on the weekend of the great barbecue. Connie explained that with getting things straightened out at home and the four-hour drive, she wouldn't get in until well after lunch. Shipley told her that would be fine. He could still get out to the yard for the special meal and would still have lots of time to get up to V&C. "Once you get parked," he said, "just go into the visiting area. You'll have to tell them who you want to visit with and let them know that I'm out in the yard. They'll call me on the speaker, and it'll take me less than five minutes to get up there. My God, I'll run all the way! As soon as workup is done and I get back to my cell, I'm gonna write you another letter. God Almighty, this is just so great."

Connie replied that she was going to write him another one also. "I still can't believe this; after all these years, we're finally going to be together again." With that, they both hung up.

Christ, my first job tomorrow will be to get up to V&C and give them an application for Connie to come in for the visit. Jeez, if I don't do that,

Vern Thibedeau

they won't let her in. Christ, wouldn't that be just ducky? After making that mental note, Shipley started down to recreation. He figured he'd better fill the supervisor in on his phone call and then get back to work. *Jesus H. Christ, I feel like I could dance all the way to work. I can't wait to see my sister again; I've just missed her so much.* Once again, Shipley was a little teary—so much for being a big, tough con. It was nice that at least for the time being, they were both happy.

Of course, most things did not last forever, and the world continued to move on.

By the time Shipley made it down to work, he'd calmed down somewhat, and after a few minutes, he found the supervisor. He told his boss all about the phone call and how great it had been to talk to his sister again. Once he finished telling him all about his sister, Shipley explained that he had been friends with Joe Dominic and asked his boss if there was any new information on what had happened.

"To be honest, I don't really know much about it. But apparently, the cause stems from a problem out on the street. But at least we know everyone who was involved, and all four of the buggers are locked up in the hole and will be charged with murder. It's too bad this happened; Dominic seemed like an OK guy."

"Yeah, he was. We came in on the same bus, and he got me out of a few problems just by talking to a couple of heavies. How come it seems like the nice guys end up dead, and the assholes keep on going? Don't seem right, does it?"

"I know what you mean. I've been in this business for about eighteen years. I worked in the units for several years, and then I took this position, and I still don't understand it. Well, that's enough yapping. Guess we'd better get back to work."

Shipley finished the rest of the day in an emotional turmoil. He felt up when he thought of Connie and their upcoming visit and crashed down whenever he thought of Dominic being killed. Then, when he remembered how Owen had been acting, he became concerned. He couldn't help but think back to his neighbour Bentley's suicide and wonder how he may have been able to help the guy. For about the hundredth time, he thought, *Christ, instead of ignoring him, I should've talked to him about what the hell was going on in his life. I might have been able to help him. Shit, I have to get a hold of Jim and see if he'll sit down and talk to me. I know Joe would've done the same for me.*

Eventually, the workday ended. Shipley and dozens of inmates left their work areas and shuffled back to their units for the count and the supper meal. Shipley, as he walked back to the unit, continued thinking about his escape plan. He was positive it would work. He still hadn't had an opportunity to have a chat with any of the guys working in the receiving area, but he had firmly decided to manage, one way or another, to get chummy with one of them. *Christ, I have ta find out if I can talk one of them into giving me a hand. Then I have ta figure out a way to get some money or drugs in. I can't go on in this fucking place. I have to get the hell out.*

Shipley was just about to turn into J unit, when he spotted one of the inmates who had originally come in on the bus with him. Shipley, once he noted that the inmate was looking his way, said, "Hey, Jim. How the hell's it going? Haven't seen you for ages. You still going to school?"

Shortly after Shipley and the other inmates had arrived at Mountainview, they had been informed that they had to have a job. It was either that or being lock in their cells during working hours. Shipley and Hall had talked over the different options, not that there were many. One option was going to school. They had been told that certified teachers came in and held regular classes, and attending school was a regular paid job. In fact, if an inmate stuck with it, he could end up on top pay—not that it was a great fortune. But apparently, an inmate, if he was willing to work at it, could earn the equivalent of his high school diploma. They'd also been told that several inmates had continued on and earned university credits. Shipley had thought about taking classes for about two minutes and then said, "To hell with it."

Shipley and Hall hadn't seen each other often for quite a while because Hall had been sent to E unit, while Shipley had gone to J unit, and they seldom bumped into each other in the yard or gym. On top of that, they just moved in different circles. But they did get along and spoke whenever they were together.

Hall replied to Shipley, "Hey, Mac, it has been a while, hasn't it? Yep, still in school; in fact, I'm about to start my grade eleven. I really don't know why in hell I didn't do all this stuff when I was a kid. It would have been a hell of a lot easier."

"I can tell you one thing, Jim: now that you're J unit and I see you once in a while, even I can see a hell of a change in you. When we were on our way here, you were one of the noisiest pricks on the bus. But look at you now; school must be agreeing with you."

"Oh, it is. I'm gonna stick to it. Even going to keep it up when I get out."

"Way to go. Talk to you later, Jim." Shipley turned and started down his range.

Once he reached his cell, he immediately sat down at his little desk to formulate another letter to Connie.

Chapter 22

Paul Raymond was on his way in to work. He wasn't happy about working the weekend, but he figured that was life. However, he was a little happier at work now that he had been placed on the tower squad. Since he'd been assigned to that particular squad after Shipley's screw-up at the hospital, Paul kind of wished he had messed up on one of his escorts years ago. *Christ, some punishment—no cons and no corporal staring over my shoulder all the time. Just me and the tower. God, it's great. That screw-up Shipley doesn't realize it, but the fuck sure did me a favour.*

His private life wasn't going quite as well, though. About two days after Shipley tried to take off from him at the hospital, he got home from work, parked the car and headed in. As soon as he stepped into the apartment, he spotted several boxes stacked up at the door. Looking up from the boxes, he saw his wife standing by the kitchen door. "Hey, what the hell're all the boxes doing here?" he asked.

"Damn it, Paul. Any other time, you'd have stopped for a couple of beers. I was gonna leave you a note, but now I'll just tell you in person. In about five minutes, my dad is coming to pick me and my stuff up. You know as well as I do that we haven't been getting along; in fact, we hardly even speak to each other anymore. In any case, I've had it. I'm leaving, and you can just sit here all alone and talk to yourself! I'll phone to let you know when the rest of my stuff will be picked up."

Vern Thibedeau

And that was the end of Raymond's marriage. He wasn't overly upset about his situation; in fact, it only took him a week or so to settle in and get the hang of being single again. *What the hell?* he thought. *Just about every second guy I work with is either divorced or separated anyway; it's sure nothing new.* Plus, he now had the whole apartment to himself. If he wasn't working, he could sleep or go out whenever he wanted to. *Hell, what more could a guy want?*

So that nice, sunny Saturday, Raymond went in to work and was not even really upset about it. He checked in for roll call and found out he was in tower three, which was the one that overlooked the exercise yard. He was about to head out and catch the mobile to get his ride around to the tower, when the sergeant stopped him by saying, "Hey, Paul, hold up for a second."

Raymond turned around and, with a questioning look, walked back toward the sergeant.

"I just wanna remind you to keep your eyes open up there today. The institution is having that barbecue in the yard this afternoon, so it's going to be busy. If anything happens, you make damn sure you're on your toes and spot it right away. OK?"

"Oh crap, that's right. I'd forgotten all about it. Don't worry, boss. Anything goes down, I'll spot it and get right on the radio." And away went Raymond to meet the mobile. *Oh hell. What a day to get stuck with tower three. Barbecue day. Christ, a once-a-year thing every con in the place comes out for it, and I have to be in that damned tower.*

Raymond, and most of the tower squad, didn't care for that particular tower. Tower three was the one that overlooked the exercise yard, and if something was going to happen, the chance was high that it would happen during yard-up. He didn't care for tower one much either. That one overlooked the front entrance, and the gates had to be opened every time someone went in or out of the prison. It seemed people were always coming and going. Tower two was OK, though. At least in that tower, he just had to make sure no one climbed the fence and took off, which wasn't likely to happen. Tower four was almost as busy as tower one. It overlooked the sally port, and every vehicle had to be let in and out. On top of that, if it was a truck, the guard had to check the roof to make sure some idiot con wasn't lying on top, trying to get a free ride out. *Oh well*, he thought. *You can't win 'em all.*

In any case, Raymond relieved his buddy in the tower, dropped his kit onto the floor and checked the equipment assigned to that tower. That was one duty he always made sure to carry out. There was no way in hell he wanted to be up there for any length of time and suddenly realize he was missing some ammunition, the rifle or revolver wasn't working properly or the binoculars were gone. Once that little chore was completed, he took his lunch out of his kit bag and put it into the little fridge. Then, after a slight hesitation, he pulled his pocket book out. It was a good one, and he was about halfway through it. As usual, it was a western, and the hero had been shot in the shoulder and was stuck out in the desert. It looked as if he might not be able to get out of his fix, and Raymond hoped to finish the book before the end of the shift. He figured he could get some of it read before the inmates came out to the yard to set up for their big barbecue.

So there he sat, leaning back in the chair with his legs up on the little table, reading his book. He was facing the yard, though, and he kept glancing up from his reading to make sure nothing was going on. He saw nothing yet.

* * *

Bill Richards was supposed to be spare on the 7:00 to 3:00 shift. However, the day before, as he was heading out to the parking lot to go home, the sergeant waved him over and said with a slight grin, "Hey, Bill, you're spare tomorrow, and we're having that damned barbecue in the yard. We were wondering if you'd mind coming in nine to five to help look after the thing. Heck, there's only a couple of hours' difference."

"Sure, that's not much difference. Hell, I can even sleep in a little longer."

In fact, Bill thought it was a good idea. This was his and Shirley's big night out. They'd been planning it for some time. The tickets for the show had been bought, and the sitter had been lined up, but then management had lowered the boom by changing the schedule around: instead of being off, he was working the day shift. But it had been too late to change their plans. He'd even thought about booking sick on the

Saturday, but once Shirley had spoken to him about it, he'd had a change of heart and decided maybe he should go in. He had been concerned about going in to work so early, because he had known it was going to be a late night. Now that was all looked after. *Well,* he thought, *great timing. You'd think I planned it.* Little did he know.

It was a nice, sunny Saturday morning, and Richards, as he pulled into the parking lot, took his usual scan, looking for any police cars, and threw a glance up at the flag. Thankfully, he noticed that all was normal. It had been a great evening—in fact, one of their best ones yet—but he didn't even feel tired. Maybe a little hungover but not all worn out. Of course, coming in to work at 8:45 rather than 6:45 certainly made a difference. *Christ, I think I'd love to work this shift steady; it's great.* After checking in with the sergeant taking the roll call, he headed to the gym area to see how the barbecue set-up was coming along.

He was just passing J unit, when he spotted the day corporal going in. He decided to go in with him and have a coffee. He figured they didn't need him down in recreation yet. He was pretty sure the workers knew how to set up a barbecue without his help, and the cons were staying in their cells a little later than usual to give the staff a chance to get the barbecue equipment out to the yard. Once that was completed, he knew they'd be let out of their cells but allowed to go to the gym only—no yard until the noon count was in. But he realized he'd be damned busy once they were let out after the count. He figured just about every inmate in the place would be heading for the yard and their yearly barbecue.

Corporal Stevens saw Richards just as they were both heading through the unit barrier. Stevens acknowledged Richards with a "Hey, Bill. What the hell you doing in the unit? Can't get enough of the place, eh?"

"Nah. Spare today, so they stuck me with that damned barbecue that's on this afternoon. Think I'd much rather be in the unit, doing my regular job. Kind of thought I might as well have a coffee before heading down." Then, with a grin, he looked at Reg and asked, "Say, you wouldn't wanna change places, would you?"

Reg gave him a look and replied, "Ha, you're a real comedian this morning, eh? Thanks anyway for the great opportunity, but I think I'll just stay here and put up with the usual bullshit."

"Don't blame you, buddy. It won't be a lot of fun down there. Just hope to hell nothing happens today. Had an episode last year, and they thought about cancelling the damned thing. Just too many cons in the yard at the same time; you can't really see dick-all. Hell, even if something does go down, you can't usually spot it. Well, let's go grab a coffee, and we'll hope everything goes smoothly. It likely will."

About 20 minutes later, after much chatting and settling many of the world's problems, Richards headed out of the unit and was on his way to the recreation area. He couldn't help but think back on the evening he and Shirley had enjoyed. *Jeez, if we do much more dancing, I'm gonna have to start back at the gym and get into shape again.* He felt a little stiff. *Boy, oh boy, that was a great evening. We're going to have to do it more often; I sure don't think Shirley would mind.*

Soon he was in the recreation area, and things got busy.

* * *

Shipley woke up the Saturday morning of the barbecue, and his first thought was of his sister coming in for the big visit. *Hell, if she could get here earlier, I wouldn't even mind skipping the yard this afternoon. Hell, they could stick the barbecue.* But he also realized she had other responsibilities and had a lot of arranging to do before she could get away.

The cell doors slammed open, signaling that it was breakfast time, and Shipley, still thinking of Connie and the visit, bumped into his buddy Owen. "Hey, Jim, sorry about that. How the hell you doing? Haven't seen you around much lately. Everything OK with you?"

Owen, with a bit of a stutter, replied, "Oh yeah. Morning, Mac. Yep, ah, for sure all good here, bud; nothing new in this place. You doing OK?"

"Oh yeah. Same old, same old. Hey, remember I told you about my sister and how I got a hold of her? Well, she's coming in for a visit this afternoon. Jesus Christ, Jim, I can't wait till she gets here. Other than our little chat on the phone a while back, this'll be the first time we've talked, let alone seen each other, in fucking years. Christ, I almost feel like dancing."

Owen, with a little jerk and a concerned and penetrating look, stared at Shipley. "Christ, that's great, Mac. Hell, you're not gonna miss the barbecue, are you? God, that'd be a shame; we only have it once a year, you know."

"Oh no, I'm gonna make it. Connie can't get here till later in the afternoon, so I'll be there. She's even planning on staying in town overnight so we can have another visit again tomorrow. I'll tell you, Jim, this is the best thing that's happened to me in years. Christ, she really looked after me while we were growing up. I know I wouldn't have made it without her. It was a hell of a rough time, you know. Christ, I still shiver when I think about it."

Shipley and Owen continued chatting as they headed to the servery to pick up their first meal of the day. It wasn't difficult to listen to each other, as most of the inmates, as usual, were a little grumpier in the morning and were a lot quieter during the breakfast meal. Shipley continued the conversation by saying, "It's great talking with you, Jim; it seems like we hardly ever get together anymore. You having some problems or something? Anything I can do to help you out?"

"Nah. Nothing special. Hey, how about we head out to the barbecue together this afternoon, and I'll fill you in? It's not really anything big, but I may ask you to do me a favour."

"Sure, Jim. If there's anything I can do to give you a hand, just let me know."

They sat down at a table and, while eating, continued their conversation. But Shipley did most of the babbling, and of course, it was mostly about his life and how great his sister had been. "Jesus, Jim, I can't wait to see her. I'll tell you again, with that old man of mine and with my mom just sitting there and not saying a word about anything, I wouldn't have made it without Connie."

"I'm really glad you and your sister got back together, Mac. I can't even imagine what you must be feeling. Well, I'm gonna head back and have a bit of a snooze for a while. Once they open up after the noon count, I'll meet you on the range, and we'll head out to the yard together. Sound good?"

"Sure thing, Jim." With a little laugh, he added, "You stay off that booze, and I'll see you later, buddy."

Shipley took his tray back to the servery and started back to his cell. *Jesus, Jim sure does look a lot better. I wonder what the hell his problem is. Oh well. Maybe I'll find out after the count. Just glad he didn't do anything stupid like hanging himself. I wonder if I'll be able to help him out a bit and make things a little easier for him.*

Of course, Shipley didn't realize it, but he was going to help Owen get out of a serious and possibly even deadly problem.

* * *

Owen didn't go straight back to his cell; he had to make a stop on the way: he needed his modified ice pick that afternoon, so he had to pick it up from its hiding spot. He had talked himself into accepting the fact that he didn't have a choice and had to do the job. He had also decided his best bet was to do it during the barbecue. Because of his acceptance, it wasn't bothering him nearly as much as it had been. After all, preservation of his own life was, naturally, his main consideration. However, he had almost crapped himself when Shipley told him he was going to have a visit with his sister that afternoon. *Holy Christ*, he thought, *if I had to go back and tell Slug I had to change plans again, he'd tear my fucking head off.*

A few days prior to the barbecue, Owen had solidified his great plan. It wasn't really complicated, but he did have to tell Slug about it and request his assistance. His general idea was to walk out to the yard with Shipley, and right after entering the yard, he would do his thing. However, he hoped to talk to Slug to see if he could set up some kind of a distraction; after all, he wanted to get away with it and not end up doing a life bit. This problem was scary enough that he'd sworn off gambling, and he hoped to get out of Mountainview and get transferred somewhere to a medium-security joint.

Owen lucked in. On his first attempt to talk to Slug, he caught up to him just as they entered the yard. Slug spotted him walking toward him, and when Owen hesitated, Slug signaled him to approach. "What the fuck you want now, goof? There's no way you're getting an extension; just get the fucking job done, or else."

Vern Thibedeau

"Oh, I'm gonna. I have a plan all worked out. I just need a little help with it. It's really no big deal."

"What the hell do you want? Me to do the job for you? 'Cause I ain't gonna, you know."

"No, no, nothing like that. I'm gonna do it just as we walk out to the yard for the barbecue. I was wondering if you could arrange some kind of distraction for about half a minute or so—just a pretend fight or something. I really don't wanna get caught, you know."

"That's easy enough to do. Maybe it'll help give you some guts. Just remember: it's him or you. So just get it done. I'm sick of you whining around about it. It should've been done two fucking week ago, asshole."

That ended the discussion. Owen walked around the yard, careful to stay away from Slug and his crew, and then went back to his cell at the next changeover. In his mind, he was all set to go.

Chapter 23

Raymond jerked his head up and looked out at the yard. Thankfully, for him, not a thing was going on. He saw a couple of recreation officers and four or five of their workers busy setting up several barbecues and hooking them up to propane tanks. *Christ, I'd better stand up and move around a bit. I think I may have dozed off for a minute or so.* He bent down and picked up his book, which had fallen off his lap and landed on the floor. Then he stood back up and gave a huge stretch. While stretching, he gave the exercise yard another look and paid much closer attention to what was going on. *God, I should've passed on those last couple of drinks and gone home a little sooner. If I had smartened up, maybe I wouldn't feel so wiped out. But God, it was a great night, and that Annie is a good-looking woman. She sure does like her booze, though, and can she ever put it away. But now I'm just about broke till payday.*

Raymond, ever since his wife had left him, was getting out to the bars a little more often than he used to. But he was noticing a difference in his spending: his money didn't seem to last as long. Last night at his favourite bar, he'd met a lady named Annie. He had seen her there a few times, and last night, he wasn't sure how it had happened, but they'd ended up sitting at a table together, and he'd had a great time. They even had made plans to meet again. She was a great-looking girl, and even though she had a kid, she was still fun to be with. But she was having a bit of a rough go. Apparently, the kid's old man had taken off, and she had lost her job, which had put her on welfare. But she had another job lined up, so things were looking better for her.

Annie was interested in Raymond and how his wife had left him. She was a good listener and couldn't understand how any wife could do something like that to a husband, especially to a nice guy like him. Annie was also curious about where Raymond was working and how he was managing in an apartment all on his own. She was a sympathetic person, and Raymond was quite taken with her. In fact, he was looking forward to their next meeting with a great deal of excitement.

Raymond completed his stretching, gave his head a shake and, looking down from the tower, noticed the workers heading back inside. That told Raymond it was getting close to the noon count, and a glance at his watch verified that fact. *Thank Christ the noon count will be in pretty soon, and it'll get a little busier. Hell, I might even get lucky and my relief will be in early; God, that'd be nice, but I sure won't hold my breath.*

* * *

Shipley, once he finished breakfast, made it back to his cell and thought a little snooze sounded good. So he flopped onto his bed and closed his eyes, but sleep wouldn't come. The thought of seeing Connie after all these years kept swirling around in his head. *God, I hope she remembers to bring pictures of her family. I'm sure she will; I reminded her a dozen times or more. God, I wonder if the kids—my God, they're my nephews—will look like me. Her husband must be a nice guy, or she would've left him, wouldn't she? I'm sure she would have. He sounds like a hell of a nice guy, though. I sure hope so, because Connie deserves nothing but the best.*

Then memories of his past life started to creep in.

He recalled Father driving him to the store and calling him a little thief, shoveling the driveway, Mother just sitting and watching him out the window, his sister sitting with him before walking away and waving, the old guy who should've gotten out of the way when he was running out of the bank and the old judge banging her stupid gavel. Memories kept swirling around in his tired head. He finally managed to doze off, but as soon as he did, there was his sister, waving at him again. Then his eyes were wide open, and he was back to staring at the ceiling.

Shipley figured that since he couldn't sleep, as soon as the doors opened up, he might as well go to the gym to pump some weights. *At least that'll give me something to do until the noon count. Christ, I wish Connie could come in this morning. I sure wouldn't mind missing that stupid barbecue. Hell, who cares about it anyway?*

Within moments of that thought, the cell doors noisily opened, and Shipley headed out. As soon as he stepped onto the range, he looked for Owen, but he didn't see him or Godwyn, so he figured he'd head down on his own. He still appreciated not having to work during the barbecue. The staff were aware of his upcoming visit and what it meant to him. After all, since the visit had been set up, that had been about all he talked about to anyone who would listen. Eventually, he'd been told to take the day off and just enjoy himself. That was exactly what he would do—or so he thought.

* * *

The car was bombing along the highway. It was a nice car, only a couple of years old and in excellent condition. The baby-blue colour seemed to suit it. The pretty young lady driving it was intent on what she was doing. Connie had been on the road for around two hours and was so deep in thought, thinking about the visit to see her brother, Mac, that she had lost most of her concentration—that was, until she heard a siren behind her and, looking in the rearview mirror, saw flashing lights and a police officer waving her to the side.

She immediately pulled over, turned the ignition off and shakily sat there, waiting for the officer to approach. While she sat there waiting, all thoughts of her brother faded away. Finally, the officer approached and said, "Good morning, miss. Are you in a hurry to get somewhere? You were certainly going over the speed limit."

"Oh no. I didn't realize how fast I was going, sir." Connie explained the circumstances of her trip and concluded her story with a sweet smile. "I'm so sorry, Officer. I've never had a ticket in my life."

The police officer took her license, went back to the squad car for a few minutes and then returned and handed Connie's license back to her. The radio had informed all patrol officers of a situation at Mountainview: an inmate had been seriously injured or possible killed.

Vern Thibedeau

He was about to tell Connie of the problem and say she might not be able to get in for a visit, but then he changed his mind. Instead, he said, "Ms. Patterson, I'm not going to give you a ticket today, but please remember to stay within the speed limit. The next time, you may not be so lucky."

"I will, sir. Thanks very much; I do appreciate the favour."

"You're welcome. Good luck with your visit; I hope it all works out." With that, the officer retreated back to his vehicle.

For the rest of the trip, Connie stayed almost within the speed limit. She didn't go more than a little over the limit. However, that was enough to make her arrival later than she had expected. But maybe that was a good thing.

During the drive to visit her brother, she couldn't help going over the life they'd had as children. She also reflected on how lucky she was. She knew if she hadn't bumped into Al that night, she could've had the same problems Mac was having. *God, thank you for small mercies.* She had repeated that statement to herself and to Al many times in her life. She still couldn't believe how fortunate she was.

However, there were many times, especially now that she had reconnected with her younger brother, when she wished she had gone back and taken him away from that hellhole of a family life. She couldn't help feeling guilty that she hadn't done so. *Hell, I bet he wouldn't be where he is now if I'd just gone and grabbed him.* That was another statement she repeated to herself and to Al often.

Even with the excitement of visiting her long-lost brother, she couldn't help thinking about being away from home and being concerned about her children. Al's sister had promised to babysit during the day until Al got home from work, but this was the first time she had been away from them for any length of time. Even though they were being well looked after, she knew no one could do that fun job as well as she could.

As thoughts of her past life, her present life, her children and meeting her brother again swirled through her mind, her foot got a little heavier on the gas pedal again. But lucky for Connie, there didn't appear to be any more police on the highway, at least not in her area.

* * *

Richards made it down to the gym area and, since there wasn't much for him to do, spent most of his time chatting with the staff who were there. Even the recreational staff didn't have a heck of a lot to do; after all, there were several inmates working to set everything up, and all they really required was some guidance. In fact, Richards said to one of the guys, "Jeez, Jim, I've never seen the cons work this hard down here. What'd you guys do—threaten them with a beheading or something?"

"Nah. This is the one time they don't mind working. They all do their share and pull together. It's this barbecue thing; they all enjoy it. We just hope some idiot doesn't fuck it up for everyone."

"Yep, I agree with you there. Management even cancelled the punishment for a few inmates and let them out of disassociation early just so they could come down for it. Boy, it sure is a big thing for them."

"Yep. I wish they'd work like this all the time." With a look toward an inmate dragging a propane tank toward the door, the recreation officer hollered to him, "Hey, MacDonald, take them both out! No sense in making two trips."

Just then, Richards noticed Shipley coming into the gym. With a look at the officer he was speaking to, Richards said, "There's Shipley. He's a little late in getting to work, isn't he?"

"Not really. He's getting a visit from his sister this afternoon. Apparently, it's the first time in years that he's seen her, so we gave him the day off. Christ, it's all he's been talking about—much easier to just give him the time off. At least it's easier on our ears. He probably came down to do a workout and burn a little energy off."

"I don't blame you a bit for giving him the time. He also has been carrying on about it in the unit. Hope it works out OK for him; he is really excited about it. Might just do him some good; you never know."

"Well, I'd better get outside to see how the cons are coming along. It's damned near count time, and they have to go in for it. I just have to make sure they're done before then, or there'll be hell to pay. Talk to you later, Bill." With that, the recreation officer headed for the yard.

Richards was going to go to N area to see if he could give a hand to the staff up there but then decided he'd stay around the gym until count time. He figured he should hang around because that really was his job. *What the hell? Not likely anything to do up there anyway.* He spent most of his time just hanging around and chatting with the staff while wishing he was on his regular job in the unit. He thought, *Holy God, anything would be better than this hanging around doing dick-all.*

Finally, the word came to send the inmates up for the count. Once they were all clear of the yard and recreation area, he headed up to give them a hand in the unit. Richards and the other staff realized there wouldn't be a lot of time for them to eat their lunch, but they figured that came with the job and knew they'd manage one way or another.

* * *

As soon as the inmates were told to head back to the units for the count, Shipley didn't waste any time and started right out. He figured the sooner the count came in, the quicker they'd be out in the yard, and the faster that happened, the sooner Connie would be there for their visit. *God, I still can't believe I'm really gonna see my sister again. I can't even remember the last time we actually saw each other. Oh my God, this is just great!*

He was busy thinking of his visit and praying that it would be a two-day visit, when suddenly, a sharp pain struck him in the shoulder. His immediate thought was that someone had stuck him with a shank. However, he soon realized he had walked into a barrier. He hadn't even noticed it until he felt the pain in his shoulder. He let out a yelp, grabbed his shoulder and, while looking around, spotted a couple of inmates standing there who had watched him walk into the barrier. They were looking at him and shaking their heads but also grinning, and that relieved Shipley's mind a great deal. Shipley, as he felt the pain in his shoulder, realized he had been careless. He had been so wrapped up thinking about his sister's visit and his newfound nephews that he had not been watching his back. He kept walking, but it was a wake-up call for him, and he immediately went back to watching everything going on around him.

Saying, "Hey there. How you doing?" to inmates he knew, Shipley entered his cell. Because of the all-important visit, he decided to get cleaned up a bit and have a shave. He immediately removed his shirt and proceeded with his plan. He heard a screw walk by his cell and knew he was counting the inmates, and with any luck, he figured the count would be in shortly.

He had just finished his chores, when the speaker announced the count was in, and recreation would be called in a few minutes. As he stood there waiting for his cell door to open, he kept glancing around his cell. Eventually, his eyes came to rest on a photograph taped to his wall. It was what he considered a perfect picture of Jennifer and Timmy. In fact, it was the only picture he had of the two of them. As usual, when he looked at the picture, his vision immediately became a little blurry. He had not had any communication with Jennifer since the phone call, not even a letter, and he wasn't really expecting any. But every time he glanced at that photograph, he couldn't help wondering how they were doing and praying that everything was good with them. He also couldn't help daydreaming. In fact, for some reason he didn't understand, he was daydreaming about them more all the time. He couldn't help wondering what life would have been like if he hadn't gotten into this jackpot and if they had managed to stay together. *God*, he thought, *I hope everything is OK with them. I wonder if he looks like me. I sure hope so. That'd be great! Those goddamn parents of hers—it's all their fault. Christ, we were doing fine; why in hell couldn't they just mind their own business and leave us alone?*

Then he heard the doors on the range above him open, and the usual noise and yelling started up. Within a couple of minutes, the doors on his range opened, and he stepped out of his cell. He looked up the range and spotted Owen coming out of his cell. Owen gave a wave and started toward him, and Shipley, with his mind still on Jen and Timmy, returned the wave.

Owen walked up to Shipley and said, "Hey, Mac, let's get going. We don't wanna be the last ones out for the great meal."

"OK, let's go. I'm getting hungry, and I'm not sure how long it'll be before my sister gets here. What the hell you doing with that jacket on? Christ, it's pretty warm out there; you're gonna cook."

"Nah, I feel like I got a cold or something coming on, and I've been a little chilly." Obviously, Owen didn't tell his buddy that he had an ice pick shoved in his pants and didn't want him or the screws to spot it.

The two of them continued chatting as they started off the range. Owen, who was walking on Shipley's right side, knew he had to get over to Shipley's left side. He figured that since the disturbance, if Slug

Vern Thibedeau

kept his promise, would be to their right, he should be on the left. Not a dummy, he didn't want to be between Shipley and the disturbance. Owen figured if Shipley was looking in his direction while trying to see what the disturbance was, it would spoil his great idea of having a distraction. After all, the distraction was to get Shipley to look in the opposite direction, not toward Owen. If the plan worked out, he could get the damned job done, get it done right and then get the hell away from the area without being spotted.

Shipley and Owen, while continuing their discussion, made it out of the unit and continued down the corridor toward the yard. Owen managed to move over to Shipley's left side.

The move earned a questioning look from Shipley. "Hey, Jim, you nervous about something? Hell, you're bouncing around like you have a date with a broad or something. Oh, by the way, you mind if we wait till after my visit and get together tonight to talk about whatever's bugging you? I still want ta help if I can, but my mind is kinda on my sister's visit right now."

Owen, with a glance toward Shipley and allowing his elbow to brush his side to ensure the ice pick was still there, replied, "Sure, Mac. There's no big rush. Tonight'll be fine."

They turned the last corner, and from the far end of the corridor, they could see the bright sunlight streaming in from the yard. "Holy Christ, Mac, it's going to be great out there. Sunshine instead of rain, a barbecue—what the hell more can a guy ask for, eh?"

Owen kept looking around and was thankful the corridor was filled with inmates. He knew that the more guys crowded around, the more difficult it would be to spot the incident he hoped was going to go down in a short time. At least he hoped so. While looking around, he spotted a couple of Slug's goons about to step out into the yard. Just before they disappeared into the sunshine, one of them looked back and, seeing Owen, stared into his eyes and gave a short nod. Owen figured, or at least hoped, that was the signal that the distraction was all set to go.

* * *

Raymond, who was wide awake now, looked down from the tower toward the yard entrance and saw a bunch of inmates storming out of the building. He put his book down on the table, stood up and made sure the rifle and binoculars were within arm's reach. *Oh well. At least I have something to do now. It's a hell of a lot better than sitting there fighting to stay awake. Christ, I hope nothing goes down; I wanna get to the bar later, and maybe Annie will be there. Jesus Christ, I hope so; she's one sweet chick, and she thinks I'm really something.*

* * *

Richards was standing in a control centre, watching the inmates rush out to the yard. Smith was assigned to the control and was watching the inmates as closely as Richards was. "Holy hell," Richards said with a quick glance at Smith, "you'd think they were getting day parole or something, eh? They always like this for the barbecue?"

"Oh, you can bet your last dollar on that, my man. It's the same mess every year. I wish to hell they'd cancel the fucking thing; it's nothing but a pain in the ass. There're just way too many cons out there at the same time. And after that episode last year, I would've bet a day's pay they were going to cancel the damned thing. Goddamned management!"

"Well, I lucked in last year; I was on two weeks' leave and missed it. From what I was told, it was pretty bad. Wish to hell I was on leave again this year. You're sure lucky you didn't bet anyone about cancelling it, though; you would've lost a day's pay.

"Oh, there goes that Shipley out with his buddy Owen; they're both in my unit. I didn't think he'd be going out to it. His sister's coming in for a two-day visit, and he hasn't seen her for years. Christ, it's all he's been yapping about for the last week or so."

"Yep, you're right about that; I would've lost a few bucks. For sure I know all about Shipley and that damned visit. I'm not even in your unit, and it's all I've heard. Gotta admit, though, he's not really a bad con, and I hope it works out for him. If it does, it might just give him something to work toward."

"You got a point there, Jim. Guess there's always hope, eh?"

* * *

Vern Thibedeau

Shipley and Owen made their way along the crowded corridor on their way to the barbecue, and eventually, they finally made it to the sunlit yard. As soon as the crowd of inmates entered the yard, they immediately dispersed. Several went off to the left, several more kept going straight ahead and a few swung right toward the yard fence. Shipley looked over at Owen and commented on how bright it was. "Christ, that sun is bright; I can't see a damned thing. There's not even a breeze, and you've got that stupid jacket on; God, Jim, you're gonna cook. It's good weather for Connie, though; it'll be a great trip for her. I just wish she could've brought her kids with her. Jesus, that'd really be something."

They took a few more steps into the sunlight, and Owen, who was looking off to their right, said, "Holy Christ, there's a big fight over there. Look at the fuckers going at it!"

Shipley, as soon as he jerked his head over to take a look, suddenly felt a tremendous serge of pain in his neck. He turned his head and tried to speak to Owen, but all he could do was emit a low gurgle, and then another huge pain struck him. There was a third shot of pain, but luckily or unluckily, Mac never felt the third one at all. He didn't know what to do or what was happening. In fact, he couldn't have done anything about it anyway. He managed to raise his hands to his throat and felt something wet and sticky, and then, suddenly, everything started to get dark. Also, he suddenly started to feel very cold. He felt himself falling but couldn't figure out why he would have been doing that. The darkness and the cold continued to envelope him.

In the narrowing cone of light, he was certain he could see his sister standing off in the distance, waving to him. As strange as it seemed, he was sure she had sparkles glinting in her hair. He couldn't fathom how she could have been out there. He tried to ask, "Hey, what on earth are you doing here?" but realized the words wouldn't come out. However, in his mind, just before complete darkness swooped in, he imagined— in fact, he was sure—he waved back. Then everything went black. He thought he felt something slam him in the chest and face area, but that was just a guess, and it was his last conscious thought.

If he'd had time before the darkness consumed him, Shipley might have thought perhaps this was going to be his successful escape.

Chapter 24

Raymond was no fool. Maybe he was not a great officer, but he was no fool. As soon as he saw the inmates storming into the yard, he never took his eyes off them. He was concerned something could happen, and if an incident did go down, he didn't want to miss any of it. He figured he'd been in enough trouble lately and knew damned well it didn't make any difference if it was his fault or not—at least in his mind, it didn't seem to make any difference.

Holy Christ, he thought to himself as he watched the inmates pouring out of the building. *That looks like that screw-up Shipley, who got me into the mess at the hospital.* Raymond grabbed his binoculars to get a better look and to make sure it was Shipley. He put them up to eyes and finally got them into focus, and sure enough, it was Shipley, walking and chatting with another con Raymond recognized as the brewmaster from J unit. Raymond was so busy staring at Shipley and thinking his dark thoughts that he missed the fight going on just out of his narrowed-down view.

Just then, his radio crackled, and a voice asked, "Tower three, what the hell's going on? Is that a fight over by the west fence?"

Raymond was just about to glance over in that direction, when he spotted a few unusual movements in the area of Shipley and Owen.

He was watching Shipley strut out into the yard, when he noticed Owen, who was right beside him, unzip the jacket he was wearing. The

jacket caught Raymond's attention because the day was fairly warm—
certainly too warm for one to be wearing a jacket. At the same time, he
noticed Shipley jerk his head to the right to take a look at something.
At that moment, Raymond spotted Owen quickly yank something out
from his waist area, reach up and make two or three jabbing motions
toward Shipley's throat. Shipley immediately reached up with both
hands, grabbed at his throat and started to collapse. Raymond couldn't
miss seeing a dark fluid spray out of the same area. Strangely, Shipley's
right hand left his throat and weakly waved a couple of times in front of
his face. For half a second Raymond, knowing it was ludicrous, had the
impression Shipley was trying to wave off a fly or something. He also
noticed that Owen, once he competed the thrusting motions, tossed an
object of some kind to his left and quickly walked away from Shipley.
As usual when there was an incident of any kind, the other inmates in
the vicinity, whether they knew what had happened or not, immediately
started to scramble out of the area. Raymond had been around long
enough to realize that the dark fluid he'd seen shooting out was blood;
there was no doubt in his mind.

Raymond, breathing heavily because of what he'd witnessed,
grabbed his radio, keyed the mic and, in an excited voice, said, "Holy
Christ, there's been a stabbing!" Then, calming down a little but still
with a stressed-out voice, he rekeyed the mic and barked into it, "This
is tower three. We have a stabbing at number-two yard entrance. We'll
need staff and medical help as soon as possible." Raymond shoved the
radio into his pocket and jerked the rifle out of its stand. He lunged for
the tower door and, just before shoving it open, grabbed the microphone
for the speaker system. He stepped out onto the parapet. Raising the
microphone, he yelled into it, "All of you, get the hell away from that
barrier, and move over to the fence! Do it right goddamn now!"

He stood there watching the inmates as they stared up at the
tower and slowly started to shuffle toward the fenced area. Raising the
microphone once again, in a pissed-off voice, Raymond yelled into it,
"Last warning, assholes! Move your asses, or I'm firing!" He immediately
dropped the mic, raised the rifle and jacked a round into the chamber.
About all he received for his instructions were more catcalls, fists waving
up at him and several uncomplimentary screams directed toward him.

Raymond aimed his rifle in the general direction of a group of inmates who were making the most noise, and being careful to ensure no one was close to the centre of aim, he pressed the trigger.

Apparently, the inmates hadn't really thought he'd pull the trigger. As soon as the rifle crashed and the bullet threw up some dirt when it plowed into the ground, the inmates stopped yelling at him and started to run out of the area. They beat it over to the fence and stood there milling around and looking over at the inmate sprawled out on the ground and not moving. The inmates who hadn't witnessed the incident thought he had been hit by the bullet. But once they started talking, that belief was soon put to rest.

Raymond remained out on the parapet with the rifle at the ready and used the radio to inform staff that it was safe to enter the yard. He also used the radio to advise everyone that it was Shipley who had been injured and that he didn't appear to be moving. Raymond, within a few seconds, couldn't help thinking that maybe he should have fired the round off much sooner than he did. In those situations, one immediately started to second-guess himself.

Sergeant Patrick was unlucky enough to be in charge of the prison for the weekend and had just finished his lunch, when he heard Raymond's radio call informing staff of the problem in the yard. Patrick grabbed his radio, rushed toward N area and, at the same time, keyed the radio and ordered all barriers closed. "Inmates still in the building are to be returned to their cells, and the units are to be secured. No inmates are to leave the yard until this mess is sorted out." Patrick returned the radio to its holster and continued striding toward N area.

Raymond, not wanting to broadcast over the radio exactly what he had witnessed but wanting the staff to be aware of what to watch for, pulled the radio out of his pocket and pressed the switch. "This is tower three. Someone contact me via phone right away." Within a second or two, the tower phone rang. Raymond grabbed the phone and spoke into it. "Tower three here."

"Raymond, this is Richards. I'm still in S control, but I'm just leaving for the yard. What the hell's up?"

"There're a couple of things you have to be aware of. First off, I know who did the stabbing; I saw it clear as a bell. It was Owen from J unit.

Secondly, I'm pretty sure I spotted him drop the knife or whatever the hell it was, and I know exactly where it is. When you come out, it's about ten feet straight ahead from the barrier and about five paces to your left. You shouldn't have any problem spotting it. It was just dropped, and I didn't see anyone around it. Also, Owen is standing among a bunch of the cons over by the west fence area."

"OK. Thanks for the info. We'll see how everything goes, but I think we'll likely let Owen return to his cell, and we'll scoop him later. Right now, there're just too many cons out there. Just make sure you don't give him any reason to think we know it was him."

* * *

Owen was milling around with the other pissed-off inmates and making as much noise as the rest of them. But his stomach was a mess. Between acting tough with the other inmates and carrying on as if his biggest problem were the loss of the barbecue, he had to take deep breaths so he wouldn't throw up. He certainly wasn't accustomed to stabbing people, especially perceived friends. But he was sure that no one had spotted him stabbing Mac and that he had gotten away with it. But he had never stabbed anyone before, and it was starting to bother him. *Christ, Mac was a good guy. He was willing to help me out of a problem before he even knew what the hell it was. Goddamn it to hell. Oh God, what a fucking mess; I'll never gamble again.*

But then the thought of not being in debt any longer and not having to worry about Slug or his buddies leaped into his thoughts and caused him to calm down somewhat and start breathing more or less normally. He started to feel a hell of a lot better. He even was on the verge of being happy for the first time in a long time.

After about his fifth time looking down at his hands and checking his clothing for blood, Owen came to believe there was none on him. He thought, *I just have to wait for the screws to do their thing and then head back to the range with everyone else. Holy Christ, it's gonna be OK.* He glanced over toward the group hanging around with Slug and received a brief affirmative nod, which helped him feel better yet.

* * *

Richards completed his conversation with Raymond in the tower and hung the phone up. He briefed Smith on what had transpired and instructed him to log the times and the incident into his notebook. By that time, the inmates who had filled the corridor while on their way to the yard had been turned around and sent back to their units. Looking up the corridor, Richards was happy to see several staff rushing down toward him and happier yet when he spotted Sergeant Patrick leading the pack. Richards stepped out of the control, and the staff gathered around him. He filled them in on everything he knew about the incident and was relieved when the sergeant took over.

Sergeant Patrick started his instructions by saying, "I agree with leaving Owen alone until he's in the unit and the place is locked down; no sense in asking for more problems. The nurse is just waiting for my word, and I'll let her know when it's all clear to come into the yard. Tom, you wait here for her and the gurney. The rest of us will get out there and see what's going on, and we have to make damn sure the area around the injured inmate stays clear. As soon as the nurse has Shipley on his way into the hospital, we'll get the rest of the inmates out of the yard and into their units. Remember, guys, this may be difficult, but don't pay any more attention to Owen than you do to the rest of the jerks."

Looking toward Richards, he continued with his instructions. "Bill, you keep one guy with you, and your only concern is to find that weapon. Remember, don't touch it with your bare hands; use a cloth or get gloves from the nurse. We may luck in find fingerprints on it. Also, make damn sure you don't get any blood on you; you never know what may be in it." With a look around at the staff, he asked, "Everything all clear?" Not receiving any questions, he continued. "OK, guys, let's get going. Just watch yourselves out there; we don't want anyone getting hurt."

As they all hurried toward the entrance, Richards heard Patrick on the radio, informing tower three that they were on their way out to the yard. He also instructed Raymond to stay out on the parapet with the rifle at the ready.

As they were entering the yard, Bill looked at Ernie and told him to stay with him. "Remember, let the other guys look after the cons and Shipley. Our job is to find the weapon, and that's it."

Vern Thibedeau

As they entered the yard, everyone checked to make sure the inmates were well back by the fence and not about to interfere with them. Bill took a quick look up at the tower and spotted Raymond standing on the parapet with the rifle pointing into the air. As soon as he saw that, he was pretty damn sure there would be no problems with any of the inmates, and at least with that assumption, it turned out he was correct.

Besides taking a quick glance up at the tower and toward the inmates at the fence, Richards was also counting his paces as he entered the exercise yard. As soon as he counted 10 steps, he turned to his left and continued walking for another five paces. As he was walking and counting, his eyes continued to sweep the immediate area, and he lucked in. Just before taking his fifth step, he spotted the weapon. It was only three or four paces in front of him and just lying there on top of the packed-down dirt, appearing undisturbed. He could tell it was the weapon he was looking for, because it was covered with blood.

Richards glanced at Ernie and said, "There it is. I want you to watch what I do, note the time and log everything into your notebook." Richards took a brown paper bag and a cloth out of his pocket, bent down, picked the weapon up with the cloth and dropped it and the cloth into the bag. He marked the exact spot where he had found the ice pick, and then they walked over toward the sergeant.

Just as they approached him, Richards heard the sergeant instruct S control to allow the nurse into the yard. Richards and Ernie looked over toward the barrier, saw the nurse and her two helpers rushing toward them with the gurney and scrambled out of their way.

As he watched the nurse do her thing, Richards sidled over to the sergeant and informed him that he had the weapon secured in an evidence bag and that it looked as if it hadn't been touched. While he was explaining that news to Sergeant Patrick, the nurse looked over and said, "I'm not sure I'll be able to help him, but I'm going to get him to the hospital. An ambulance will be here momentarily. You never know; we may just luck in."

While the nurse was explaining her plan, the helpers loaded Shipley onto the gurney, and they took off for the barrier.

The rest of the job in the yard was relatively simple. Staff had to remain in the area to ensure no one disturbed the crime scene. They also had to log each inmate's name into a book and give him a quick frisk before allowing him through the barrier and back to his unit. The job went much faster than staff had imagined it would. Of course, having Raymond standing on the parapet with a rifle pointed in their general direction certainly helped the situation, especially since he had already fired one round off. Sergeant Patrick and Richards stood off to the side and watched as the inmates were cleared to head into the prison. Patrick looked up toward the tower and gave Raymond a little wave to let him know he was aware of his being up there with the rifle and doing his job. Then Patrick looked over at Richards and said, "I'll tell you, Bill, Raymond did a hell of a good job up there this afternoon. I don't know how he happened to spot the problem as quickly as he did, but I'm damned glad he managed to."

"Oh yes, he sure did. I have to admit I'm a little surprised, though. Maybe I judged him wrong. Hope so anyway."

"OK, I have to get to the hospital and see how things are going. By the looks of the blood, I wouldn't think Shipley will make it, but hey, we've been wrong before. You just never know, eh? I'm gonna take that evidence bag with me and lock it up in the security safe. You stay here until everything is clear, and then make sure a couple of staff stay in the area to guarantee that no one pokes around. The ambulance should be here any minute, and I don't doubt the police will be right behind it." With that, Patrick headed in to see how things were going.

Richards watched Patrick walk away and was happy that Patrick, not he, would have to do the paperwork and answer all the questions. With that happy thought, Richards walked over to help keep an eye on the few remaining inmates being checked out. He watched the staff write the names and their institutional numbers down and then give them quick frisks, and that was about it.

Once the inmates were cleared from the yard, he picked three staff members and told them they'd have to stay out to keep the area clear until the police arrived. "And that means very clear. On top of that, make sure you keep those damned birds away. It wouldn't take very long, because of all that blood, for the whole frigging area to be covered with the little buggers. If that happens, you guys'll have to explain to the cops how that mess came about." With those instructions and a wave, Richards started inside.

* * *

Sergeant Patrick, once he finished his instructions to Richards, left the yard area and started in to see how everything was proceeding inside. He figured his first stop would be the hospital. He had to try to make damned sure Shipley was sent downtown. He had been in enough situations to know that even if Shipley didn't make it, he had to try to talk the nurse into sending him down. If they could get him on the way to the downtown hospital and off prison property, then whether he was alive or dead, it would make things a lot easier for everyone—no coroner or that damned wagon of his coming in, just the police. He figured that would be enough work as it was. *Hell, I hope he does pull through, though. The guys say he seems to be turning out OK.*

He reached S control and stopped long enough to instruct the officer to contact J unit and tell them he wanted Owen locked up in segregation immediately. Once that job was completed, he turned and started down toward the hospital. As he entered the hospital, he was surprised to see the nurse sitting in her office, filling out a logbook. As soon as she heard Patrick, she looked up and said, "He's already left in the ambulance. I can't believe how quickly they made it here. One of your guys went with them as the escort. Hope that was OK."

"Hell, I didn't think they'd be here for another twenty or thirty minutes. Yep, that's great. I must've missed the radio call; it was rather noisy out in the yard for a while. Christ, I'm glad you sent him downtown. Saves me a ton of work. How was he? Think he'll make it?"

"Well, to be honest, I couldn't even guess. I did everything I could possibly do, but he's in really bad shape. Whoever wanted to dump him sure made a good attempt at it. Guess we just have to hope for the best, but at least it's their problem downtown. Any idea who did it or why?"

"We've got a pretty good idea of the who, but the why is open to debate. Anyway, I've a million things to do, so I guess I'd better take off." With that, Patrick left the office.

On his way out of the hospital, he stopped at the security office. He gave a glance at Allen, the security officer, and said, "I have to use your phone for a minute to call Raymond in tower thee." The officer made a move as if to get up and leave, but Patrick waved him back into the chair and dialed the tower.

Raymond answered the phone on the first ring. "Tower three. Raymond here."

"Raymond, it's Sergeant Patrick. I just want to compliment you on the job you did up there this afternoon. I don't know how you tripped to the incident as quickly as you did, but it was a hell of a good job. I also want to let you know that I'll be remarking on it in the report. Anyway, I'm going to have you relieved shortly so you can write up your incident report. When you're done, make damned sure you get it to me. See you in a while."

Patrick hung up. He then said, "See you later," to Allen and headed back toward S control. He knew Allen would tell several staff about his phone call to Raymond, and it wouldn't take long for the whole shift to be aware of it.

Patrick stepped out into the corridor and received a radio call informing him that the deputy warden had arrived. A relieved Patrick acknowledged the call and made his way up to N area. *Thank Christ he made it in. Be nice to have some help in here.* Patrick had contacted him by phone shortly after he was informed of the incident. He hadn't expected the deputy to make it in so quickly, but he was happy he had. The deputy would take a lot of the pressure off his shoulders, and that made Patrick a happy sergeant.

* * *

Owen, when it was his turn to be checked and cleared to leave the yard, stood there with his arms out while he was patted down. He looked over and spotted Corporal Richardson supervising the search. Once he was cleared to go in, Owen noticed Richardson glance his way, and he gave Richardson a nod. *Jesus Christ. The idiots have no clue I did it. Christ, look at them all, standing around like they know everything, and they don't know dick-all. Guess I might as well get in and have a sleep. Sure won't be any yard or gym tonight. Holy God, I'm free and clear, and I don't owe that goof Slug a thing. Christ, life is great!*

Vern Thibedeau

Owen headed in toward his range with a couple of other inmates. They chatted about the incident as they went. Owen didn't say much; he just more or less listened to them go on and on about it. But he couldn't help giving a little smirk every once in a while. *Christ, they think they know everything; they're just like the pigs. Don't know bugger-all.*

Just as they were entering the unit, one inmate said, "Christ, the poor fuck must be dead. A guy couldn't lose that much blood and pull out of it."

The inmate beside him replied, "Ah hell, Jake, you never know. I seen plenty of this shit and seen lots of them survive when they should be dead. You just never know. I kind of hope he lives. I'm pretty sure it was Shipley who got it. He's the guy who's been talking about his sister or somebody coming in to visit him today. Guess that visit's kinda screwed. Also, tell you something else. That asshole who did him could've waited till after the barbecue. Christ, the pigs only give us one a year. Now that's fucked up! Christ, he deserves to get his nuts kicked in." Looking toward Owen, he added, "Christ, you're fucking quiet. Blood turn your stomach or something?"

"Nope, just thinking about having a sleep once I get home." At the same time, Owen was thinking, *You stupid jerk. You don't know dick-all. If you knew what I'd just done, you'd probably throw up. Yeah, real fucking know-it-all!*

Owen reached his cell, walked in and, as soon as the door slammed shut, flopped onto his bed and hoped he could drift off for a while. But he knew he likely wouldn't be able to. He was still running on adrenaline and couldn't help going over and over in his mind what he had just done.

He rolled off the bed and grabbed a Coke. He wished he had some brew left, but no such luck. He fired up a smoke, when suddenly, his cell door crashed open. The sudden noise made him jump, and he slopped some of his Coke on the bed. He spun around, and his stomach dropped when he saw four staff members rushing through the door.

"Get your face and hands up against the wall, asshole. In case you haven't guessed it yet, you're on the way to the hole. The cops will be in shortly, and you'll be charged with murder, you fucking hero. And please try something, will you? I'd love to use this mace."

Owen, who immediately realized the trouble he was in, turned to face the wall, put his arms up as far as he could and just stood there shivering. He didn't say a word, not even while the guard roughly patted him down, but his mind was going full steam. *Oh Christ. One of the pricks must have seen me do it. God, I'm done for. I'll never get out of here. Christ, I hope I die.*

One of the officers instructed Owen to turn around and hold his arms out. Once he did as instructed, handcuffs were slapped on, and he was escorted to segregation. Once he was there, per the usual practice, the cuffs were removed, and he was strip-searched, given a change of clothing and then secured in a cell.

One of the staff, as he locked the cell door, looked in at Owen through the window and said, "There you go; you're all set now. Enjoy your stay, tough guy."

Owen looked around the sterile cell and, in a haze, noted that it contained nothing but a bed, a blanket, a sink and a toilet. He spread out the blanket that was lying on the bed and flopped on top of it. About all he could do was lie there and stare at the ceiling—and that was exactly what he did. That and think about the mess he had made of things. While shivering, he kept saying to himself, *Christ, I should've gone to Richards and told him what was going on. God Almighty, I really fucked up this time. Jesus, I'm screwed.*

* * *

Raymond was happy to see the last of the inmates on their way inside. He noted that three staff were staying behind, and he knew they would be there until the police arrived and would likely stay until the cops finished doing their thing. He had just stepped back inside the tower, when his phone rang. He picked up the receiver and answered with the usual statement. As soon he heard the sergeant's voice, he thought, *Oh Christ, it's about firing that round off. I bet I'm gonna wear it for doing that. God, I had to, though. Just no choice.*

Once the conversation was completed and Patrick hung up, a relieved Raymond almost felt like dancing. In fact, he did a little jig. *Holy Christ. Thank God I used the binoculars to see if it was that fuckhead*

Vern Thibedeau

Shipley coming out. If I hadn't done that, I likely wouldn't have seen a thing. Thank God for small mercies!

Richards left the yard and figured he might as well go up to N area to see if he could give them a hand in locking and counting the cons. He knew there was no sense in going back to the gym. The equipment was all outside and wouldn't be coming back in until the police had finished doing their job. He also thought he might have to give them a hand in locking Owen up, if they hadn't already done it.

He reached N area and looked around, and the only officer he saw was the corporal in charge of the area. Richards said, "Hey, it's awfully quiet. Where the hell is everyone?"

"My guys got stuck with taking that Owen to the hole. They should be back shortly. I guess they're pretty sure he's the one who did Shipley, eh?"

"Oh, for sure. There's absolutely no doubt. Don't know how Raymond did it, but he actually saw the con do the stabbing. Kind of amazing that Raymond was on the ball like that. It's also good that he had the balls to get a shot off."

Just then, three officers approached, and one, with a little laugh, said, "Well, that idiot's in the hole. I'll tell you, he was one shocked con. He really thought he got away with it. I can also tell you that he's not really very happy right now. In fact, the guys in the hole said they're going to keep an eye on him just in case he tries to top himself."

Richards replied, "I'm not surprised he had no clue about what we knew. He was just hanging around with the other cons over by the fence, acting tough and giving staff a hard time. And I'll also tell you all something else: we sure couldn't tell just by looking at him that he had just stabbed one of his buddies. We really checked him over while clearing him to come in, and there was absolutely no blood on him at all. That's kind of surprising because there sure was a hell of a lot of the stuff on the ground."

*   *   *

Shipley had lucked in, though; the ambulance arrived within minutes of his reaching the prison hospital, and he was quickly loaded into it. While that chore was being carried out, a corporal instructed Shelly, one of the officers who had helped to push the gurney back inside, to grab a radio and go with the ambulance as an escort. "Radio us when you get there, and fill us in on how everything's going. Depending on how long everything takes down there, either we'll get a relief for you, or someone will come down to pick you up." In other words, if Shipley lived, they would send him a relief; if he died, he didn't need an escort, and they would send a vehicle to bring Shelly back to the institution.

So the unlucky Shelly jumped into the ambulance, and they headed for the sally port. Shelly radioed the sally port to say that he was in the ambulance and that they would be there shortly. Upon arrival, without any fanfare, just a wave from Shelly, and with the siren screaming, they were on their way to the downtown hospital.

Shelly, with nothing to do and knowing there was no reason to handcuff Shipley, just sat there in the ambulance and watched the medics work on him. It was almost a straight run to the hospital. Every once in a while, Shelly could tell the ambulance driver had to tap the brake to slow up slightly, and Shelly guessed they were rushing through an intersection. A few times, he had to grab the bench he was sitting on when the ambulance rocked as they tore around a corner while hardly slowing down. In Shelly's mind, it appeared that just before those things happened, the siren would screech. The screeching made Shelly twitch more than once, and he noticed the medics give each other a grin every time he twitched. Once things seemed to calm down a little, Shelly, looking at one of the medics, asked, "What do you think? Any chance he'll make it?"

"Oh, that's not for us to say. We do what we can in here and then let the doctors do their thing. They'll let you know as soon as they know. But to be honest, it doesn't look all that good for him."

After about 15 minutes, they squealed into the hospital emergency entrance. The medics, with the assistance of several hospital staff, unloaded Shipley and, with Shelly following, rushed inside. On the way in, Shelly couldn't help noticing several people standing around or sitting in chairs. With one quick glance at them, he knew they were waiting their turn to see a doctor. It appeared to Shelly that they seemed to become more alert when they noticed his uniform, the radio bouncing on his hip and the handcuffs hanging from his belt. Partly to give them a show, he keyed his radio and spoke into the mic: "This is the hospital escort calling main control. We've arrived at the hospital without a problem. Will notify you as soon as I find out what's going on. Over."

The radio immediately squawked with a reply: "Main control here. Thank you. Appropriate personnel will be notified. Over and out."

Chapter 25

Sergeant Patrick received a radio call informing him that the police had arrived, and he immediately left his office to meet them. He arrived at the front entrance, saw four police officers waiting for him and introduced himself, and they started down toward the cell blocks. Patrick gave the officers a quick briefing on what had gone down and asked them if they wanted to go straight out to the yard.

"Yep. Might as well. We'll get a look at the area, and then I'll come back in and interview your staff. It doesn't really look like there's a hell of a lot for us to do; sounds like your guys pretty well covered everything. We'll make sure we take the statements and the weapon with us when we leave. But I'll have to talk to the inmate you locked up after I interview your guys. Not that I expect him to say very much, but gotta go through the steps, eh? We haven't heard anything one way or another from the hospital yet. If you get word of how he's doing, would you let me know right away?"

"For sure. Someone will get a hold of you as soon as we hear anything. Oh, by the way, the tower officer will be relieved shortly. I'll have him wait in the office, and you can talk to him first if you want. He's the one who, luckily, saw the whole thing go down through his binoculars. Not sure how he managed that, but he did. Even saw the weapon being tossed. A corporal picked it up, and I have it locked up in my safe."

Vern Thibedeau

The sergeant and the police arrived at N area, and one of the first guys Patrick spotted was Richards, who was standing there talking to a few of the staff. Patrick, with a wave toward Richards, said in a bit of a raised voice, "Hey, Bill, come on over here for a second, will you?"

Richards looked over toward Patrick, looked back at the group he was talking to and said, "Hell, I should've known enough to get out of sight somewhere. Guess I'd better get over there and see what the hell I'm gonna get stuck with now."

Once Richards made it over to Patrick, he was introduced to the police officers, and Patrick continued with his instructions by saying, "Bill, I want to take these guys out to the yard and show them where all this crap went down. Once they've finished out there, just bring them up to N area, and we'll see what else has to be done. Oh, just to let you know, as of yet, we haven't heard anything about Shipley from the hospital. Oh, and one other thing: make sure you take a radio with you in case something else comes up."

"Will do, boss. Well, let's head out, guys. There's not really much to see or do. We did leave a few staff out there to protect the area and make sure nothing gets disturbed."

Once they reached the yard, Richards pointed out where the incident had taken place and pointed to the tower Raymond was in. One of the police officers said, "Holy Christ, that's a long distance. How in hell did he spot the stabbing?"

"He lucked in. Just happened to be using the binoculars and watching the inmates come out and spotted Owen doing his thing. Boy, talk about being lucky. Normally, when something like this happens, we don't even know about it till it's over and done with."

Richards told the staff protecting the area to hang around until the police were done and then head up to N area. "Believe me, you're better off out here, guys, than back in the nuthouse. The cons are rather noisy; guess they're getting hungry. God forbid something would interrupt their meals."

The police hadn't been kidding when they said they wouldn't be long. They just took some pictures, measurements and several blood samples from the ground, and that was about it. In less than 30 minutes, they were all trooping back inside.

Richards used the radio to inform the sergeant that they were on the way back in and that two of the officers had to go into the dissociation cells to interview Owen.

"I expected that. You might as well take them in to do that little job; you're in that area anyway. Tell the guys who are with you to come up to N area to give a hand. We're gonna have to feed them as soon as the stewards get a meal ready."

"Will do, boss. I'll let you know as soon as we're done in the hole."

Richards looked toward the guys who had been out in the yard. They'd overheard the sergeant's comments, so they gave Richards a wave and kept on going. Richards then looked toward the police officers and said, "We might as well go over to segregation, and you can do your interviewing now if you want."

"Sure, let's go. The sooner that's finished, the sooner we can get the hell out of your hair."

Richards, using his radio, informed the staff in segregation that he was on the way with a couple of officers from the pen squad and that they had to interview Owen.

It only took a couple of minutes to reach segregation, but even so, the door was open, and a staff member was waiting to escort them in. "Hey, Bill, things getting back to normal yet?"

"Yep, we're getting there slowly but surely. Can you bring that idiot Owen out to the interview room for us?"

"Yep. The corporal's bringing him out now. Want me to hang around?"

"Nah. If he acts up, I'm sure we can handle him. I almost hope he does."

Just then, a couple of staff and the inmate, who was handcuffed, entered the area. Owen was escorted directly into a room that held nothing but a small desk and four chairs. For safety reasons, each individual item was bolted to the floor.

The two police officers followed them in. The staff placed Owen in a chair on the far side of the table and told him to stay there and not move a fucking muscle. Then they nodded to the police officers, and one of them said, "He's all yours." Then they turned around and left.

Richards followed them out, and they all stood outside the door in case Owen acted up. Richards didn't want to get involved with the interview, because it would just be one more item to keep track of. Plus, so far, he didn't think he would have to testify in court, and he wanted to keep it that way.

The corporal looked over at Richards and asked, "Hey, Bill, any word on Shipley yet? I've heard it looked pretty bad."

"Nope, not a thing yet. And it was bad. Christ, I haven't seen that much blood in a long time, and I hope I never have to again. That fuckhead say anything yet?"

"Nah. Hasn't opened his mouth. In fact, he's pretty shook up; he sure got in over his head. Can't see him doing it on his own. Him and Shipley kinda hung out together."

"That they did," replied Richards. "Does seem kind of weird, don't it? I'll tell you, wouldn't be a bad place to work if we just knew what the hell was going on with these idiots. Most of them are just a fucked-up bunch of know-nothings."

Just then, the door opened, and the police walked out. One officer said, "We're done with him for now. But I'll let your sergeant know that he'll likely be charged, so you'll have to keep him locked up."

With that, Richards and the police officers headed up front.

* * *

Owen was escorted back to his cell, and after the handcuffs were removed and he received a quick pat-down, he was locked in. He had remained stoic thus far, but once his cell door was slammed shut and locked, he started to shake and was barely able to keep from screaming out loud. During the interview, the police had informed him in no uncertain terms that he would likely be charged with either murder or attempted murder. *God Almighty. What in hell did I do? I should've gone to a guard and asked for protection. I never thought something like this would ever happen. Christ, poor Mac. That damned Slug and his bunch— it's all their fault. I should never have listened to them. Oh my God, I'm done like a turkey. Oh God, on top of everything else, I'll end up in a supermax. Christ, I never thought of that. I wish I had a razor blade; it'd all be over, and I wouldn't have to worry about a fucking thing. Oh Christ.*

It was likely a good thing that Owen was on a suicide watch. He had reached the end of his rope.

The one happy person was Slug. He had accomplished what he had been instructed to do, and there would be no comeback on him. And he hadn't even had to raise a finger. What more could he have asked for? He couldn't help thinking, *Jesus Christ, life is sure good.*

* * *

The phone in tower three rang, and Raymond, who was still keyed up and pacing around the tower, answered with the usual "Three tower. Raymond here."

"Raymond, this is Sergeant Patrick."

As soon as Raymond heard who was on the other end, from force of habit, his stomach immediately dropped, and his first thought was *Oh shit, what'd I do now?* But then, in a flash, he recalled that he was sort of a hero, and he relaxed somewhat.

"Just want to let you know that there is a relief on the way up to you. As soon as he takes over, I want you to report to the front interview office to give your statement to the cops. I would assume you noted the incident, the times and all that stuff? You doing OK?"

"Yeah, I'm fine. I'll head in as soon as he gets here."

As he hung the phone up, Raymond, giving himself hell, grabbed his notebook and, while trying to recall exactly what had happened, the order in which it happened and the times, started to write. *Damn. How in hell did I forget to do this? Christ, I hope I get it right.* Luckily, one thing helped him sort out the times: when he'd spotted the ambulance roaring in, he had noted the time of its arrival while thinking, *Shit, how in hell did it get here that fast? It must have been parked around the corner or something.* Many other staff had shared that first thought. He was also amazed at how quickly it had taken off for the downtown hospital. His next thought had been that Shipley must still have been alive, or the vehicle wouldn't have torn out with the siren and lights blazing the way it had.

He didn't have long to work on his notes, as he spotted the mobile coming around the corner just before receiving the radio call that it was on the way. *Hell, that wasn't even five minutes. I thought I'd have more time than that. Christ, what the hell do they expect from us?*

Vern Thibedeau

The mobile pulled up, and Raymond lowered the key down to his relief. The relieving officer unlocked the barrier, entered the tower, relocked the barrier and started his climb. Once he reached Raymond, they did the usual changeover while discussing the incident and filling each other in on their involvement. Once that was completed, Raymond headed for the ladder to start down to the mobile. Just as he started down, his relief asked, "Hey, Paul, how in hell did you manage to get an eye on the con who did the stabbing? Boy, that was good work."

With a bit of a grin, Raymond looked up and replied, "Ah, you know me, Jerry. Just my usual alertness."

"Oh sure, I can just imagine" was the sarcastic reply.

Raymond didn't hear the reply, not that he would've cared anyway. He climbed down, locked the barrier, hooked the key onto the rope so Jerry could pull it back up and climbed into the mobile. Away they headed for the front entrance.

Raymond made it through the ID building, through the gates and into the front entrance. Giving a wave to the control staff, he turned the corner, and upon reaching the interview room, he knocked on the door. Upon receiving a "Come on in," he opened the door and walked in. He spotted two guys dressed in civvies behind the desk, and Corporal Richards sat in the corner.

Richards made the introductions and told Raymond that the sergeant had asked him to remain while he gave his statement to the police. "I think the sarg just wanted me here to help answer any questions that may pop up. He was going to be here himself but got a phone call about something or other, so I'm stuck with it."

Raymond sat down and filled the police in on everything that, at least in his view, had gone down. Some of his times weren't quite right, but with Richards's help and some talking back and forth, everything worked out.

When they were about halfway through the interview, one of the officers said, "Paul, that's a hell of a distance to be able to spot something that happened so quickly. We were just wondering how on earth you managed to do it."

"Well, you're right about the distance; it is a long way. But just as a group stepped into the yard, I noticed one inmate—I couldn't really recognize him, but I could tell he was wearing a jacket. My immediate thought was, *Why in hell would anyone have a jacket on when it's this warm out?* I sort of thought that something may be up. I grabbed the binoculars, and as soon as I used them, I recognized that damned Shipley." Looking toward Richards, Raymond continued. "I knew him right away because of that episode at the hospital, when I stopped him from escaping."

Richards just nodded as if he agreed with everything Raymond had said. But his thoughts were a little different. *You goddamned goof. Hospital security stopped that escape. You were just screwing around. Christ, if it'd only been up ta you, he would've been long gone. You're nothing but a damned useless jerk.* But Richards wasn't sure, once the interview was finished, if he should mention to the police what had actually happened. *Aw, to hell with it. Won't make any difference in the grand scheme of things anyway.*

Once the interview was completed and the officers thanked Raymond for doing an excellent job, Richards looked toward him and said, "Hey, Paul, before you head down to N area, the sergeant wants to see you in his office."

Raymond certainly knew where the sergeant's office was located. After all, he had been there more than once—and usually not for a happy chat. This visit, thankfully for Raymond, didn't take long. Sergeant Patrick just wanted to compliment him again.

"That was an excellent job, and it will be noted in your file. Also, the inmates are locked up for the rest of the day, and we have lots of staff on duty, so you may as well take off early. You certainly earned it today, my man."

Raymond gave him a quick thank-you and was out the door in a matter of seconds. It didn't take him much longer to reach his car, and within 10 minutes or so, he was on the highway and on his way to his apartment. He couldn't help thinking about his day at work. *Jesus Christ, am I ever lucky I used those binoculars. Hell, I'm a fucking hero. Even the cops think I am, and I sure know that I am. By God. If Shipley hadn't tried to screw me at the hospital, I wouldn't have paid any attention to him or that Owen jerk when they came out. Well, ain't that something? Boy, oh boy, you just never know how things are gonna work out. Christ,*

Vern Thibedeau

I thought I was done when I fired that shot off, but jeez, I'm a real hero! By God, I'm gonna use some of that rent money to go to the bar tonight. Hope to hell Annie is there; she'd love to hear about the shooting and what all went down. Hot damn, I'm all set for a big night!

With those thoughts and a few more, Raymond reached his dark, empty apartment, and as he entered it, he once again thought, *Jesus Christ, this place is too big for me. I've gotta move to a smaller one; might as well save some money.*

Chapter 26

Richards remained with the police while they finished up their work and gathered all their stuff. Looking at Richards, one of them said, "I guess that's about it for us. No doubt someone will be back and forth a few times, but there's not much more we can do right now. If you'll walk us out, I don't think we even have to bother the sergeant again. But just in case, while we're finishing up a couple of things, would you give a call to see if he wants us to stop in? If not, we'll just head right on out."

Richards did as requested, and the sergeant told him it was OK with him if they wanted to take off. Then Patrick said, "Once you've escorted them out the gate, would you stop in at the office for a couple of minutes? I just want to go over a few things."

"Sure thing, boss. Be back in a few minutes or so."

Richards was right; he was sitting in the office, talking to the sergeant, within five minutes. There wasn't much to go over, and their chat was completed in under 15 minutes.

Sergeant Patrick finished their conversation by saying, "That was a good job everyone did today. And you did a hell of a good job; you really took a load off my shoulders. Also, everything is pretty well wrapped up; you might as well take off and go home. Oh, and don't forget to have a drink for me."

Vern Thibedeau

"You talked me into it, Sarg. Don't worry; I may even have two for you. And I'm really glad I could help. Anyway, I'm outta here. See you tomorrow." With that, Richards started out to the parking lot.

Richards, who was happy about being allowed to leave early, made it out to the parking lot and was just about to jump into his car, when a car pulled up almost next to him. Richards couldn't help but notice the nice-looking young lady who opened her door, stepped out and gave herself a big stretch. She noticed Richards glancing her way and gave him a tentative smile.

Richards couldn't help admiring her car. It was a couple of years newer than his, but it was a nice baby-blue colour almost the same colour as his own. The lady, who continued looking toward Richards, hesitantly opened a conversation by saying, "Good afternoon, sir. I would assume, by looking at your uniform, you work here?"

Richards took a couple of steps in her direction and replied, "Yes, I do. Is there something I can help you with?"

"Boy, I certainly hope so. I've never visited a place like this in my life. I must admit it is really scary. Anyway, I'm here to visit my brother, and I would certainly appreciate some help. Jeez, I don't even know where to go to find this V&C place he told me about."

Richardson gave a little jerk when the lady mentioned visiting her brother and wasn't sure if he should say anything about the incident or not. He decided to take the easy, or maybe smart, way out. He figured it wasn't his job anyway. "Sure, miss, I can help you out with that little problem. To be honest, you certainly aren't the first person to run into this difficulty." As he pointed toward the ID building, he said, "Just go into that little building over there. Once you get in, tell the officer you are going to V&C, and he'll explain how to get there. It's really easy. Once you come out on the other end of the building, just stay on the sidewalk, and that'll lead you to the gates. As soon as they open, go right on through and into the main building. The officer in the main control will direct you to the V&C area. Heck, you'll be there in a couple of minutes."

"Oh, that sounds really simple. I can't wait to get in for the visit. I haven't seen my brother in years. This is going to be so great. I've even been thinking that maybe I should've brought my kids with me for the visit." With that little note and a thank-you, the lady turned and started out for the ID building.

Richards was shaking as he entered his car. *Oh Christ*, he thought, *that must be Shipley's sister. I can't go back inside. Hell, she'd be in before I made it in anyway. I'd better phone the main control to tell them to give V&C a heads-up.*

He grabbed his cell phone and dialed the main control. As soon as he received an answer, he said, "Gene, this is Richards. I'm out in the parking lot. There's a lady on her way in wearing a light red jacket. She's coming in to visit her brother. I'm about a hundred percent sure she is Shipley's sister. She was supposed to come in for a visit today. You'd better phone V&C to give them a heads-up. And as soon as you've done that, let Sergeant Patrick know she's on her way in. Someone—I imagine it should be the sergeant—has to sit her down and tell her about her brother. Don't waste too much time; she's going through the ID building now. Not really sure who'll actually get stuck doing the notification, but good luck to him. She seems like a really nice lady." With that, Richards hung up.

Christ, what a job that's going to be. I'd guess it'll be the sergeant doing it. God, I don't envy him having to tell Shipley's sister about Shipley getting stabbed. Why the hell did this have to happen, especially today, of all days?

With that thought, Richards put his car into gear and started out of the parking lot for the drive home. He was a little worn out. After all, the night before had been a late evening, and he wasn't used to the late nights and all that dancing. On top of that, it had been one hell of a hectic shift. All in all, he didn't plan on doing much once he got home. *Jesus, I don't imagine Shirley made any plans for tonight; I'm sure she must be as worn out as I am.* All the way home, Richards struggled to keep his mind on the wonderful time he had shared with Shirley and on what they would do that evening. For the most part, he was successful, but every once in a while, the day's episode would slip in.

Richards made it home, pulled into the driveway, eased out of the car, took a couple of deep breaths and entered the house. Shirley had heard the car pull in and met him at the door. She gave Richards a deep look, walked over and gave him a tight hug. After a minute or so, she whispered into his ear, "What the hell happened this time, Bill? You are OK, aren't you?"

Bill, knowing he would have to sit down and give a full explanation, swallowed a couple more times and said, "Oh sure, I'm fine, hon." Taking Shirley's hand and leading her toward the sofa, he continued. "Nothing physical at our end, but …"

* * *

Sergeant Patrick and the deputy warden were sitting in the sergeant's office, discussing the events of the afternoon.

"Have you heard anything from the hospital yet?" the deputy asked.

"Nope, haven't heard a thing from the hospital—or the escort, for that matter—about anything. I'm sure that as soon as they know, we'll know. If the hospital doesn't phone us, what's-his-name doing the escort sure will. You can bet your bottom dollar he'll want a relief as soon as possible or a ride back if Shipley doesn't make it. In any case, we'll know pretty quickly.

"Oh, also, I guess you noticed that I told Raymond he could leave early. Since the inmates are locked up, we have all kinds of staff. It's kind of strange, though; it wasn't very long ago that I had Raymond in here and reamed him out for screwing up on an escort. In fact, he's been chewed out several times by myself and by a couple of other supervisors. But I have to admit he sure earned his pay today. I can't figure out how he spotted the stabbing as quickly as he did, but I'll tell you, I'm sure happy as hell that he did."

The deputy and sergeant were in the middle of another subject, when the phone rang. Patrick picked it. "Patrick here. What's up?" He listened for a minute or so and, before hanging up, replied, "Oh crap. Today, of all days. Christ, I'll be right out; don't let her into V&C." Patrick hung up the phone, stood up and answered the deputy's questioning look by saying, "Hell, that was the main control. Shipley's sister is on her way in for a visit. I'm gonna have to bring her in here and explain the situation. Depending on her reaction, I may have to assign someone to drive her down to the hospital. Shit. Not enough going on. You gonna wait here or take off?"

"Ah, I'll just sit here in the corner and look the reports over. At least if I'm here, I can give you some input if you need it."

Walking quickly, Patrick left the office and started out for the front entrance. He arrived there just as he saw a female wearing a red jacket enter the building. Knowing who it was because there was only one person entering and also because of the red jacket and having been informed of her name, he approached her and said, "Good afternoon, Ms. Patterson. I assume you are here to visit Mac Shipley?"

"Oh, ah, yes, I am. Is there some kind of a problem? I was told—I'm sure I was told to go to V&C."

"My name is Patrick. I'm the sergeant in charge. Do you mind if I call you Connie?" Once he received an affirmative nod, he continued. "Oh no, Connie, you certainly haven't done anything wrong; I didn't mean to give you that impression. But I do have to have a chat with you. If you'll just follow me to my office, it will be much more comfortable than trying to talk out here."

Once they arrived at the office, Patrick waved her in and, pointing to a chair, said, "Just have a seat over there, Connie, and I'll fill you in." As she sat down, Patrick looked over toward the deputy and introduced him. "This is Jim Faraday; he's the deputy warden, and he had to come in due to an incident that happened in the yard." Patrick was just about to continue the conversation, when Connie interrupted.

Connie, who wasn't nearly as intimidated as she had been when she first arrived, asked, "What is going on? I just travelled here to visit my brother, and I don't understand what the difficulty is."

Patrick, with an uncomfortable glance toward the deputy, clearing his throat, commenced his explanation. "Ms. Patterson, I'm afraid there was a serious incident in the yard this afternoon that involved your brother. Your brother did absolutely nothing wrong, but unfortunately, he is the one who was injured. He was—"

Connie interrupted him by asking, "What do you mean *injured*? What's going on? My God, this is the first chance we've had to see each other in years, and now you're trying to tell me he's been hurt. Where is he? I want to see him right now!"

"You will, Ms. Patterson. But I have to explain his injuries to you and let you know where he is. We also have—"

Once again, Connie cut him off. "Tell me where he is? You mean he's not here?"

Patrick, figuring he'd better get right down to it, replied, "I'm trying to explain to you, Connie, that he is in the downtown hospital. He was stabbed in the yard and was sent down by ambulance. This just occurred a short while ago, and as of this moment, we haven't heard anything back from the hospital. But I can assure you he is getting the best care possible."

"Oh my God. I have to see him. How do I get there? How long will it take? Can someone draw me directions? I have to get going!"

"I know you are upset, Connie, and I can understand that. I assume you are not from around here?"

"God no. It took a four-hour drive to get this far. Is the hospital far from here? Can you give me directions? Aw God, I wish Al had come with me; he'd know what to do."

"We'll do everything we can to help you. You can leave your car in the parking lot, and I'll have an officer drive you downtown. The only thing is, he can't stay, and you'll have to bring a taxi back. That'll cost around twenty dollars or so. Is that OK with you?" Patrick asked as he reached for the phone.

"Oh yes! Thank you. Thank you so much!"

"OK. I have an officer waiting out front. He'll take you out to the ID building. Just wait there, and a vehicle will pick you up in a couple of minutes."

Patrick stood up, and Connie followed him out of the office. Patrick gave the officer his instructions and went back into the office to arrange for Connie's ride downtown. With a look toward the deputy, he said, "Well, that went better than I thought it would. I just hope Shipley makes it."

* * *

Connie and her escort were waiting in the ID building for only a couple of minutes before a penitentiary vehicle pulled up, and the escorting officer waiting with her said, "There's your ride, miss. Good luck to you. I really hope everything turns out OK."

"Thank you, sir," Connie said. She then hurried out and opened the car door, and when the uniformed officer gave her a nod, she climbed in. The ride downtown was mostly quiet, and it was also a tense ride. The officer was uncomfortable with the situation and didn't know what to say to Connie. He was not accustomed to dealing with family members of inmates in any type of situation, let alone a situation like that one. To him, Shipley was just another con who'd gotten himself into a jackpot and couldn't get out of it. Also, he thought, *Maybe he got what he deserved. Who the hell knows what's going on with them in there?*

Connie didn't know what to talk about either. Her mind was obsessed with her brother. But she did try to start a conversation a couple of times.

"Do you have any idea what happened to my brother? When I was in the office, they didn't really tell my anything. I just don't know what's going on."

The driver wasn't sure what he should say. He had been posted outside when the incident happened, but he had heard all the radio calls and had a good idea of the events. He also realized he couldn't give out much information; on the other hand, after all, this was the sister of the con.

"I can't really say much because I was working outside the fence, and I wasn't really involved. But I do know there was an incident in the yard, and an inmate—I guess it was your brother—got injured and was taken to our hospital and then taken downtown by ambulance. The police were called, and I was informed that an inmate is locked up in the hole. I don't know if there have been any charges or not; it is really too soon to know that. I can tell you one thing, though: most of us really hope everything works out for him. He really isn't a bad inmate, and staff are pulling for him." The officer was mostly just being polite. He didn't really know Shipley and wasn't overly concerned about whether he made it or not.

Connie managed to hold back her tears while her mind went back several years to the life she and her brother had lived. *Oh my God, after Al and I were married, we should have gone back to the house and taken Mac with us to live. I'm sure I would've been able to track him down, and it would have been so much better for both of us! If I'd just done that one little thing, he wouldn't be in this mess. Oh my God, this is all my fault.*

She started to clench and unclench her hands while those thoughts and others raced through her mind.

Her hand-clenching startled the officer, and he just about went through a red light.

In a relatively short time, though it seemed like hours to Connie, the vehicle pulled up at the hospital entrance. Connie opened the door and, looking at her driver, said, "Thank you very much for the lift; I would never have been able to find the place on my own."

"You're very welcome, ma'am. Oh, I also want to let you know again that I and a lot of the other guys are wishing you well." He didn't know what else to say, and he thought that was the best way to say goodbye to his passenger, who appeared to be stressed out.

Connie closed the car door and, almost at a run, disappeared into the cavernous entrance of the hospital while thinking, *Oh God, please let Mac be OK. He doesn't deserve this. Oh, please.*

The driver waited until his passenger disappeared into the hospital, and then, with a mental shake of his head, he checked for traffic, did a U-turn and started back to the prison. He reached for the radio to inform staff of that fact. *Christ, I'm glad that job is done with. It's too bad; she does seem like a really nice person. But at least it was a change, and I'm not dealing with goddamn cons.*

Jeez, it'd be great if my relief makes it in a little early. I forgot we have to go out for a couple of things and then get groceries on the way back home. God, that's one job I hate. Oh well. What the hell? It's gotta be done.

Connie rushed up to a counter that had a couple of hectic-looking people behind it. Within a second or two, one of them approached her, but before the nurse could ask her a question, Connie, in a stressed-out voice, explained her circumstances.

The nurse quickly gave Connie directions to the surgical unit, and just short of running, Connie took off. She hustled down a corridor, hoping it was the correct one, and took an elevator up two floors. She exited the elevator, turned left and entered a large room. As she headed for the counter, she couldn't help but notice several people in the room. Most of them appeared to be stressed, and those speaking were doing so in hushed voices. Upon reaching the counter, Connie once again explained her circumstances, and she received a reply of "Please have a seat over there, and I'll find out whatever I can and get right back to you."

With a nod to a couple of folks, Connie did as instructed. But she had a difficult time constraining herself to a chair, and within moments, she stood up and began pacing. Suddenly, a thought struck her: *My God, I haven't even told Al about Mac being in the hospital. I have to phone him right now!* She dug her phone out of her purse while rushing out to the hallway and pressed her husband's cell number with shaking fingers.

It only took two rings for Al to answer. "God, Connie, I've been waiting for you to phone. Is everything OK? What's happening?"

Connie replied, "Oh, Al, I'm OK. But ..."

She explained what had happened at the institution and informed her husband she was at the hospital. She also explained that so far, she had no idea what was going on, how badly her brother was hurt or even if he was still alive. "God, Al. I just don't know anything!"

Al immediately asked Connie if she wanted him to head out. "Jeez, babe, I can get Mom and Dad to look after the kids. I know the boss will give me time off for something like this, and I can borrow Mom's car. I could be there in a few hours."

After much discussion, they decided Al would stay home with the kids for now. Connie ended the phone call with "As soon as I know anything, I'll call, and we'll decide what the heck we're going to do. I love you, hon, and I'll call as soon as I find out what's happening." She then hung up and rushed back into the waiting area.

After what felt to Connie like an hour or more but was only several minutes, she saw the nurse approaching. Before Connie could ask a question, the nurse said, "You are certainly in the correct area. Your brother is in surgery, but so far, there is no news. As soon as the team is finished, one of the doctors will be out to bring you up to date on your brother's status. Until then, about all you can do is have a seat. If you want, I'll be happy to bring you a coffee or a glass of water."

Connie replied, "Thank you, but I'm fine." She continued her pacing, not knowing she was in for a long wait.

Chapter 27

Owen sat by himself in his lonely cell, staring at the walls in a more or less catatonic state. He wasn't sure how long he'd been locked in the cell, but he knew he was in a world of trouble. He had found an old, thin plastic dinner knife with a serrated edge lying on the floor just under the bed. Such knives were issued, along with plastic forks and spoons, with each meal. Staff, naturally, were instructed to ensure each utensil was retrieved at the completion of every meal; however, there were times when the odd one was missed. He didn't know how long it had been lying there under the bed, but it was covered in dust and had bits of food stuck to it, so he assumed it had been quite a while. But that was the least of his concerns.

Owen continued sitting on the edge of the bed, staring at the solid steel door and contemplating his life and what he had just done. *God, Mac was my buddy. What in hell did I do? I should've ratted to a pig. Christ, that Richardson seemed like an OK guy. At least I'd just be a PC con and not locked up in a special handling place for years. God Almighty, it'll be a murder charge; I'll never get out of this fucking mess! Aw, Mac. I'm sorry, but I didn't have a choice; you must know that. Hell, you're likely up there looking down and thinking how you're gonna get back at me. Jesus Christ, after everything you did for me, I pulled this stunt. I'm sorry, Mac. I hope you're still alive, but I guess that's not very fucking likely.*

Just as that thought flashed through his mind, he felt a sharp pain in his thumb. He gave a little jerk, and looking down at his hand, he spotted some blood oozing out of the thumb. He realized he had been rubbing his thumb over the edge of the plastic knife, and the serrated edge had cut his thumb and caused it to bleed. As he sat there looking down at the blood, he thought, *Oh my God, that hardly hurt at all. Fuck, that little thing would lay my arm wide open! Christ, I wouldn't have to worry about Slug or the SHU or anything; hell, I'd just go to sleep, and everything would be all over.*

Just then, he heard footsteps coming down the range toward his cell. He remained in the same position, but he eased the plastic knife up under the cuff of his coveralls.

* * *

Corporal Johnson, who was in charge of the diss. cells, was sitting in the office with the other two staff on the shift with him. He looked over at one of the officers and said, "Hey, John, take a quick walk down the range, and check the cons. Be sure to take a good look at Owen; he's in number fifteen. He looked a little shook up when we locked him in the cell, and I'd hate to have a hanger on our shift. Christ, we'd be here for ages, filling out paperwork!"

John stood up from his chair, started for the office door and replied, "Sure thing, boss. Good idea. You sure are right about not having a hanger. I want to get the hell out of here as soon as I can; my wife and I are having a big night tonight."

John left the office and started his walk. As usual, whether there was an inmate in it or not, he glanced into each cell. Usually, an inmate would just look up at him, look back down again and not say a thing, but once in a while, one would ask a question, such as "What time is it, boss?" or "Is it yard time yet? I wanna get out of here for a while."

John continued his walk, spoke to a couple of inmates and kept looking through the small windows. Once he reached cell number 15, he slowed up somewhat and took a closer look. He noted that Owen was just sitting there staring at nothing, but he did spot him give a quick glance toward the door and knew darn well Owen had seen him. "Hey,

Owen, how you doing? All OK?" Upon receiving a slight nod from Owen, John completed his walk and returned to the office.

He entered the office and informed everyone that all was quiet and that Owen was just sitting there staring at nothing. Even though there was a punch station at the end of the range, which he made sure he punched to verify that the walk was completed, he watched as the corporal noted the time and made a comment in the daily logbook. He knew the comment in the log was made just in case. Once that task was completed, he poured a cup of coffee, took a seat and joined in the conversation.

* * *

Once the guard completed his walk and passed back again on his way to the office, Owen continued to stare at the door, thinking about his past life and some of his screw-ups. He couldn't help but dwell on what was in store for him: a special handling unit for several years, court, lawyers, a trial, a conviction, and life in prison. *God, what did I do?* Suddenly, a major thought struck him: *Christ, no brew in a supermax. Holy God, I never thought of that!*

While Owen thought, he unconsciously rubbed his thumb against the edge of the plastic knife again. In the back of his mind, he felt the throbbing in his thumb, but that was not enough to cause him to even glance down at what he was doing. He kept thinking about his future, the life he could have had and what he had done to his buddy Mac, and within minutes, his eyes became wet, and he realized his life was useless and as good as over. Once again, he glanced down at the small amount of blood oozing out of his thumb and thought, *Hell, that doesn't even hurt!*

Owen took another quick glance toward the door and, naturally, didn't see anything. He didn't bother to stand up but just eased down onto the floor and crawled over toward the toilet. Once he reached the toilet, he sat there with his knees pulled up almost to his chin and continued to stare at the wall. Then, without even realizing what he was doing, he pulled the sleeves of his coveralls up. He continued to sit there dreaming about his life. Eventually, he looked down at his hand, saw blood and proceeded to absentmindedly rub it over his inner wrist until he could hardly see the skin. He looked back up again and continued to stare blankly at the oppressive door. Unconsciously, he took a solid grip on the plastic knife and pressed the blade as hard as he could against his inner wrist. Still pressing with his thumb, he slid the knife up his arm toward his elbow. He was surprised there was little pain, hardly any at all. He didn't watch what he was doing; he continued to stare at the door.

In a short time, he did feel some pain. He looked down at his wrist and thought, *Oh God, what did I do?* Things started to become hazy for Owen. He slumped down ever farther and sort of started to doze off.

* * *

Corporal Johnson and the two staff were just sitting around the office, discussing world affairs. The corporal suddenly glanced at one of the officers and said, "Hey, John, take a stroll down the range, and take another check on cell fifteen. I feel a little uneasy, and I just want to be sure all is good down there."

The officer said, "Sure thing, boss," and he stood up and headed out.

He was only out of the office for a couple of minutes, when the staff heard him yell, "Hey, at fifteen! Need some help! And get the nurse!"

Chapter 28

There sat Connie, trying to rest and looking around at everyone. She imagined they were waiting, just as she was, for news of a loved one. They all looked tired, frazzled and worn out. She imagined they felt exactly how she was feeling. Connie felt drained from the stress and from strutting around the hallways, and still, there was no word regarding her brother. *Oh my God, is he even alive? What can be taking so long? They must know something by now; it feels like I've been here for hours. How did Mac ever get into a mess like this? I should've been there for him. Oh God, why didn't Al and I try to find him? Everything would've been so different.*

As Connie sat there thinking her thoughts, half in tears, she heard the doors that led into the scary place where the surgeries were performed slide open. Everyone jerked his or her head toward the sound and stared at the person walking toward them. The stranger, who was dressed in a green gown and had a white mask hanging down under his chin, looked around and turned toward a couple sitting on chairs on Connie's right side. Connie could not hear what was said, but watching the relieved faces of the couple, she knew they had received welcome news. The couple stood up, shook the stranger's hand and, holding each other's hand, happily followed him through the doors into that scary place.

Watching that interaction, she couldn't help thinking, *Oh God, I wish that person was speaking to me. I can't take this much longer.*

Not having any choice, Connie continued sitting. She was just about to stand up and take another relieving walk around the area, when she spotted a woman come into the room. The lady looked around and, spotting the empty chair beside Connie, walked over and sat down.

After a couple of minutes, the newcomer looked at Connie and introduced herself. "Hi. My name is Joyce Herald. You look like you are all by yourself."

Connie introduced herself, and the two of them had a little chat for a few minutes. Connie thought how nice it was to have someone to chat with rather than just sitting and staring around. Joyce then said, "My husband is in there, having an operation. Luckily, it is only minor. Are you waiting for someone in there too?"

"Oh yes. My brother is having major surgery. It seems like he's been in there forever. I don't even know if he is going to live or not, and no one's come out from that back area to tell me what the heck is going on. God, all I can do is sit and wait."

"I'm so sorry. I wish I could do something to help, but I'm more or less in the same boat. Was he in an accident or something?"

"Ah, no, I wish it was something like that, but it wasn't. He's doing a sentence at that place up the highway called Mountainview, and an inmate stabbed him in the throat with something. It's really bad."

With a bit of a shocked expression, Joyce replied, "Oh, I'm sorry to hear that. That must be really rough."

Connie noticed the lady suddenly seemed a little uncomfortable; in fact, she started to ease over in her chair, putting more space between herself and Connie. She also appeared to suddenly take an interest in something on the other side of the room and didn't seem to be interested in continuing their conversation. Connie didn't know what she had said to upset her, but then it struck her: *My God, it must be because my brother's an inmate. Maybe I shouldn't have mentioned that little fact.*

* * *

Shipley opened his eyes. He wasn't really aware of the fact that he did, and he didn't know where he was or what had happened. He was just lying on his back and looking up at the ceiling. Because the ceiling was white, in his dreamy state, he thought he was looking up at the sky and thought the ceiling was a large, fluffy white cloud floating along.

He didn't feel any pain or notice the tubes that had been put into both arms. He was lucky the medication was working, or he would have felt only pain. His throat was stitched and bandaged and also had a tube inserted just above where he had been stabbed.

A nurse noticed that he had opened his eyes and waved to a doctor, who hurried over. After glancing at Shipley, he looked at the nurse and said, "Holy crap, I really didn't expect this! Maybe he will make it!"

Shipley just lay there looking up at his clouds and almost dreaming. For some reason, he had a fleeting thought about his sister. He couldn't imagine why he would have been thinking of Connie. Then he spotted movement up in the clouds, and glancing toward the disturbance, he spotted those damned black birds again. They seemed to be swooping toward him, but strangely, this time, they were silent. There was no sound at all, just a weird silence. He stared at the birds for what he thought was an hour or so but really was only a few moments. Then they hesitated and just seemed to fade away.

At that moment, someone in the far distance waved to him, and without another thought about his sister, Mac gave a little twitch and drifted off.

* * *

Connie was sitting in a chair again. She had been up pacing for several minutes, but after tiring of that, she'd found a chair in a corner by itself and made use of it. Within a few minutes, she spotted a doctor come out of that strange place and look around at everyone left in the area. Most of the people who had been waiting had received their news, both good and bad, and had left. The doctor looked in Connie's direction and started toward her. Connie tentatively stood and apprehensively waited for the doctor to approach. She noted that the doctor was not smiling; in fact, he appeared rather grim-looking. *Aw,* she thought, *stop being silly. He's just having a hard day.* But at the same time, Connie clung to the back of her chair and once again wished her husband, Al, were by her side.

The doctor, with what appeared to Connie to be a sympathetic look, approached and said, "I assume you are Ms. Patterson, and you are waiting for news regarding Mr. Shipley?"

Connie, with a hesitant voice, affirmed that he was correct.

The doctor continued with his sympathetic look and voice. "Ms. Patterson, I assure you we did everything we could for your brother; however, I'm afraid there really was no chance he could survive his wounds."

Normal Weekday Schedule in Most Prisons

Please be aware that all prisons have their own routine. However, most maximum- and medium-security institutional routines are fairly similar. That said, please note that times will vary. Minimum-security institutions have a completely different environment, and their goals as well as routines are also different.

I'm going to start at breakfast time and go through to the next morning. Afterward, I'll list a weekend and holiday routine.

- 0700 (7:00 a.m.)
  Cells are unlocked for breakfast. If the inmates wish to eat, they go to either a servery or a kitchen and dining area. Once they receive their trays, depending on the institution, they eat in that area, in a common room or in their cells. If they're in segregation or dissociation, meals are delivered to the cells.

- 0800 (8:00 a.m.)
  Cells are unlocked for workup, and inmates go to their work areas. Inmates working in the kitchen or servery will already be at work. Some other work areas include cleaning within the institution, outside ground work (but still inside the wall or fence), canvas and boot repair shop, machine shop, school, recreation work, metal shop and more. There are too many jobs to list.

- 1130 (11:30 a.m.)
  All work areas are cleared; inmates return to their cells for a formal count. All inmates in the institution must be accounted for. Nonworking inmates must stay in their cells during working hours.

- 1200 (12:00 noon)
  Once the count is certified correct, cells are unlocked for the noon meal.

- 1300 (1:00 p.m.)
  Inmates return to their work areas.

- 1600 (4:00 p.m.)
  Inmates return to their cells for another formal count.

- 1700 (5:00 p.m.)
  Once the count is certified correct, cells are unlocked for the supper meal.

- 1800 (6:00 p.m.)
  This is the start of recreation time. Inmates have the choice to remain in their cells. Some institutions have televisions on the range, and they can stay there and make coffee or go to a common room to do the same thing. They can also go to the gym, go to the yard if it is light outside, go to a group (which usually includes outside visitors) if they've joined one, or go to a hobby and craft area to work on a hobby or craft or have evening visits with family or friends.

- 1900 (7:00 p.m.) until 2200 (10:00 p.m.)
  All cells are unlocked every one and a half to two hours for approximately 10 minutes, and inmates have an opportunity to leave the area they are in and go to any of the other above areas. This is called changeover.

- 2300 (11:00 p.m.)
  Inmates are returned to their cells, and another official count is taken. Inmates are locked in their cells for the night.

Notes

During the day, in addition to their regular jobs, inmates have interviews with their parole officers, work board and institutional court and visits with family or friends. There are also visits during the evening. Also during evenings, several outside groups enter an institution and meet with various numbers of inmates. Included in these groups are AA, different religious orders and several other groups.

Several prisons have another official count at 2100 (9:00 p.m.).

During the midnight shift, staff patrol the ranges at least once an hour. Also, there are usually two official counts during this shift, with the last one being just before breakfast.

Normal Weekend and Holiday Schedule

- 0800 (8:00 a.m.)
  Cells are unlocked for breakfast.

- 0900 (9:00 a.m.)
  Cells are unlocked for recreation, and the routine is similar to the weekly evening routine.

- 1200 (12:00 noon)
  Inmates are returned to their cells for an official count. Once the count is certified correct, inmates are released for their noon meal.

- 1300 (1:00 p.m.)
  Recreation starts again with the regular changeover.

- 1600 (4:00 p.m.)
An official count and the supper meal occur.

- 1800 (6:00 p.m.)
Evening recreation begins with the normal changeover.

- 2300 (11:00 p.m.)
Inmates are returned to cells for the night, and an official count is conducted.

Glossary

CMO, or parole officer: Several inmates are assigned to this person. He or she formulates rehabilitation and release plans for the inmates.

dissociation: A secure area within segregation. Also called *diss cells* or *the hole.*

heavy: An inmate who carries a lot of unofficial power among inmates within an institution.

inmate clothing: Green pants and shirt worn during working hours. Different-coloured polo-type leisure shirts may be worn during recreational hours. Also, blue jeans are now standard.

IPSO: Institutional preventive security officer.

OP: Off privileges. This is a minor disciplinary action in which an inmate is not allowed to go to the yard, the gym and so on for a short length of time.

PC: Protective custody institution or inmate.

pen squad: A small squad of city police officers who investigate serious incidents in the institutions.

sally port: An entrance and exit for vehicle traffic, usually a double gate. The vehicle enters the first gate, gets checked out by staff and is then allowed to enter or leave the institution.

seg: Segregation. An extra-secured cell area within an institution.

shive, or shank: Homemade knife.

SHU (special handling unit): A supermaximum institution or a unit within a maximum institution for inmates who have committed serious crimes while under sentence.

skinner: An inmate sentenced for a serious sexual offence.

tossing cells: Searching cells.

V&C: Visits and correspondence department. This department regulates and observes inmate visits and sorts and delivers inmate mail.

About The Author

Vern Thibedeau, at the age of 17, enlisted in the Canadian Army. After three years of service, he returned home, worked at odd jobs, married Sheila and eventually returned to school. Once he earned his teacher's certificate, he became a heavy-equipment operator in the hope of paying off his student loan.

In 1973, at the age of 33, he joined the Correctional Service of Canada, which involved moving himself, Sheila and their three small children from a small northern Ontario town to Kingston, Ontario. In total, he worked for the service for 26 years and served in five different prisons. At that time, due to many incidents he was involved in, which included physical injuries, abduction at gunpoint and several hostage situations, his stress level was rising. Finally, at the urging of his wife, after many discussions, he retired.

Once retired, Vern and his wife travelled for several years in an RV, and eventually, they moved back to Kingston. Shortly after retiring, prior to writing this fictional novel, he published his memoir, *The Door: My Twenty-Six Years Working inside Canada's Prisons*.

The Door was well received. Vern received many responses from the general public, including from officers, retirees, students and even lawyers. The responses were surprising and much appreciated.

Any comments or suggestions may be sent to, vernthibedeau@ hotmail.com

Printed in the United States
by Baker & Taylor Publisher Services